THE **THINGS** THAT AREN'T **THERE**

THE **THINGS** THAT AREN'T **THERE**

A Vic Lenoski Mystery

by Peter W. J. Hayes

LEVEL BEST BOOKS

Copyright Page

The Things That Aren't There
A Vic Lenoski Mystery

First Edition | July 2018

Level Best Books
www.levelbestbooks.com

Trade Paperback ISBN: 978-1-947915-06-0
Also Available in e-book

Printed in the United States of America

To Sono and Jason, who for longer than I can count have kept me honest, happy and whole.

ACKNOWLEDGEMENTS

Write any acknowledgement and you know within seconds that the idea of a writer suffering alone in her garret is selfish garbage. Books, by definition, are living proof of the enduring strength of community. It takes a community to form a writer, a community to help the writer create and complete a book, and after publication, links a new community of readers. My own experience is no different. *The Things That Aren't There* simply would not exist without everyone who offered their time, advice, support and—when needed—well-meant criticism of the manuscript.

Where to start?

Without doubt with Robin Walsh, who, like me, is a member of Pittsburgh's Mary Roberts Rinehart Sisters in Crime chapter, and who read the entire manuscript and offered intelligent and succinct advice on the plot and characters, including a few important criticisms, all of which I took to heart. I can't thank Robin enough. But of course there were others. The idea for the book was hatched in the kitchen of Howison Schroeder, a longtime friend and long-ago teammate. A colleague from an earlier career, the artist and filmmaker Andy Spanoudakis, provided invaluable advice on how to deconstruct a key character's video alibi and on the capabilities of video streaming, all of which are critical to the plot. My Wexford writer's group, led by MaryAlice Meli and populated by fine writers in their own right, provided helpful advice on multiple sections of the manuscript. However their contribution has more to do with how they helped me—with humor and friendship—see my own weaknesses as a writer and learn to improve. I look forward to our meetings every month. And, of course, my enduring thanks to Verena Rose of Level Best Books, who read the manuscript and snapped it up for publication in an astounding three weeks, dragging me out of my own garret into an exciting and impressive community of readers and writers who I will do my best not to let down.

"Everyone has a plan until they get punched in the mouth."

~ Iron Mike Tyson

CHAPTER 1

Vic Lenoski hated Sundays. He had a list of reasons why, but as he ducked under the crime scene tape the one that came to mind was the day his wife, Anne, enrolled their eight-year-old daughter in Sunday school. He'd gone along in a show of support, but quickly grew disgusted with the minister's sermon. Twenty years as a cop had taught him that when someone asked him to take something on faith, the lies had already started. He and Anne argued about it driving home, their daughter silent in the back seat.

As he walked the length of the carpeted office he thought about how he regretted that argument, even more than his hangover and the way his mouth tasted like sour milk. He stopped in front of a man splayed dead on the floor beside a large wooden desk.

"Jesus," said his partner, Detective Liz Timmons, her voice loud in the high ceilinged office. Vic's mind tilted back to that drive home from church all those years ago and he couldn't help himself, he glanced over his shoulder to see if his daughter was there. She wasn't. He snapped his head around, his anger vibrating like a bright tuning fork. *This is what I do now*, he thought, *I look for things I know aren't there*. He didn't understand why. It was as if he'd let go of everything he knew and trusted and didn't care that he had. He blinked, letting training and habit force his attention onto the victim. He tallied what he saw, ticking down each fact like an abacus bead. Male victim. Caucasian. Early fifties. Twenty stab wounds? Neatly trimmed sandy-colored hair and eyebrows. Cashmere sweater, or what was left of one. Buckles on the loafers—that made them Ferragamos, five hundred dollars a pair. Enough blood to have filled Pearl Harbor.

"It's something, isn't it?" said a man standing nearby, his belly sagging over the waist of his hospital scrubs, an unshaven look more slovenly than stylish. In his anger Vic tried to remember the medical examiner's name and failed. On Sundays the Pittsburgh Bureau of Police borrowed staff from the local hospital system to give their full-time coroners a day off. He watched the ME tilt his head from side to side as if he was appreciating a work of art. Vic's anger vibrated harder and he stepped in front of the man.

"*Something* doesn't help us. You get that? We need a time and cause of death. Right now."

The ME straightened and blinked, his lips moving before words came out. "I need to do an autopsy. Then, time and cause of death, I can let you know."

"You don't want to go out on a limb and say he was stabbed to death?"

"I need to confirm that." The ME shuffled back a step.

Vic moved with him. "OK, let me help you. See those three lower stab wounds, the ones just above the belt line? Cuts are horizontal. That means the perp held the knife near his own waist and stabbed him three times fast." He bumped the ME's soft belly with his closed fist three times, mimicking the movement. "Hard to defend against, that's why his hands have so few defensive wounds. The other wounds are slices. Means after the first three stabs the perp changed how he held the knife, started stabbing downward." He leaned closer and dropped his voice. "Started hacking. That's why the slices are so long. The knife deflected off the ribs and slashed down the body. It's why there's so much god damn blood."

"Anger," said Liz, from his shoulder. "Someone with a grudge."

"Rage," breathed Vic, knowing from the taste that he was

blowing day old whiskey into the ME's face.

Again the ME edged back, his eyes down. "I'll determine how it happened once I've done the autopsy."

"We need a time window for when this happened. We can't test alibis until you give us one. Today. You understand?"

"I know. They told us that in the course I took."

Vic felt as much as saw Liz roll her eyes. The ME waved his hands as if he was trying to clear a smell. "I'll look at everything." He ducked into his medical satchel for something. Vic guessed it was his pride. He looked at Liz, his mind still bright with anger.

"Photos?"

Liz's dark copper-colored skin looked washed out in the fluorescent lights, but there was no mistaking the message in her half-hooded eyes. Vic guessed it went something along the lines of 'why the hell are you doing this to him?' She wagged her cell phone in front of his face. "Only if you get out of the damn way."

Vic stepped back to give her room, musing about how his anger had got away from him, but feeling better for it. He focused on the immediate vicinity of the body, his mind registering the details. Everything matched the expense of the man's clothes and grooming. A mahogany desk five feet wide and four feet deep, its matching leather executive chair flat on its side. A hand carved wooden cigar box gaped open, thick cigars littering the desktop.

"I got it," said Liz, pointing her phone toward the cigar box. "Right handed," she added.

Vic turned to the ME, who was finally kneeling beside the body but seemed unsure how to start. "You hear that?" He heard gravel in his voice and felt his anger cooling, leaving an odd hollowness.

The ME looked up, his brown eyes fragile. In a kind way Liz said, "Wounds are more on the left side of the vic's body. Suggests the perp was right handed."

The ME nodded, a flush rising to his cheeks as he lowered

his head.

Vic surveyed the rest of the office, looking for something, he didn't know what. The windows behind the desk overlooked an Allegheny River swollen from spring rains. Along the facing wall was a row of cupboards and shelves that held books, acrylic mementos, and framed photographs of local political figures, businessmen and athletes, including the mayor. Everyone was smiling and most held golf clubs. His eyes fell on a metallic, cylindrical object perhaps ten inches long with a bulging black plastic nose. Rubber versions of the kind of treads you might see on a World War I tank were attached to the sides. It was mounted on a slab of wood, and he stepped closer and read the engraved brass plate set in the wood.

Big Bullet (Prototype III)
The Future of Robotics from PipeMine
January 22, 2017

Liz broke his train of thought. "Good to go. Techs will get the official photos. We can go through the office after that. Interviews?"

He nodded vaguely and looked at the ME, who seemed to be checking vital signs. He bit back a comment and said, "Everything I asked for will be today, right?"

The ME didn't answer, but Vic couldn't bring himself to say anything more. He turned and followed Liz across the thick carpet. As they approached the door a pot bellied, white-haired sergeant directed a pair of crime scene technicians into the office. He looked down a bent nose at him.

"Can't believe nobody shot you yet, Vic."

Vic was five eleven with his shoes on, Wroblewski perhaps six feet, but there was something about Wroblewski that made him seem larger.

They shook hands. "I'm too nice a guy, Sarge." Twenty years earlier, during Vic's rookie year, Wroblewski's undercover work had led to the bust of one of Pittsburgh's most violent drug gangs. Vic still remembered paramedics carrying Wroblewski out of a stash house during one of the raids, compresses on two bullet wounds, while he shouted to the other officers not to let anyone escape. But the memory slid away from him, as if he had dropped a file folder of documents and it was just another piece of paper on the floor.

Wroblewski stepped closer to him, his eyes boring into him. He spoke softly, so it was only between the two of them. "You doin' all right, Vic? After what you went through?"

"What I *went* through? You telling me it's over?"

Wroblewski searched his eyes, stepped back and nodded toward the ME. "New guy. Look at him. Ain't like the old days." He rocked on his heels. "Sundays. Jesus."

"Yeah," said Vic, almost spitting it out. "Worst damn day of the week."

CHAPTER 2

Still feeling hollowed out, Vic tagged behind Liz along a row of low cubicles toward a glass-walled conference room in the far corner of the floor. A young woman with a short blonde ponytail and a female officer sat at the conference table, white Styrofoam cups in front of them. As he entered, Vic's eyes were drawn to the windows overlooking a bend in the river. In the swift-moving center a single thick branch reached upward, waving sluggishly back and forth with each underwater tug of the current. It was as if something hidden below the waterline was trying to get his attention. He tugged his eyes away and met the gazes of the woman and uniformed officer.

"I'm Detective Vic Lenoski. Pittsburgh Bureau of Police, Homicide." He nodded to his partner. "This is Detective Liz Timmons. I'm the lead investigator." He met the woman's blue eyes, aware of how Liz cocked her head and stared at him. He had never announced himself as the lead investigator before and wasn't sure why he did it now. "Mind if we sit?"

The woman shrugged, her eyes never leaving him. Despite her youth she radiated competence and confidence. Vic settled at the head of the table, Liz across from her. As the female officer left the room he asked if he could record her preliminary statement. When she nodded, he pressed the record button on his phone screen.

"Okay, Erica Lauder, right?" He narrated the date, case and address. "So, just take us through it in your own words. How you found the victim, Mr. Drake Monahan."

Erica turned her eyes to the window, her fingers tight around her cup. Vic followed her gaze and saw a flock of swifts veer across the sky like a handful of thrown buckshot. He looked at her hands and saw that her nails were perfectly manicured and gleamed in the fluorescent lighting. She wore no rings or jewelry, only small earrings with blue stones.

Erica pulled her eyes from the window. "I came in at nine. I had to get a presentation ready for tomorrow. I worked about forty minutes and then went to Mr. Monahan's office to ask him a question. He said he would be in by nine-thirty. When saw him beside the desk, I called 911."

"Which phone did you use?"

"The one at his secretary's desk. I didn't want to go near him. I just wanted to get away from there."

Hearing her tone Liz cut in gently. "It's an unpleasant crime scene. Did he often ask you to work Sundays?"

"Saturdays. Sundays. Stay late, come in early. It's that or you don't make the A team. I can't believe I worked forty minutes with him lying there."

Vic nodded. "Were the office doors locked? Anything out of the ordinary for a weekend?"

"The front door of the building was locked, so was the office door."

Vic glanced at Liz.

"Office has auto locks," she said, knowing his question. "Building front door is a deadbolt system."

He nodded, impressed that Liz noted the door locking mechanisms as they entered the building. He couldn't remember exactly what he was thinking when they arrived. He turned back to the girl. "Was the door to his office open or closed?"

"Closed. Which was weird. He normally only closed it when he was discussing something confidential."

"So what did you do?"

"I knocked. No one answered, and like I said, he told me he would be in. If he says he'll be in he usually is. So I opened the door and looked."

"And you saw him."

She nodded. Vic pointed at his phone and she leaned forward. "Yes, I opened the door, looked inside and saw him."

"And did you go inside the office?"

"I didn't need to."

Vic sat back, aware of the distant rumble of voices from the crime scene technicians. "What is it your company does?"

"Monahan Partners? We're a VC. Venture Capital. We have a fund of forty million dollars. We invest in start-up companies by giving them cash so they can develop their products. In exchange they give us an ownership piece of their business."

Vic rearranged himself in his chair so his gun no longer stuck into his side. It reminded him that he tipped the scales heavier than two years earlier.

"Do you know if anyone threatened Mr. Monahan lately? Is anyone angry at him?"

"You mean apart from all of the companies he invested in and everyone who works here? Oh, and the people who put up the forty million?" Her anger rippled through the room.

"Perhaps you could expand on that a little." Liz's voice was careful.

Erica's eyes flashed. "Monahan made Scrooge look like Mother Theresa. He worked everybody hard, paid badly and drove disgusting deals. You have to understand, these small companies? He would take them for everything he could get. In a lot of cases he ended up owning more than the entrepreneur who started the business. Sometimes he stacked the company's board so he could vote out the founder as soon as the company was profitable. He didn't want to help companies, he wanted to take them for everything he could get. That's what turned him on."

"And you?" Liz probed.

"I worked three unpaid internships here during and right after college. Because unpaid internships are the kind he likes. In the last unpaid internship, I pitched a company and he put two million into it. He walked away from that company a few months ago with his money back, plus interest, plus a fifty-two percent ownership stake worth two and a half million dollars in stock. You know what I got when I asked him for a piece? He pinched my cheek. Said I was cute." Her eyes clouded in disgust.

"But you're still working there." Liz leaned forward, her eyes bright and full lips pressed together. Vic liked the question. Anyone who stayed at a job they hated needed a strong reason.

"Sure. Monahan has done more deals than anyone in town. I work five years and any other VC in town will hire me. Since I started full time, I've pitched him five companies and he's invested in four of them. All of those investments are panning out." She sat back. "And he was dead wrong on the one he turned down. Dammit, I just needed one more year and then I could have told him to go jump in the river. I would have found another VC and outplayed him."

Vic thought his own daughter might have looked like Erica one day. She had the same blond hair and fierce concentration. It could have been her sitting at this same table ten years from now. From his peripheral vision he saw Liz glance at him, a look of expectation on her face.

He picked up his phone and turned off the recorder. "Include the internships."

"What do you mean?" Her blue eyes searched his face.

He couldn't get the image of his daughter out of his mind. "You don't need five years. You found good companies while you were there so you've proven yourself."

Her forehead smoothed. "What are you, my damn guidance counselor?"

He caught himself and pushed aside thoughts of his daughter. "Just the guy deciding who's angry enough to kill Mr. Monahan. Or if someone would stay at a job they hate just for the chance to take him out." He rose slowly, holding her gaze, then dropped his business card in front of her. "Call if you think of anything else. We'll be in touch." He slid his phone into his pocket and nodded Liz out of the conference room.

They took the elevator to the lobby in silence. At the

double doors that led into the office building they stopped and Liz examined the door's deadbolt system, her eyes sharp.

"Yeah. One door stays locked all the time, opened by those two levers. The other needs a key. From both sides." She tested the permanently locked door and it didn't budge.

Vic studied the building lobby. A grey tile floor led to a receptionist's desk of stained wood. The wall behind the desk was stone. He checked the walls. "And no CCTV." He walked back to the receptionist's desk and looked behind it. "Yeah, no monitors. Confirm that, okay?"

Liz nodded. "When we pulled up I saw another door. Grey metal access door on the loading dock. No handle on the outside. Pretty sure there was a bubble camera above that door. We can check on the way out."

"So the fire escape stairway leads outside through the loading dock." He walked over and pushed open the stairway door beside the elevators. "That looks like it."

They exited the lobby and crossed to their car. As they pulled away Liz said, "You worry me, Vic."

Vic closed his eyes briefly. "What the hell now?"

"Dump on the medical examiner, all sweetie pie on the blonde. Until you jumped on her."

"She needs to learn how to shut up around cops."

"You dismissed her as a suspect already?"

"Not until we check her alibi. But she doesn't care if we know she hated the guy. You know people with something to hide don't talk that way." The reasoning slid out before he could stop it, the same way the memory of his daughter had confused his questioning of Erica.

Vic stopped the car at the side of the building. "Smart you. Okay. There's the fire escape door. It does have a camera."

They stared at the grey door. It was in the corner of the building, a loading dock in front of it. About twenty feet away a small chain link enclosure held two dumpsters.

Vic pointed toward the door with his chin. "You're right. No outside handle. It's an exit only, no entry."

"So why do you need a camera?"

Vic smiled. "Good question. Bet the camera doesn't work, bet again there isn't even a camera?"

"I ain't taking that bet."

"See? You're smarter than everyone says."

"Well yeah. I'm a black woman. That's two strikes. Because I'm a woman I gotta be five times smarter than you old white guys to get the job, and five times smarter again because I'm black. So, yeah."

"Okay, smart woman. Which way to Monahan's wife?"

Liz pulled out her phone and swiped through some screens. "North. Sewickley Heights." Disgust shrouded her voice. "Of course."

"Anyone break the news to her yet?" Vic only knew that he didn't want to.

"Coupla Heights officers. But they promised not to question her until you get there because, you know, you're the lead investigator and all."

He clenched his mouth closed to make sure he thought about what to say next. After a moment he said carefully, "Well, technically, I am."

Liz was silent for a moment. "Vic, the only reason I lasted this long with you is you never gave a shit about stuff like that. You could have run the department if you'd just gone to the trouble of applying when the job opened up. And look who we got. I still haven't forgiven you for that. Your only benchmark is how well a detective closes cases. It almost makes you color blind. Almost." She looked at him, her brown eyes probing. "You changing that?"

He drove for a few moments and then glanced at her. "No. I'm too damn old."

Liz smiled, her eyes on the road. "Shit. I coulda told you that ten years ago."

CHAPTER 3

As they drove, Vic and Liz split the responsibility of who would review Monahan's telephone and banking records, and his appointment book. When they entered the village of Sewickley, they drifted into silence. Vic checked each person on the sidewalk, his eyes automatically jumping from person to person. He couldn't help himself.

"Must be a nice life," Liz said, pointing at the high end boutiques on each side of the main road. "You been here before?"

"Yeah. There's a PI has his office here. Levon Grace. Good guy. I been out a few times to talk to him."

"Rich people got their problems too. You know I got a great uncle buried here?"

Vic glanced at her, interested. Liz had migrated to Pittsburgh from New Orleans after hurricane Katrina destroyed her home, but somehow he never asked why she had chosen Pittsburgh.

"Didn't know that. You have other family in Sewickley?"

"No. They moved to the East End. My great uncle got his name on a memorial here for the Tuskegee Airmen."

"He flew for them?"

She shook her head. "Lotta guys from around here did, though. Six or seven from Sewickley, maybe a hundred from around here. He was a mechanic. Went overseas with them."

"And I thought this was a white bread town."

"Yeah. Well. Someone had to keep all that white bread

fed, make sure their houses don't leak and their gardens look good."

Vic saw the set to her mouth. She stared straight ahead, her skin oddly dull in the overcast light of the day. As always her hair was cropped short, she wore no makeup and despite several piercings in her ear, her only earring was a small gold star. Combined with her white blouse and dark slacks, everything about her spoke to efficiency and commitment. He liked that about her. He pulled his attention back to the car and steered onto Blackburn Road, following the rise and tight turns into Sewickley Heights.

He tried to gather himself. "We got anything on the wife?"

"Nope. No idea how this is gonna go."

The GPS system warned him to turn left and he guided the car between a pair of stone pillars overhung by hundred year old oaks. They followed a long driveway flanked by maple trees, the branches a latticework over their heads. About two hundred yards ahead a rambling colonial of field stone appeared on the far side of a gravel parking area, a Sewickley Heights police cruiser parked near the front door.

Inside they shook hands with the two uniformed Heights officers, who led them through the house and out the back door, toward a glass structure that reminded Vic of a huge and intricately designed greenhouse.

"How's she doing?" asked Liz as they trooped across the grass.

The two officers glanced at each other and the younger one said, "Oh, she's good, she's fine." He stretched out the last word and the sergeant smirked.

The door opened to a rush of humid air and the tang of chlorine. A large swimming pool stretched away to the right, its surface perfectly smooth. To the left, a woman in a single piece white bathing suit sat motionless on a barstool, her eyes locked on a television screen embedded into the woodwork above the bar. A black and white movie played on the screen.

"Mrs. Monahan," said the uniformed sergeant.

She raised a finger for them to stay quiet, her eyes locked on Lauren Bacall as she leaned against a door and spoke to Humphrey Bogart. They all waited until Bogart whistled. Finally the woman swiveled on her stool, took a sip from a tall glass and inspected them.

"So you brought the real cops?" She directed the question at the sergeant.

Vic calculated her age, aware of how tightly the bathing suit clung to her curves. He guessed mid thirties, perhaps twenty years younger than her husband. "Mrs. Monahan, I'm Detective Lenoski and this is my partner, Detective Timmons. Pittsburgh Bureau of Police, Homicide Division. We're sorry for your loss." The last word stuck in his throat for a split second. "We're the lead investigators." He glanced at Liz to make sure she heard him. "Obviously, this is a suspicious death."

Mrs. Monahan gave her perfect shoulder length brown hair a tiny shake, her brown eyes settling on him. "Apparently so."

Something about her eyes jolted him and he hesitated, trying to stay focused. Liz stepped in to cover his silence. "We realize this is a difficult time, but we'd like to get some information from you."

Mrs. Monahan waved her hand for Liz to continue and sipped her drink. Liz explained their need to know which telephone and banking companies her husband used. Mrs. Monahan provided the names and slid off the barstool. Vic sensed the two uniformed officers tighten as she presented a shapely backside on her way around the bar. She stopped and turned to them. "Can I help you with something?"

They both shuffled in place trying to find somewhere to look.

Vic understood the young officer's earlier comment and it annoyed him that he would joke about her on the day her husband died. He said quickly, "Mrs. Monahan, can you tell me if your husband received any threats lately, or if he had any enemies?"

She added ice to her glass and filled it three quarters of the way to the top with vodka, finishing with a splash of tonic water. After a quick stir she took a sip. "Lots of enemies. No threats that I know of."

As she circled back around the bar Vic saw how she presented her body, as if she wanted the men to stare at her. It felt calculated to him. Her large brown eyes confirmed it. She was looking right at him and he could almost hear her evaluating. *Six feet? Not quite. Thick middle, thin hair. Jacket and pants as worn as his face. Washed out blue eyes. Huh.*

Her appraisal annoyed him, but it interested him as well. He was used to denial from family members, or shock, but she was sharply self possessed and the way she carried herself was almost aggressive. He wondered if she was angry about her husband's death and wanted a confrontation.

"Gee," he said, "what a nice place you have here." He let the sarcasm build. "You're so very lucky."

She stopped, her hand on the back of the bar stool, her head cocked. "Luck has nothing to do with it. Maximizing assets does." She said it in a way that sounded like a threat. Vic knew he'd guessed right. She was angry and wanted an outlet, someone to challenge her.

He waited a few seconds then responded. "Okay. Maybe you could explain, Mrs. Monahan. Being that I'm just a dumb, poorly dressed cop."

Something flickered in her eyes. "Why of course, Officer...?"

"Vic Lenoski." He saw no point in repeating his actual rank, he knew he would sound too desperate to impress her.

She hopped onto the bar stool, her breasts rising and settling with the motion. The younger cop failed to hide a gasp. Her gaze remained on Vic. He returned her stare, her expression again reminding him of something that he couldn't quite place. She blinked and he knew she had made a decision.

She turned to the bar, put the TV on mute and ran a manicured finger around the rim of her glass. "Maximizing assets is what my husband did for a living." She turned and looked at the group. "That's what afforded us this house. Now, let me answer the questions you really want to ask, because…" She focused on Vic as if they were alone. "Because I get the feeling that you don't distract easily, Officer Lenoski. Or was it Detective?"

"Lieutenant or Detective Lenoski," Liz cut in.

Mrs. Monahan took a long pull on her vodka tonic. "Okay, Detective. Yes. I'm the second wife. Yes. I'm much younger than him. Like him, I used my *assets* to get here, as our local officers over there have spent so much time evaluating." She waited to make sure they all understood her point. "I swim every morning, that explains the bathing suit and why I'm out here. But my husband and I understood each other. We got along. He told me he would be home by eleven last night. I called him when I got home and he didn't pick up. That was about two fifteen. You'll see it in my phone records. And his. I woke up this morning and put on my bathing suit to go swimming, called him again, and then these police officers arrived at my door. At some point I expect you will ask me for an alibi. I was at the country club. In the bar." She sipped her drink. "Until two."

Liz cut in again. "We'll ask for your alibi when we're ready to."

Mrs. Monahan ignored her, watching Vic. "There's one more question you want to ask, isn't there, Lieutenant Lenoski?"

Vic liked her bluntness and found that it calmed him. He felt more pulled together. "There's more than one, Mrs. Monahan, but, yeah, there is one big one."

She nodded and Vic thought he saw a smile in the corners of her mouth. "Then let me help you out. My husband maximized assets, as I said. To do that you can't *share* your assets. That means I signed a prenup. My lawyer can give you the details." She looked at Liz and told her a name, waiting while she wrote it down. "This house, his company and his investments go to the children from his first wife. He did name me as a beneficiary on a life insurance policy. I'll get fifty thousand dollars."

Having guessed right about her anger, Vic pushed a bit harder. "A prenup and such a low dollar insurance policy makes me think you didn't maximize your own assets very well."

He expected a sharp answer, but a smile crept into her eyes and she sipped her drink as if she was actually tasting it.

"I like you, Lieutenant. A statement like that might set some women off. Make them say something they don't mean to. Which I bet is what you want. But you got right to the core of it, so I'll give you an honest answer. Yes. I did sell myself a little short. But I was playing the long game. If we stayed married for fifteen years the prenup went away. Too bad we only made it five. But what I got right away were introductions to a specific group of people and a certain lifestyle." She waved her hand at the pool house. "My husband and I both knew what we were doing. It's why we got along and why I'll miss him. But it's the long game that matters. You'll understand that when you ask for my alibi and I tell you who I was with in the country club last night."

"Until then," said Vic.

"I'll look forward to it, Lieutenant." She emphasized the word Lieutenant and Vic heard no sarcasm in the word. She waved her hand at the two uniformed officers. "And next time, there's no need to bring those two. They bore me."

Vic eyed her drink, which was already three quarters gone. "Can you do me a favor, Mrs. Monahan?"

She studied him, waiting.

Vic nodded at the glass. "I'd appreciate it if you chose not to swim today. I think it might be better for your health."

She swirled the ice in her glass and a full smile twitched her lips.

"The drinks were to soften the news. However I will stay out of the pool. And I'll do that specifically for you, Lieutenant, because you were kind enough to ask."

CHAPTER 4

Vic and Liz arrived at their yellow brick offices on Western Avenue thirty minutes later. Vic parked behind the building and together they crossed to the front door.

"Maybe Crush stayed home today," said Liz as they swiped their ID cards and moved through the metal door that led to their unit.

"This is the kind of thing gets him up in the morning."

"Maybe he ran out of blood to put on his cereal. Had to go kill something with them meat cleavers he calls hands."

Vic smiled to himself, remembering Crush's right hand worrying an orange during one of his first staff meetings, when, frustrated with the glib way his detectives were answering his questions, he slammed his oversized fist onto the conference table. The orange exploded, splattering the two nearest detectives and leaving bits of pulp on Crush's shaved and shiny skull. Within a day he was known as Orange Crush, the nickname shortened to Crush soon afterwards. But now everyone answered his questions with zeal.

They entered the tennis court sized room that housed the force's investigations units. Fresh from reading a managerial book, Crush had grouped together each of the eight investigations units. Homicide was the first, a cluster of eight low walled cubes separated by an aisle that led to a small window set high in the back wall. Vic had long since decided that if there was a single cloud in the sky, it would be within view of that window.

He placed his Glock in the upper right drawer of his desk,

settling it carefully on top of two thickly stuffed files held together by a rubber band. Across the aisle Liz shrugged out of her
leather jacket.

"I'll start the murder book," Vic called to Liz, referring to
the binder where all documents and reports related to the case
would be kept. Two years earlier, again at Crush's insistence, the
department had adopted a new software program designed to
keep case files on-line, and while Vic and Liz were required to
maintain an electronic file, Vic still printed out all the reports
and notes and kept them in a three ring binder. He liked to flip
the pages and think about the information, rather than scroll
through screens on his computer. Somehow the case felt more
real to him when he could actually touch the documents. Liz
maintained the electronic file so they satisfied departmental requirements, but she also spent a lot of time with the binder. Vic
liked her better for it.

"I'll call that Sunday ME," said Liz. "Maybe he'll respond
better to someone being polite."

"Won't help. Look at him and you know the guy can't
even find a razor. He won't know his own cause of death when it
happens." Vic scanned his emails, the buzzing of the fluorescent
ceiling lights in the low ceiling distracting him. He clicked on
an email and frowned. "Crush is in. Wants to see us ASAP. Lorna
sent the email, so he must have dragged her in on a Sunday as
well."

Liz sighed and they both rose and walked to the aisle
that ran the width of the room and separated the glass walled
offices from the investigations units. The offices faced south,
their large windows overlooking the parking lot, and beyond,
Pittsburgh's football stadium and casino. In the gaps between
the buildings the Ohio River ran muddy and sluggish toward the
Mississippi.

Outside Crush's office Lorna looked up from her secretary's cube. Technically she was a resource for the entire department, but when Crush changed the layout of the floor he moved
Lorna across from his office. Predictably, through no fault of

her own, she provided less and less support to the detectives and more for Crush. Crush had called the move "resource alignment," and it fooled no one.

Lorna smiled at Vic and gave her permed red hair a little shake. She was about forty, newly divorced, and seemed to own an endless supply of tight blouses and skirts that highlighted her broad hips and large chest. When Vic heard about her divorce he had genuinely wondered why her husband would leave her, but soon afterward she was linked to a series of detectives and deputy chiefs, so he guessed she was happier unattached.

"Glad you made it," she half whispered to Vic as they approached.

Vic leaned over the low wall of her cube and asked, "What kind of mood?"

Lorna rolled her green eyes. "For him, pretty good. Mayor knew your victim and his wife, so he called the chief, who called Crush and told him to come in. Mayor wants updates."

"Oh great," Liz said under her breath.

"Vic! Liz!" The shout from Crush's doorway sounded like a bulldozer starting up. Liz cut right and entered his office, Vic trailing. Crush stretched up to his full size of six feet two.

"What'cha got?" Crush rumbled. "Chief is all over this one."

Vic and Liz each took one of the chairs that faced Crush's desk. He sat down as well, his right hand, closed in a fist, pumped rhythmically like a heart. Vic glimpsed silver near Crush's thumb and realized he was exercising with a grip strengthener. Usually Crush worked out daily at the gym, but he never seemed to think it was quite enough.

"We barely got started," said Vic. He explained the murder scene and what they had learned from their interviews with Erica and Mary Monahan. Crush stared at the wall between them as Vic talked.

"She got a prenup," Crush repeated, when Vic was finished. He still didn't look at Vic. His hand pumped. "Need me to call this ME?"

Peter W. J. Hayes

Liz cut in. "I was just about to call him. He's a young kid. Vic did a good job getting him focused. I'm gonna try being nice. See if that helps."

"Okay. Good." He smiled at Liz. "What you got next?"

"Alibis," said Vic. "Once we get a timeline for Monahan's last hours and a window for time of death we'll start testing alibis. I'm guessing that Mary Monahan will come out clean, but this Erica who found the body might be a possibility." He sensed Liz glance at him. "And when the crime scene jockeys are done we'll go through the office again."

Liz cut in. "Vic and I ain't had time to talk about this, but this Erica girl said that Monahan liked to screw the people he invested in. I'm thinking that we need to interview those folks, see if one of them is mad enough to go after him. The attack looked like the person was real angry."

Crush nodded his head so hard it looked like a head butt. "Good thinking, Liz. Let me know the time of death window when you get it. TOD is critical. Like I said, glad to call this ME and get him moving if you need it."

"I was planning to ask Freddy to take over tomorrow when he gets in," Vic said, referring to their full time pathologist. "If the mayor is interested, then we want everything by the book. No mistakes."

"Right." Crush tossed the grip to his left hand and started pumping. "One other thing. Press. No talking to the press on this. No leaks. Approved statements only. Everything goes through me. We clear?"

They both nodded.

"Okay. Let's run this mother. Interviews with the people Monahan invested in and get Freddy going. Keep me updated."

They both rose, but before Vic could leave the room Crush called, "Vic!"

When he turned Crush was standing behind his desk, staring at him, his eyes hard. He stopped pumping his hand. "Vic, you up to this? I got the mayor and chief all over me." He thumped the flat of his knuckles on his desk.

Vic nodded. "Yeah. I got this."

"Then get your head in the game. We need to clear this fast. Victim was a major player in the business community. Those startups he funded are putting Pittsburgh on the map. The mayor told me that. We need to show we can handle it. This is exactly what we talked about in your end-of-year review. Close this case and it'll kick start your career. Do you read me?"

Vic's was suddenly angry. "My career? My career's fine. In my review you talked about my career, but it sounded more like you were talking about your career, not mine. Remember you told me to transfer?"

The top of Crush's head flushed red. "I never said that. I said you should consider all your options."

"I'm fine where I am. I told you that. You're the one who hasn't been promoted in the last two years. I'm guessing you think that's because of me. Look, I got this. And when I close it you'll look good, which is what this is all about." He pivoted and stepped out of the room before Crush could say anything more.

Outside Lorna waved him over, her eyes wide. "Vic," she leaned toward him but he avoided the spectacular view down the front of her shirt. "That sounded terrible, is there anything I can do? I'm available."

He studied her, decompressing, taking in her round face and high cheekbones. Her eye liner and green eye shadow flirted with being overdone.

"No thanks, all good," he answered.

"Well. Just thought I would ask." She smiled and blinked at him.

Liz waited for him a few steps down the hall. When they reached their cubes she looked at him and fluttered her eyelids. "Vic, anything I can do for you?"

"Don't even start."

"That girl spends too much time getting herself ready for work."

"Just call the ME and tell him we want Freddy doing the autopsy. Get him lined up to do it tomorrow." He cocked his head. "Glad to call the ME and get him moving if you need it."

"Don't *you* start," said Liz as she settled into her chair.

"And the crime scene guys. Make sure they fingerprinted all the doorknobs and locks. Still doesn't make sense how someone got into those offices."

"They're already on it. Unless you want to go back and do it yourself?"

Vic stared at her.

"Yeah," said Liz carefully. "Didn't think so." She leaned back in her chair. "And that's what Crush was talking about at the end of the meeting. Nobody knows where your head is at."

^^^

That night Vic circled the first floor of his house again and again, his hand clutching his fifth whiskey, moving through the living room, dining room and kitchen. Sunday evenings alone. Another on the list of reasons he hated Sundays.

Worse, he couldn't get the image of the branch sticking above the river out of his head, the way it waved at him as it moved.

He knew why.

On a grey spring Sunday like this, almost two years ago, his fifteen year old daughter, Dannie, had left home for a friend's house and never arrived. The branch today felt like a sign. Dannie somewhere, reaching out to him. Letting him know. Something.

The idea was utterly false, he knew, but he wanted to believe it. It was that wanting to believe that angered him, that kept disorienting him. But he couldn't stop himself.

So he walked.

Through the dining room, barren except for one wall haphazardly covered with reports, photographs and interview transcripts from the task force's search for Dannie. Department policy had kept him off the team, but it hadn't stopped him from copying their findings. Now he didn't even bother to turn on the dining room light. Without looking at the wall he moved into the living room, past the armchair and the packing box topped by the television. In the kitchen, he stopped in front of the card table rescued from the basement and stared at the litter of takeout containers and half-filled bottles of whiskey and scotch.

Before Dannie disappeared he rarely drank. Now he didn't know how not to.

While the task force was operating he vicariously followed every lead they turned up, consumed by it, ignoring his cases, so warped by it that he couldn't sleep until beer and whiskey sealed his eyes. Five months later, when the leads ran out and Crush disbanded the task force, it was as if someone had cut his anchor line. Liz stoically returned as his partner, he guessed out of guilt. But he knew how the failure to find Dannie still dogged every meeting Crush attended with the deputy chiefs, the district attorney and mayor. Crush's upward movement through the department had stalled. And from their conversation that afternoon, he knew it was only a matter of time until Crush figured out a way to transfer him.

The branch waving slowly in the current came back to him.

He finished his whiskey and poured himself another, the ice cracking as the liquid sank to the bottom of the glass. He swigged. "So here I am," he said out loud. He wanted to go out. To get in his car and drive, as he did most nights now. He knew where he would go, but he forced himself to dismiss the idea. Too much to drink. He sipped, flipped off the kitchen light and resumed walking through the darkened first floor. He had to. It was all that would get him to Monday.

CHAPTER 5

It was eight a.m. when Vic parked his car on Penn Avenue and entered the long medical examiner's building. He nodded to the security guard and passed through the metal detector. As he picked up his badge, gun and keys from the basket on the other side of the gate, Liz materialized from the gloom of one of the hallways.

"Freddy got my message. He's cutting now." She started toward the elevators that led to the basement and Vic followed, his head feeling as if someone had landed a couple of roundhouses on him the night before.

Downstairs their footsteps echoed along the narrow, fluorescent-lit hallway. At the double doors that led into the autopsy room they both tied on surgical masks from a box on a shelf next to the entryway and tugged on paper robes.

The tiled room was organized around four metal tables, each with a large sink at the head and a light above. Monahan's nude body lay on one of the tables, the long Y incision already complete, with Freddy and the Sunday ME standing over the corpse. Freddy's real name was Franz Englund, but he had won the nickname when someone realized that Franz's last name matched the name of the actor who played Freddy Krueger in the *Nightmare on Elm Street* slasher movies. Given Franz's trade, the nickname stuck instantly. But unlike the movie character, Freddy was short and wiry, with a booming voice saturated with the hard consonants and the precisely pronounced words of his native Berlin. As Vic stepped into the room, Freddy peered at him through horn rimmed bifocals, the bottom of his face hidden by a surgical mask. He stopped his explanation of how to use the power saw to remove Monahan's skull cap. The Sunday ME, swathed in blue disposable robes and wearing a large plastic face protector that looked like a dollar store version of a welding mask, looked up as well.

Freddy lowered the saw. "Detective Lenoski." He pronounced the final *ki* in Vic's last name so hard that the sound bounced off the white tile walls. He gestured to their Sunday ME, his white latex glove giving his hand a ghostly momentum. "I understand you gave our ME a difficult time? You will be more cooperative next time?"

Vic glanced at the ME, who was suddenly intensely interested in Monahan's Y incision. "Not everyone is like you, Freddy. Sometimes people need some help getting started."

Freddy raised the saw. "You do that again *und* I use this on you." He turned to the Sunday ME. "Okay. On *und* off button here. Then around the skull where I marked. You must press hard when starting the cut." He glanced at Vic. "Pretend it is the skull of Detective Lenoski." He flipped the button, the whir of it drowning out their voices before Vic could respond, and handed it to the ME. Freddy stepped aside and the young man carefully lowered the saw to the skull. Vic gritted his teeth as the whir became a screech. Freddy pantomimed the cut to help him along. For the time it took the ME to complete the procedure, Vic kept his stomach muscles tight so last night's whiskey would stay in place. He was glad he had delayed breakfast and coffee until after the meeting.

When silence flooded the room, Freddy motioned Vic and Liz over to some X-rays clipped to a light box. He pointed at a couple of long grey lines in what Vic guessed was an abdomen. "So. Easy to identify cause of death. Stabbing. First few cuts just above the belt line, they angle upward. Two sliced the liver, the third the aorta. See this?" He traced the lines with a long gloved finger. "Forceful stabs. Top of the scale."

Liz breathed out. "Fits with the number of wounds, someone angry and committed."

Freddy nodded and adjusted his mask. "But this is unusual. Blade is very wide. Very wide. Four or five inches. This is why so much damage inside him. No ridges. How do you say? Not serrated." He peered up at Vic to make sure his point was communicated. "Those three stabs, he hemorrhage very much. His life ends. A very nasty knife."

"He would've passed out pretty quickly?" asked Vic.

"Of course. Conscious for less than a minute. Then blood pressure drops. That can save your life if treatment is quick, but liver cuts bleed. The die is cast, as you say." He barked a laugh, throwing his head back. "That is good. The die? You understand? Die? Dead? Not dice? I must use this again."

Vic closed his eyes, trying to think.

Liz spoke almost to herself. "Stabbing is personal. You gotta get right up next to the person."

Vic opened his eyes and looked at Freddy. "Time of death?"

"Saturday night. From lividity, no later than one a.m. That is best I can do."

Vic nodded. "Okay. So we know he left for the office at eight p.m. So between eight and one. You know what I keep thinking about?" He turned to Liz. "Erica said she found his office door closed. So this guy walks in, which Monahan doesn't seem to have a problem with because he lets the guy walk all the way down that long office to his desk, the guy assaults him, puts him down and stabs him lots of times because he's major angry, but when that same guy leaves he carefully, really carefully, closes the door behind him, soft and polite."

Liz nodded. "Doesn't reconcile. Angry and controlled at the same time."

"Or there were two of them."

Liz tilted her head. "One to stab and one to cover Monahan?"

"Maybe. Might explain the closed door and why he was at the side of his desk. Suppose one of them holds a weapon on

Monahan and orders him out from behind the desk? Other guy stabs him."

"If it's two we got a conspiracy."

"Maybe. Still doesn't feel right. I don't get why he was next to the desk, not behind it. First reaction to a threat is defensive, he'd stay behind the desk."

The room was quiet except for the shuffling of the young ME and the buzz of a machine.

"Anything else stand out?" Asked Vic, turning back to Freddy.

Freddy shrugged. "Yes. Brown stains on the clothing around the wounds at belt level. They prove those were the first stabs. But I cannot help much. The brown is oil, although there is metal dust mixed in it."

"Metal dust?"

Liz spoke up. "Like sawdust, just from cutting or grinding metal. You'd find it in a shop doing metal work. I was in my great uncle's shop when I was a kid. Those days you tooled replacement parts yourself because they actually fixed engines, they didn't just replace parts. You tool metal, you get dust."

"So we need to find a tool shop?"

They all fell silent again. Freddy glanced at the wall clock. "Okay. More questions? I must get back to work. I will email my preliminary report today. I do more analysis on the oil, but that will take more days, *und* tox screens are three weeks. But you will unlikely find anything there. Victim was very healthy. Except for being dead." He barked out a laugh again.

"Okay, thanks, Freddy." Vic turned to the door, hearing Liz say something to the Sunday ME.

Outside they dumped their surgical masks and gowns in the receptacle. As they walked the long hallway to the elevators Liz asked, "You solid on this two person thing?"

Vic shook his head. "Not yet. It's one way to make sense of it, but two people means a plan...and two people who hated the guy enough to kill him?"

"But it's a possibility."

"Yeah. Don't mention it to Crush, or he'll have us searching the city for two suspects."

"Them locked doors bother me."

"Someone had a key."

"Only one kind of person should have a key."

Vic nodded. "Yeah. Someone who works at Monahan's or is connected to the place." They were both quiet as they stepped into the elevator and started the rise to the first floor.

"The width of the blade is something. A knife that wide isn't common," said Vic thoughtfully. "That might mean a tool shop. Plus we need to know where everyone was until one a.m. that night. You had a good idea. We test Mary Monahan and Erica on their alibis, then we start on the companies they invested in. How many was that? Sixteen?"

The elevator doors opened and they stepped into the lobby.

"Can't wait," said Liz. "I'm guessing that you want to take the pissy Mrs. Monahan and I'll check Erica?"

"Well, sure, if you want to play it that way. I can force myself."

CHAPTER 6

Vic was just finishing checking another alibi when Liz placed a paper plate holding two pieces of pizza on his desk. She added a bottle of water. He glanced at his computer and realized groggily that it was almost one in the afternoon.

"Catch up on where we are?" she called to him as she settled into her chair.

Vic studied the pizza slices, but they didn't make him hungry.

"Should have bank records tomorrow, but we got to think this out," said Liz, biting into a slice of white pizza.

"Yeah. So here's something." Vic pushed one of the slices around the plate, hoping that it might trigger something inside him. "Mrs. Monahan's alibi checks out. But the guy she was drinking with at the country club? One of the owners of the Steelers. He confirmed Mary's alibi. Seemed excited about it. Or about drinking with her."

Liz broke a string of cheese connecting the pizza slice to her paper plate. "Lots of guys would be excited to spend a few hours drinking with her. Guys like being seen with good looking women."

Something about Liz's cube caught Vic's attention, but he couldn't sort out what it was. He heard himself saying, "You know that country club started in Allegheny City, on the north side, then moved to Sewickley Heights in the early 1900s?"

"Ain't you Mr. History."

"Good to know where things come from. How about Erica?"

"Date. She was at some bar with a guy and some friends. Checked out. You know what I was thinking? How come Monahan was even in his office that night? Maybe that explains the doors. Maybe he was planning to meet someone and left the front door open for them."

As she spoke, Vic studied the walls of Liz's cube. Something was missing, he just couldn't remember what. When she paused he said, "Nothing in his appointment book about a meeting, and I asked his secretary. She didn't know of any meeting."

"Still, a possibility. Explains how someone might have gotten in without a key."

Vic nodded and took a tentative bite of pizza. His stomach churned and turned hot. He sipped from his water bottle and watched Liz pop the last of her slice into her mouth. He didn't understand how she could do it. He swore her stomach was made of Kevlar.

"Hi, Vic."

Lorna stood beside his cube, her skirt so tight he didn't know how she could walk in it. Today her red hair was perfectly flipped at the ends.

"Lorna, does Crush want us?"

"No. But you have a phone call." She pointed to a blinking light on his telephone. "I just wanted to make sure you took it. Sewickley Heights police. They said it was important. I hope I did the right thing?" She pouted. Across the aisle Liz clapped a hand to her mouth to cover a smirk.

"Lorna, all you do is the right thing. Thanks for walking all the way back here to tell us."

"Anytime." She smiled happily and squeezed her arms against her sides so her breasts stood out even farther, then turned back up the aisle, walking slowly. Vic was drawn to the sight of her but caught himself and turned to the telephone, knowing Liz was watching him. He picked up the receiver. Two minutes later he dropped it into its cradle and stood up.

"Let's go," he called across the aisle.

Liz leaned back in her chair, one eyebrow arched, waiting.

"Monahan's house just got robbed. That was Sewickley Heights police, they wanted us to know. They said the place is a mess."

Liz rose and shrugged on her short leather jacket. "I thought you talked to Mary Monahan this morning?"

"I did." Vic opened his desk drawer, retrieved his Glock and holster from its resting place on the file folders and clipped it to his belt. He took his time pulling on his sport coat to let Liz get ahead of him. As she headed down the aisle he swung by her desk, seeing a short stack of folders and a pair of framed photographs tucked into a small space next to her computer. And then he knew why her cube looked different. When Liz arrived from New Orleans she brought her three year old boy with her. He was a seventh grader now. She had never discussed the boy's father and Vic had let that go, figuring she would tell him when she was ready. But, for as long as he could remember, two photographs of the boy hung on the wall of her cube, facing across the aisle toward Vic. She had moved them to her desktop. Vic wondered when. And why.

As he caught up to her he said, "Apparently after I talked to Monahan she went out to run some errands and the house got hit."

"She okay?"

"Yeah. Whoever it was had left by the time she got back."

"Well, ain't all that just goddamn coincidental."

As they exited into the parking lot, Vic decided that Liz had moved the photographs out of respect for his daughter. She didn't want to remind him of children. It was the kind of thing she would do.

Half an hour later they pulled to a stop on the gravel turnaround in front of the Monahan's house. A Sewickley Heights police cruiser was parked by the front door. A chunky, blond haired uniformed officer swung open the door before they were out of their car, as if he had been watching for them, and held it open. Inside, they shook hands all around.

"Chief called and said you guys were coming. Told me to stay until you clear the scene."

"Sure, thanks," said Liz, catching Vic's eye. Vic knew she was making a point about how the Sewickley Heights Chief had unloaded the investigation onto them. Vic nodded that he understood, glancing at the drawers of the hall table upended on the floor, gloves and scarves scattered around. In the living room Mary Monahan sat on the couch, the floor around her littered with chair cushions and side table drawers. She was sitting very straight and looking at the wall. Vic turned back to the Sewickley Heights officer. "How'd they get in?"

"Garage has an exterior door with a window. They broke that and opened the deadbolt. Came upstairs."

Vic crossed into the living room. "Mrs. Monahan," he said carefully. "The Sewickley Heights police called us. Would it be okay if we took a look around the house? We'd like to understand if this is related to what happened to your husband. Did you see anything missing?"

She didn't react for a moment, then slowly turned her face to him. "They left my jewelry."

"Did they go all through the house?"

She nodded. "I never turn on the alarm system during the day. Only at night. They were all over."

"I understand. Do you mind if Detective Timmons and I walk through the house and take a look?"

She settled troubled eyes on him. "Help yourself, Detective Lenoski. I would appreciate it. Detective Timmons," she said, shifting her gaze to Liz. "Thank you for coming. Please, feel free to look anywhere."

"We'll let you know if we find anything," called Liz.

"You heard it," Vic said as he returned to the uniformed officer. "Can you keep anyone from entering? I want to preserve the scene as long as we can."

"Yes, sir. Will do."

Vic led Liz down the hall to the first door on the right, which opened into a study. The room was large, with quarter-sawn oak wainscoting that matched the wood stain of the old fashioned executive desk. Cupboards and bookshelves lined one wall, the doors open and contents spilled onto the floor. Open books were scattered about, their pages splayed open.

Vic picked his way behind the desk, trying not to step on the contents of the files scattered on the chair and floor.

He and Liz glanced at one another and he knew they were thinking the same thing.

"Upstairs," he said quietly.

They took the wide staircase to the second floor. They found four bedrooms and a master suite that Vic guessed was larger than the ground floor of his house. The four bedrooms were largely untouched, just drawers and closet doors hanging open, but the master suite was as disrupted as the study. The mattress stood upright against a wall, clothes piled on the box spring with others crumpled on the floor in a large pile. The box seat built into the bay window was open and the contents strewn on the floor.

Vic tilted his head and said, "That's something."

"Other than a mess?"

"Woman's clothes are mostly still on hangers in the closet. The pile on the bed are men's clothes."

"And they went through that pile. Some of the pockets are inside out."

"Yeah. And you saw the other bedrooms. They hardly searched them. But they trashed this room and the study."

"The places where our Mr. Monahan spent most of his time."

"Exactly."

"Yeah. Looks more like a search."

Vic nodded. "If you're stealing stuff you don't go through every book. You grab the TV and laptop and run."

Liz disappeared inside the walk-in closet and called to him over the sounds of drawers being opened and closed. "And she's right, her jewelry is still here." She rejoined him in the bed-room. "Basement? Maybe he had a man cave?"

Vic nodded. "Yeah. Although this guy would have a man castle."

Downstairs, Mary Monahan hadn't moved. Vic asked if her husband had another room where he spent a lot of time. She nodded. "Wine cellar. You'll understand why when you see it. It's through there."

Vic and Liz trooped down the wide steps to the basement. The first room was large enough to hold ping pong and pool tables plus seating around a large screen TV. Vic headed toward the far side of the room and a pair of large wooden doors. He opened them to a blast of cool air and a room the size of his living room. Floor to ceiling wine racks covered most of the walls, except for a small bar area fronted by four stools. The center of the room was dominated by leather armchairs gathered around a low coffee table. Some cabinet doors behind the bar were hanging open, but otherwise there was no sign that someone had searched the room.

"Looks just like your basement, Vic. There's what, a few hundred bottles of wine here?"

Vic crossed behind the bar and looked inside the cup-boards. Wine glasses stood upside down in rows, undisturbed. Below the bar top was a workspace that included a sink and small dishwasher. The dishwasher door was open, the wine glasses inside untouched.

"They got back here but just looked."

"No TV in here," said Liz. "I thought guys always want a big TV."

"Quit profiling."

"Oh, right." She followed him back into the game room. "Just because it happens ninety-five percent of the time but isn't politically correct to talk about."

"Exactly. And it's right there anyway." He pointed at the TV before heading toward another door near the steps. Beyond that door was a four car garage with a single empty bay. "Crime scene guys towed his car from the office to impound so they can go through it, right? I thought I saw an email about that yesterday."

"Yeah. We got the email yesterday afternoon."

"Only thing the guys here couldn't search was his car." Vic's eyes lingered on a late model red Mercedes sedan. He guessed it was the one Mary Monaghan drove.

"Or his office downtown."

He shook his head. "So what the hell were they looking for?"

"You only getting to that now?"

"I wanted to see everything first."

"Maybe the guys he invested in know. We still have to talk to them. We could ask."

As they treaded the stairs back to the first floor, a thought flitted through Vic's mind. "You know what I don't remember from his office? His briefcase. Guy like that has to have one." They reached the front hall. The Sewickley Heights uniform was standing by the door holding a mug of coffee. Mrs. Monahan was no longer sitting on the couch. Some noises from the back of the house placed her in the kitchen, so Vic headed there.

He found her sitting at a counter that overlooked a huge slab of kitchen granite, a tree-filled back yard and distant, rolling hills of leafless trees. On a counter near the stainless steel refrigerator a silver machine no larger than a nuclear reactor puffed a cloud of milky steam and emptied a rivulet of coffee into a mug.

Mrs. Monahan kept her eyes to the window. "I've called Lisa and told her to bring help tomorrow when she comes to clean the house. Tomorrow is her cleaning day anyway."

"Okay. We were wondering, did your husband usually carry a briefcase?"

She shifted positions and turned her brown eyes on him. "Why are most of my things still here? The televisions, my laptop and jewelry. I don't understand that."

"Right. My guess is this isn't a robbery. Someone was

36

searching for something. You don't know what it might be, do you?"

She was quiet for a few moments and then slowly shook her head.

"And the briefcase?"

She nodded absently. "Yes. Square leather thing. Light brown."

"Okay, we need to find that. And do you have a safety deposit box? Somewhere your husband would keep important documents?"

"Yes, a safety deposit box. It's in both of our names. I still have the key, it's with my jewelry."

"I'm just throwing out options. But it would be helpful to have some idea of what they were looking for. If you think of anything, you'll let me know?"

She nodded, slid off the stool and rescued the mug from underneath the spout of the coffee maker. She held it close to her face with both hands and inhaled deeply through her nose.

"Would you like a mug, Lieutenant?" She lifted her eyes to him and again Vic felt a jolt of recognition.

"No thank you, ma'am, but I appreciate the offer."

"Don't call me ma'am. My name is Mary. I get the feeling we'll be seeing a lot of each other in the next few weeks. No need to act like strangers."

Vic found a smile crossing his lips. "I'm Vic. Thanks for the offer of coffee, but we have to go. We'll be in touch."

Liz was waiting for him at the front door and he nodded her to the car. As they drove along the driveway Liz looked at him.

"I got a text. Crush is into this. I guess Lorna told him about the call. Anyway, he insisted that our techs go through the crime scene."

"That's good. We don't usually fingerprint a robbery. You know, there's something about Mary Monahan that reminds me of someone."

"Maybe she looks different when she's wearing clothes?"

"It's the eyes," said Vic. "She's got someone's eyes."

"Sure. That's it. Damn people went through her house looking to get their eyes back."

CHAPTER 7

Mid-morning Thursday Vic and Liz crossed a shop floor, the air filled with the whine of tooling machines and the bright and unnerving smell of electricity. It was their number sixteen. The chief executive officers of the previous fifteen companies listed as Monahan investments had been little help. Each had an alibi and none could offer an explanation why anyone would want to search the Monahan home. Monahan's briefcase, when Liz found it on the list of items collected from Monahan's office, was as boring as the fifteen interviews. It contained only a few files on potential investment opportunities, a paperback book and his membership card to a gym. Vic's surge of excitement at finding the card ebbed away during his call to the gym, once he learned that members didn't have permanent lockers.

The message from all fifteen CEOs was the same: Monahan was universally hated. That morning, the arrival of Freddy's preliminary autopsy report had offered nothing new. However, as they crossed the floor of the tool shop, Vic remembered the metal dust Freddy had found on Monahan's clothing around the first few stab wounds.

A secretary showed them into the office of Chris Leaner, CEO of PipeMine. Vic took in the jumble of machine parts, electrical components and files. The office smelled of oil. Blueprints covered the walls. Leaner himself was a slight man with black slicked-back hair and dark nervous eyes. As they started the interview, Vic saw how Leaner's hands constantly moved. He straightened desk files, then worried the components on a small motherboard before choosing to wind and unwind electrical wire around his palm.

"How about Monahan personally?" asked Vic, once Leaner provided his alibi for the night of the murder.

Leaner settled back into his cracked leather chair, the wire going round and round.

"Well, the guy was an asshole, but he was smart. Take our company. You know those bullet shaped things gas and oil companies run through their pipelines to clean them?"

"No." It was Liz who spoke, but Vic didn't know either.

"Okay, they're called pigs. They run inside the pipes and check for leaks or metal stress, clean them, whatever you need. Sewer lines need robots because they don't get pushed by the flow of whatever is inside the pipe. We make both kinds. But the difference with our pigs and bots is we've collated all the data we've found as we go through the pipes. We have industry baselines on the kinds and levels of gasses you should expect in a pipe, flow speed, pipe strength, all sorts of crap. I mean any asshole can build a bot that checks for metal fatigue or cleans the pipe. Ours also tell you what isn't there, which could mean a leak, or if you have a concentration of gasses, which means a blockage, or how far off normal your pipe is stressed. You get that? No one else does that. They just look at each pipe as a single unit. Monahan got it right away. He took the lead on our investment and put in two million. That put us over the hump. Yeah, he pretty much raped us when it came to the size of the stake he took in our business, but his lead brought in five million from other investors and put our only competitor out of business. So who cares if he was an asshole?"

Liz shifted in her chair. "Monahan's ownership stake in your company is as big as yours. That doesn't concern you?"

"Were you listening?" Vic's mind was drifting as Leaner spoke, but the retort snapped him back. He watched Leaner lean forward and glare at Liz. "Yeah, the guy's a dick. But I wouldn't be sitting here today if it wasn't for him. Cost of doing business.

So I watch him closely and pick other people to drink with."

"And you met with him regularly?" Vic asked.

"Not that much. His stake gave him a board seat, so I saw him at board meetings. I figure they'll assign someone else now but I guess his lawyers are still arguing about that. I heard there was something screwy about his will, not that I give a shit. His investment did its job and honestly I'm happier dealing with someone else on our board."

Liz leaned forward. "And you met with him no other times?"

Leaner waved his hand in dismissal. "Only if I saw him out someplace."

"What did you talk about when you met?" asked Vic.

"Sales pipeline. Cash flow. R&D. That kind of thing."

They fell silent. On the shop floor a machine whined and something thumped heavily several times.

"Okay," said Vic. "What did you hear about the will?" He felt run out, as if he was thinking about the murder the wrong way.

Leaner settled his gaze on him. "I heard his first wife is pissed."

"Where did you hear that?"

"I had lunch with my lawyer yesterday. He just mentioned it in passing. Those guys gossip more than women. I could care less."

Ten minutes later Vic and Liz sat in the parked car in silence.

"Well, he's an asshole," said Liz finally. "But I got a bad feeling about this. Everybody's alibis are tight. Erica Lauder, the wife, every one of the executives we talked to. Even his damn first wife, Clair Standish. Nothing's panning out."

Vic watched the traffic passing the side window. "Yep." He rubbed his face. "That thing Leaner said is weird. How his bots find things that aren't there?"

"I'm more interested in the will. Monahan's lawyer still hasn't sent us a copy. Or the prenup."

"Yeah. When I called Mary Monahan yesterday to see if she'd discovered anything had been stolen, she told me the lawyer for Clair Standish called and asked when she planned to move out. She was pissed about it. The lawyer reminded Mary the house is in a trust for Monahan's kids."

"Aren't you two getting friendly. You guys on first name basis now?"

Vic watched traffic speeding by. "But doesn't that seem weird to you? Clair Standish's lawyer calling up? No way the will is close to being executed. We need to see the will and pre-nup as soon as we can."

"Well, I'll tell you what *is* there with your Mrs. Monahan. Her looks. Women like that always land on their feet. Sounds like she's already got you wrapped around her finger. But focus. We got nothing."

Vic started the car. "Maybe go back to the unlocked doors. You set up an interview with the janitor who cleans the place? Maybe he knows how the doors work."

"Not yet. Called the service but they haven't reached him yet. Should be tomorrow. How about the banking records? Anything show up there?"

Vic checked his side mirror, waiting for a break in traffic. "Nothing at all," he answered, and pulled into traffic.

CHAPTER 8

That night Vic sat in his living room in the only armchair his wife, Anne, had left him. He wondered what she was doing. Six months earlier he had arrived home to a covered dinner plate and a note explaining how to warm it in the microwave. At the bottom of the note, almost as an afterthought, was an apologetic explanation that she was back living with her mother and sister. Vic remembered reading the note and nodding to himself, unsurprised and numb, before he opened a fresh bottle, drank off two thirds and stumbled to bed.

He had tried to convince her to return, but each time the lack of conviction in his voice gave him away. If he couldn't convince himself that he wanted her back, he knew she heard it also. She knew him too well.

He sipped a whiskey, watching the hockey game. He'd lost count of how many whiskeys. Four? He drifted in and out of sleep, feeling as if he was being drawn along a swollen river, floundering, Leaner's words swirling around him. Suddenly Dannie's face bobbed in front of him, blurred and featureless. He jerked awake and stumbled to the framed photograph on the windowsill. He stared at Dannie's face, tracing it with his fingertips. He had placed the photograph there a year after her disappearance, the same night his wife moved back to her mother's. He'd liked the idea of his daughter watching over him. Now he felt like the photograph was there to remind him of something.

He turned off the television and drifted into the kitchen. Before he could stop himself he was down the stairs and, careful not to look toward the far end of the basement, crossed into the garage.

Ten minutes later he parked the car on a residential street, a block uphill from a hulking red brick house similar to the others lining both sides of the street. Yellow light streamed through the ground floor windows across a concrete porch and onto a tiny lawn. He cut the engine. It was the house Dannie was headed to when she disappeared, her friend Jennie's house. He waited, watching the sidewalk and his mirrors in rotation, looking for anyone who might appear. A light rain began to fall, tapping on the roof. In time the downstairs lights switched off and a single light gleamed upstairs. Half an hour later that also clicked to black. His mouth was dry and he wished he had something to drink. Usually he did. He moved his eyes from the sidewalk to his mirrors to the opposite sidewalk.

No one left the house. No one walked by. No teenage girl with blonde hair.

The chill of the night sobered him. His mind slid to how odd it was, the house dark and still, the wet slate roof gleaming under the streetlights. He could see every detail of the house front. The dull red brick, the heavy concrete windowsills, the white frames of the storm windows. The facts of the house were there, but he saw no sign of the life inside, of Dannie's friend and her parents. But they were there. The facts of the outside of the house couldn't distract from that. His mind tacked again and he thought of Monahan's bank records and something tugged at him. Slowly, he turned his keys and started the car.

At his desk the next morning he printed out Monahan's bank records, and taking a ruler, tracked each line of the spreadsheet. In five minutes he realized what was living inside the numbers, sleeping, what he'd missed when he just looked at the fact of the amounts.

"I thought you did that already," said Liz, looking over his shoulder. The coolness of the morning clung to her. She still wore her leather jacket, her large handbag over her shoulder.

"What Leaner said yesterday, about finding things that

aren't there? First time through I was looking at the dollar amounts, looking for patterns and odd transactions. I should have looked for what wasn't there." He sat back and tapped the ruler against his thigh. "You ever get cash out of an ATM?"

Liz crossed to her desk, slid out of her jacket and sat down in a single motion. "Sure."

"Yeah, well, guess what? Monahan stopped taking money out two years ago. No withdrawals for two years."

"Maybe he used checks?"

"No checks written just for cash."

"So his wife took out the cash and gave it to him?"

"The way he kept her away from his money?" He checked his notes and dialed the Monahan home. Mary Monahan answered on the fourth ring, a burr in her voice. He hit the speaker button and Liz stepped across the aisle. He announced himself and Liz, then asked, "Mrs. Monahan, it appears your husband made no ATM withdrawals in the last two years. Did he use cash at all?"

"Mmmm," she breathed, then said, "he started to use just cash a while back. Hundreds. He said he didn't like credit cards."

"Did you withdraw money for him?"

She laughed. "Really, Detective Lenoski, do you think I had access to his checking accounts? He gave me a cash allowance and paid my credit card bills."

Vic and Liz exchanged glances. Vic saw a smile flit across Liz's lips.

"Okay, do you mind if we come out to your house this morning? We'd like to go through it again."

"It's still a mess. I cleaned up the bedroom but left everything else for Lisa. Anyway, I want to start boxing things up. I've decided to move out."

"I understand. But we think that whoever went through your house was looking for something. Maybe it was your husband's cash. Knowing this gives a better idea where to look."

"Feel free, Vic. According to the will anything inside the house is mine, so I would appreciate it if you found some cash here."

"Well, I'm not making any promises."

He hung up and looked at Liz. She stared back.

"Vic, you got the look. I been missing that look for a while."

"Oh yeah. Something smells."

"Check his office?"

"Then his house."

CHAPTER 9

V ic peeled back the crime scene tape blocking the door to Monahan's office and stepped inside, his shoes settling into the thick carpet. The tang of industrial cleaners came to him, and when he glanced at the spot where they had found the body, it appeared a lighter shade of tan than the rest of the carpet. From the offices came the low murmur of voices and the distant soft whoosh of a copier. They divided the office between them and searched carefully, but fifteen minutes later they had found no cash hidden anywhere. They stood in the center of the room, Vic staring at the Allegheny River outside. The water was still a muddy brown. The level had dropped and the river looked reduced and tired. It matched how emptied out he felt.

"Lotta nothing," said Liz.

"Yeah." He turned and scanned the room, following the shelves. A current tugged at him. "We're missing something."

"What do you mean?"

Vic crossed to the bookshelves. "He had some prototype here. Looked like a big bullet with treads on the side. It's missing."

"Room's off limits. Somebody took it?"

"Maybe. Check the office inventory list the CS guys put together. But I saw it. It was definitely here. We need to know where it went, even if that means interviewing everyone in the office. And whoever cleaned the damn carpet."

^^^

At the Monahan's a plump elderly woman answered the door, a dust rag balled in her right hand and an unused garbage bag trailing from the back pocket of her jeans. She looked them up and down and opened the door wider. Mary Monahan stood in the center of the living room, wearing skinny jeans and an oversized sweater that hung off one shoulder.

"Mrs. Monahan," Vic called to her, thinking that her clothes made her look like a college student.

She studied him. "You know, Detective Lenoski, it turns out that having someone empty all your drawers and cupboards onto the floor is a huge help. I can see what I have and what I want to take with me."

"Do you mind if we take a look around?"

She waved her hand vaguely. "Help yourselves." She looked at Liz. "Good to see you again, Detective Timmons." She turned back to Vic. "And remember, I get to keep anything that's in the house. So find all the cash you can." She gave him a smile, the first genuine one he had seen from her.

"I can't promise anything, Mrs. Monahan." He gestured to Liz and as they walked down the hall toward the office Liz spoke into his ear.

"I told you she's the type who lands on her feet."

In the study they surveyed the barren cupboards and bookshelves. Finally Vic said, "I'll take the desk," and stood the office chair upright before sitting down.

"I guess bookshelves for me, then."

Fifteen minutes later their search for a safe or hidden compartment had come up empty.

"You sure this is worth the time?" asked Liz.

"Money always takes you somewhere. Anyway, you got any better leads right now?"

Liz shrugged, pulled out her phone and swiped through a few screens. "We got the cleaning service. They tracked down the janitor who worked Saturday night. We got that."

"Set something up for tomorrow. Him or her?"

"Him."

"Maybe when he gets to the building to start work. We can meet him there."

Liz tapped at her screen. Vic looked around the office again. His mind checked off the things he saw: books, files, office supplies. He thought about what else people kept in their offices. Photographs. On the floor was a framed picture of two small children, another with Mary Monahan on a beach in a bikini. When he lifted it from the floor he thought her smile was forced and he saw a distance in her eyes.

"Good to go," said Liz. "Upstairs?"

He nodded and followed her. Twenty minutes later, finding nothing, they trooped through the basement to the wine cellar. Vic pulled open the door to the suck of cool air.

"Why so freaking cold?" asked Liz.

"So the wine keeps. It's set to fifty-five degrees."

Vic made a slow circle around the perimeter of the room, staring at the wine racks. Liz crossed to the bar and searched behind it. Once in a while Vic pulled out a bottle and studied the label, but none of them meant anything to him. He and Liz met at the bar.

"Maybe he kept the money in his car?"

Vic slowly shook his head. "No, he'd keep it closer. He was that kind of guy. He took scalps and trophies. This house, his wife. Did you notice how in all of the photographs of her she's wearing something that shows off her body? And those are the only photographs in the whole house, apart from a few of his kids. None from their wedding, or Mary Monahan's family, just her in a bikini, a tight dress, or short shorts. And that whole wall of his office was trophies. Deals he made, important people he hung out with. If he has cash he'd look at it the same way. It's a trophy and he'd keep it close."

He scanned the room. On the facing wall, about halfway up the floor-to-ceiling wine rack, sat a built-in cupboard about two feet wide and a foot high. From opening it earlier he knew it contained a shelf littered with corkscrews and bottle stoppers. But now he noticed that the first nine wine bottles directly on the right of the bottom section of the cupboard were smaller than the other bottles. He crossed to them and pulled one out. It was a half-bottle, as were the others. He stuck his hand inside the bottle's cubbyhole and quickly hit the back wall. A full-sized bottle of wine wouldn't fit without sticking halfway out.

He slid open the door to the cupboard and stared at the corkscrew and stoppers on the top shelf, then glanced at the bottom shelf. There was nothing there. Carefully, he placed his hand into the cupboard and against the wood of the back wall, below the shelf. Working through the mechanics of it in his head, he pushed the back wall toward the shorter cubbies and half-bottles.

The wood slid.

But only the section below the shelf. It revealed a space as wide as the cupboard and perhaps eight inches high and deep. Stacked in the space were bank envelopes and what appeared to be legal documents.

"What the hell," said Liz, stepping next to him.

"Photos," he said quickly. He stepped back and waited while Liz snapped photographs on her cell phone. "Go get some evidence bags and Mary Monahan." He felt his pockets, found a latex glove and worked it over his hand. Liz disappeared though the door. Carefully, he lifted the top bank envelope on the pile, cupped the edges and looked inside. It was filled with hundred dollar bills. He replaced it and waited. Less than a minute later Mary Monahan entered. She walked over and stared at the cubbyhole and its contents.

"No touching." Vic looked at her. "Did you know this was here?"

"No idea." A crease developed on her forehead and she crossed her arms.

"I bet your intruders were looking for this. The envelopes have cash in them and those are legal documents."

"This all belongs to me. It's inside the house."

"No argument, but it's also evidence. We'll document everything in front of you."

Liz arrived with a handful of evidence bags.

Liz gave Vic another glove and he removed the envelopes and spread them on the coffee table, waiting as Liz photographed each step. Carefully, he and Liz removed the cash in each envelope, counted it, and returned it to the envelope.

When they finished Liz said, "Ten thousand in hundred dollar bills in each envelope."

Vic stared at the coffee table. "I count eighteen envelopes."

"Eighteen, but one only has two grand in it. So, one hundred seventy two thousand all in, first count."

Vic met Liz's gaze. "Explains why he didn't need to take money out of an ATM." He knew they were thinking along the same lines, but with Mary Monahan present he didn't want to speculate. Instead, he picked up the legal documents.

"Your prenup and your husband's will."

She reached for them and he moved them away from her. "You understand why you can't touch these, right?"

Her eyes flashed angrily. "Of course I do. So you can check whether I've touched them already. But I told you I haven't."

Vic unfolded the prenup and scanned it, taking in the crossed out words, handwritten notations and initials next to the handwriting. He leafed through the will and saw the same kind of changes.

"Mrs. Monahan, can I ask you a question?"

"Yes." Her voice was flat and controlled, but her arms were tightly crossed under her breasts as if she was holding herself together.

"We were interviewing one of your husband's clients yesterday. He mentioned there might be problems with your husband's will. Do you know anything about that?"

"No. As I told you, I just know that Drake's first wife called my lawyer and wanted to know when I was moving out, because her copy of the will said she got the house. My lawyer told me to sit tight until all of this is worked out. But I'm leaving as soon as I can. Between Drake's death and someone breaking in I don't want to be here. She can have it."

"Okay. We'll process these documents and deliver them to your lawyer. But your husband wanted some changes made."

"What changes?" Her large eyes bored into him.

"I think that's up to a lawyer to explain." From the corner of his eye he saw Liz scoop the cash envelopes into an evidence bag. He met Mary Monahan's gaze and made a note to soften his tone. It surprised him, and he realized he was starting to like her. "We're not lawyers, Mrs. Monahan. But we will get these to your lawyer as soon as they're processed."

Her look hardened. "Make damn sure you do. I'll call my lawyer and tell him to expect them. And I wrote down how much money is in those envelopes, so don't even think about it, *Detective* Lenoski."

Vic sat back on his heels, watching how she stared at the will and prenup in their separate evidence bags.

Then something flickered through her, he could feel it. She focused on him again, her eyes steady. "I'm sorry, Detective. I have no reason to suggest you would steal that money. My comment was too quick. This shook me, that's all."

Vic nodded, aware of how intently Liz was staring at her.

CHAPTER 10

A s Vic guided the car down the driveway, Liz broke the silence. "She's an interesting one, your Mrs. Monahan. She's got a lot going on."

"Yeah. And did you notice? She was more interested in the will and prenup than the money."

"That's where the real money is. But she also never asked where the cash came from."

"The whole idea might be too new to her. Makes me believe that she didn't know about the hiding place. But I want to see what fingerprints we find." As he turned onto the main road a thought rose to him. "You know, there's one group of people we haven't interviewed."

"Who's that?"

"People who pitched Monahan but didn't get his investment money."

"But there's gotta be hundreds of them. We saw files on two of them in his briefcase."

"No, I'm thinking the ones that got far enough to pitch him personally. Remember Erica, the one who found the body? She said she recommended five companies, but he only took on four. That's one right there. People who get that close to funding then get rejected have to be pissed."

"Have to be pretty pissed to kill someone over it."

"Tell me you haven't seen people killed for a hell of a lot less."

"Jayvon White."

"Jayvon White."

They fell silent. The Jayvon White call was from five years earlier, not long after he and Liz were partnered together. Deep August, midnight on the tail of two weeks so hot that, as Vic crossed the street to the narrow front steps of a row house awash in the blue and red lights of emergency vehicles, he could feel the asphalt through his shoes. Inside, in a tiny kitchen, they found Jayvon slumped over a narrow red Formica kitchen table with the side of his face in a plate of food. It took Vic a moment to realize the table was actually white and the red was from blood that had leaked out of a slash in his neck, then down the table legs and across the floor. The handle of a paring knife stuck out of one eye. The man's wife was sitting handcuffed on a couch that dominated the living room. When Liz asked her what happened, Jayvon's wife boiled it down for her.

"He added salt to his dinner. Then hot sauce. I season my dinners right. That shit is no good. Can't buy me no air conditioner, I been asking for years, but he salt my food. It's an insult. So I stabbed him in the neck. He puts his ugly face in his plate. I ain't gonna waste my meal. It's cooked right. I ate and then called 911. While I'm waiting I decide I don't like the way he's lookin' at me. Just staring at me. So I done stabbed his eye, too."

Vic drew up to a stop sign on the edge of Sewickley village. He had to shake off the memory. The senselessness of it. "Maybe give Erica a call. See if she can put a list of names together?"

"Sure, but how does that fit with the money?"

"No idea. But it'll take a few days to get fingerprint results. Gives us something to be doing when Crush asks."

"And it gets after something that ain't there."

He glanced at Liz, surprised she made the statement. "Yeah. Funny how things are working out that way."

Liz swiped her cell phone, tapped in Erica Lauder's number, put the phone on speaker and held it close so he could speak. When she answered, Vic identified himself and said, "I want to follow up on something. You said you recommended five companies but Monahan only accepted four. Did that fifth company pitch you guys? We'd like a list of companies from the past year that pitched Monahan but were turned down. With contact names and numbers."

"Sure. The company we didn't fund was called PipeSafe. Great mechanics. CEO was David Gaspare. He's out of business now. Mr. Monahan picked PipeSafe's competitor, I never understood why."

"What was the competitor company?"

"PipeMine."

"Chris Leaner is their CEO, right? We talked to him."

"That's him. He gives me the creeps. I can text you Gaspare's information, I still have it. The other list will take some time. Is tomorrow okay?"

"That'll work. Thanks. My email is on the card I left with you."

"I still have it."

Liz thumbed the phone call off. "Okay, Vic. Out with it. What were the changes to the will and prenup?"

Vic glanced at her as they pulled up at a red light. To the right was a shabby white side door that led up some stairs to the office of the private investigator, Levon Grace. He checked the second story windows as if Levon might be looking down on him.

"Yeah. It does make things interesting. But I don't know if it will hold up."

"Cut the crap, Vic, what were the changes?"

"I guess Mr. Monahan was starting to like his new trophy wife. From what I saw he changed the prenup and will so she would inherit his business. Everything else went to the kids, the house to the first wife. But the business went to her."

"Jesus. The goose that lays the golden eggs."

"Yeah. But that means we need to figure out if our Mary Monahan was lying to us on Sunday. She said she got nothing when her husband died but fifty grand. Now it isn't looking that way. Need to figure that one out as well."

"Which is why you didn't want her touching the documents. If her fingerprints aren't on them, chances are better she didn't know about it."

"Yeah. It's not 100%, but it might help us find out."

"Okay. I like this."

They fell silent, waiting for the light to turn green. Vic's eyes drifted to the side door again. He knew Levon had grown up in Sewickley. That might be helpful, he just didn't know how. His fingers thrummed the steering wheel.

Liz shifted positions in the seat. "And here I was yesterday worrying we didn't have many leads."

As if in answer, Vic's cell phone dinged a new text message.

"If that's Erica with Gaspare's address, how about we go there in the morning?"

"Yeah." Vic shifted his left leg. "Either crush or mush." He stared straight ahead, aware of Liz's quick glance toward him. He wasn't sure why those words came out. But he knew where he had first heard them: from Levon Grace, whose office door was just a few feet to his right.

"Feast or famine, you mean?"

"Yeah. Either we got too many leads to follow, or none. Just a bunch of mush."

CHAPTER 11

V ic slurped the last of his whiskey, worked the glass into the sink among the dishes and glasses from the prior few days, opened the narrow door to the basement and, holding tight to the rail, clambered down the stairs.

He stopped at the bottom of the stairs, swaying, blinked slowly and waited for his head to clear. He pivoted and looked the length of the basement, toward the washer and dryer, his eyes drawn to the right, to the far corner, where a boxing heavy bag hung from the floor joists above, oddly weightless for something so large. It was suspended in the shadows, as black as a memory. He shuffled across the floor, his eyes on the tall white lace-up boxing shoes beneath. When he reached the bag he gently pushed it with his fingertips. It swung slow and heavy, the chain creaking against the hook, like an animal that didn't want to be wakened. It thudded back against his fingertips, compressing the joints of his fingers and pushing against his wrist. He moved his hand away, watching it sway, until the momentum was exhausted. He couldn't remember the last time he worked out on it. He started to turn but stopped, and finally backed away from the bag, watching it, until he reached the door to the garage. Only then did he turn and open the door.

His car waited, gleaming in the light. He stared at it, knowing he shouldn't drive, but launched himself into the narrow space between the cinderblock wall and the car and squeezed into the driver's seat.

A minute later he backed down the driveway, checked

that the garage door was closing and headed along the street. A block farther on and he thought to check his headlights. He flicked the switch and the road was suddenly easier to see.

He let the car drive him, following the back streets, working his way from his house through a string of Pittsburgh neighborhoods. Twenty minutes later he drifted his car to a stop in front of a large Victorian house. Light gleamed through the front window. He clambered out and walked up the front path, his mouth sour and dry. He rang the doorbell.

His wife, Anne, answered the door. She wore jeans and a cotton turtleneck, a faded green cardigan over her shoulders. She'd changed her hair, he thought to himself.

"Vic," she said softly. "What do you want?"

"Say hello." He felt himself sway.

"Should you be driving?"

"Yeah. Not too bad. Didjew do something with your hair?"

She stared at him, her blue eyes pale in the porch light. "I told you to call before you come over."

"Just wanted to say hey."

"Showing up three-quarters drunk isn't the way you do that."

The door pushed wider and Anne's sister stood in the hallway, looking at him, her face tight with disapproval. "You don't come over here unless we ask you to," she said sharply.

Vic watched his wife's face, looking for something and only finding deeper lines on her forehead than he remembered. She lowered her head and stared at his feet.

"We gotta find a way," he said.

Anne raised her head and looked directly at him, her eyes watery. "This isn't it, Vic. You know that. You can't just arrive like nothing happened every time you get lonely."

"But the date is coming up. We gotta get organized. Visit the grave."

A keening sound cut between them, falling to a guttural sob, as Anne's chin dropped to her chest. Vic stepped back, staring at her.

Anne's sister pushed between them, backing Anne away from the doorway. "You need to leave. If you don't leave right now, I'm calling the cops."

"I am the cops," he said, trying to understand what just happened, surprised at how the tone of his own voice sounded so pleading.

"And a damn crappy one. You couldn't even find your own daughter."

From somewhere inside anger flickered. He locked eyes with her, his dislike for her pouring out, his brain registering her square hard face and her haircut that looked like a helmet. She edged back in response to whatever she saw in his eyes, bumping Anne farther back into the house.

"You have no idea what you're talking about," Vic heard himself say, surprised at how well he enunciated every word.

"I know everything I need to. You couldn't even bring yourself to look for your own daughter. My sister correctly left you. Now you'll be hearing from our lawyer." Her head was tilted up to speak to his face but she still managed to look down her nose at him. Vic saw the glitter of hatred in her eyes. He tried to find his wife over her shoulder but all he saw was the sweep of her hair over the top of her head. She was still looking at the floor.

He faced Anne's sister again. "How is it your sister is so kind and you're such an asshole?"

"What did you call me?"

"I didn't call you anything. I said what you are. I came to talk to my wife. Not you."

"And she's not talking to you."

"Vic," said Anne from behind her sister, her voice hollow and distant. "It's not a grave. It's a memorial. Dannie isn't there. And we don't need to visit it together. It's just a memorial."

As he opened his mouth to reply the door slammed shut an inch from his nose. He breathed slowly, waiting for it to re-open, knowing it wouldn't. Finally he turned away and walked carefully back to the car. The night was cool. It started to drizzle. He climbed behind the steering wheel and looked back at the house. The light was out in the front room, but Vic was sure he could see his wife standing in the dark, arms folded tightly, staring through the window, watching him.

He jammed the key into the ignition and sucked in a breath. He listened to the engine turn over, closed his eyes and opened them. He had never felt so empty.

Slowly, he guided the car from the curb, knowing that Anne's sister might have called the police to report him for drunk driving. He let the car gather speed so he would be out of the neighborhood by the time they arrived. He knew they wouldn't cite him, but it would be an ugly twenty minutes.

As he drove, he thought about Anne's sister, and how she had married a short, skinny man who worked fifteen years at a local factory before being taken by an unexpected heart attack.

"Happiest day of his life," he said to the windshield. "He was probably praying for it to happen. Maybe I need to investigate that."

He was sure it was the sister who convinced Anne to move back home, who now encouraged her to start divorce proceedings. She was that kind. If she wasn't happy then no one around her could be happy either. He drove, working his tongue around his mouth, trying to moisten away the sour taste. His anger sobered him and his thinking widened. He wondered if Drake Monahan's first wife, Clair Standish, was the same way. If she held a grudge about her divorce, or had somehow heard about the changes to the will. That would explain why she wanted to move quickly and get the new Mrs. Monahan out of the house. Close out the estate while it all still belonged to her. He stopped at a GetGo and bought a bottle of water. Back in the car he drove carefully, focused on the traffic, his mind still orbiting around Clair Standish.

If she knew about the changes to the will and prenup, she had motive.

"Never get between a woman and her kids," he said to the

windshield. "Or her damn sister." He swilled water out of the bottle, lowered the window and spit it out, but the bad taste wouldn't leave his mouth.

CHAPTER 12

The next morning Vic and Liz tracked down the address Erica had given them. David Gaspare's house sat at the end of a narrow street on the South Side slopes, an older area of narrow upright frame houses clinging to a hillside above the Monongahela River. In the distance Pittsburgh's skyscrapers huddled under a sky as hard and dull as marble. They sat in the car staring at the house's faded and peeling paint. Liz's cell phone beeped and she checked the screen.

"Interesting," she said finally.

Vic waited, his mouth sour, joints heavy and dull, his stomach hot. He felt displaced, oddly fractured, and knew it wouldn't go away until he'd had a good night's sleep.

"They started processing the fingerprints on the cash envelopes. Couple of people so far. Monahan, our vic, is one, yeah, but the other one."

"So?"

"That damn ferret of a guy we interviewed yesterday. Chris Leaner. The CEO of PipeMine."

Vic tapped his fingers on the wheel. "How come his fingerprints were in the system?"

Liz swiped the screen and kept reading.

"Turns out our CEO Leaner has a couple of assault charges. Plea deal on one and the other was dropped." She fell silent, a furrow on her forehead. "Guess who dropped the charges?"

Vic was quiet for a moment, waiting for his brain to catch and fire, but he sensed something coming together. "Wouldn't be the CEO of PipeSafe, would it? David Gaspare?" He nodded toward the house. "The guy who pitched Monahan and lost?"

"The very same. Looks like Leaner worked for Gaspare, according to the charge sheet."

"Let's find out."

They got out of the car and approached a concrete front porch cracked and pitted by rain and hard winters. Two metal porch chairs near the front door were covered with rust spots. Vic knocked, trying to ignore how much the short walk had worn him out. As they waited he studied two nearby pots. Each contained the brown and brittle remains of a dead plant. The wooden handle of a trowel stuck out of the dirt of the larger one.

The man who answered was six feet tall with unruly black hair and a five day growth of beard. His grey sweatpants and blue t-shirt were spotted with stains, his eyes bloodshot and cautious.

"Mr. Gaspare? I'm Detective Vic Lenoski from the Pittsburgh Bureau of Police. This is my partner, Detective Timmons. We'd like to talk to you about Drake Monahan."

Gaspare nodded and stood aside so they could enter. They stepped into a living room that looked like it was decorated, and last dusted, sometime in the 1950s. Vic smelled burnt toast and his stomach flipped. He sucked in a breath to control it.

"Through here." Gaspare led them under an archway into a dining room repurposed into an office. Only the table remained, loaded with a jumble of electronic circuit boards, wires, and pieces of machined metal, as well as two boxy machines with small screens that Vic guessed were for testing electronic circuits. There were no chairs so they all stood.

Gaspare folded his arms across his chest. "I heard about Monahan. Got what he deserved."

Vic let the comment sit for a moment, then said, "Yeah. About that. I understand you pitched Monahan to invest in your business, but you lost out to PipeMine."

"Did you guys know that PipeMine is my technology? Leaner stole it."

Liz cut in. "Is that why you guys got in a fight?"

Gaspare barked out a laugh that shook his body. "Fight? I caught him leaving one day with one of my prototypes. I confronted him and he hit me with his briefcase and told me to F off. No big deal, I got the prototype back. But I fired him. Three weeks later I figure out he also stole blueprints and an earlier prototype. By then he was looking for investors, and I decided that if he had an assault rap then investors would stay away from him. So I tell the cops but he turns it back on me and says that I attacked him, so it's my word against his. I didn't have the money or time to go after him on that or the blueprints and prototype. I had to drop the charges."

Liz shifted on her feet. "So you must have been pretty angry when Monahan chose Leaner over you."

Gaspare squared his shoulders. "Damn right I was. I still am. I invented the technology and came up with the whole idea of how to develop an industry baseline to help with diagnostics. When I first told Leaner about the idea he laughed at me. Which is my point. The guy is as creative as a rock, except in figuring out how to steal other people's ideas. I still don't know how he stayed in business for the year before Monahan invested in him. But once he had Monahan on board he went to my customers, told them he really invented the baseline idea and undercut me on price. I lasted about six months after that."

"And last Saturday night? Where were you? Between eight and one?"

"Here."

"Anyone see you?"

He smiled with his large teeth, but didn't seem to find anything funny. "Look, my mother died ten years ago. Left me this house. This is my office now."

"Did you talk to anyone?"

"Only the god damned bot I'm working on right now."

"Nothing else?"

"I'll show you." He uncovered a laptop among the jumble on the table, lifted the top, tapped on the keyboard and swiveled the screen around so they could see a video. Gaspare's voice narrated as a rectangular box with large side treads negotiated along PVC pipe that was cut in half lengthwise, so the camera could follow the robots' movement inside the pipe. He paused the video.

"I worked on this Saturday night. You can hear my voice." He pointed at the screen. "Time stamp is there. Took me seven hours of shooting and editing to make the demo. If you check the file history you'll see that. Your tech guys can sort it."

Liz nodded at the screen, her eyes locked on the small robot as it maneuvered along the pipe. "That's crazy. What does it do?"

"Pretty much anything. There's whisk attachments so it can clean the inside of a pipe, and video in case you have blockages. Ultrasonics to measure pipe stresses. I was the one who added sensors to measure gas levels. He had some stupid idea about adding sound. For what? It had no purpose."

Vic frowned. "The monitors are at the front, behind that black plastic bubble?"

"Yeah."

"Okay." Vic glanced at Liz, who just shrugged. He wondered if she had picked up how much the robot looked like the one missing from Monahan's office.

"Anything else you want to know?" Gaspare glanced from one to the other.

bag and dropped it inside, then wrote the details on the outside.

Vic glanced around the room, taking in the clutter of electronics and machine parts. "I'm good for now. But could we get a copy of the video? I'd like to have our tech guys confirm the file was made when you said it was. So we can eliminate you as a suspect."

"Sure."

Gaspare pushed some equipment about on the table and found a flash drive, which he inserted into the laptop. A few more clicks as he opened and closed windows, then he extracted the flash drive and held it out. Liz opened an evidence

"You shot the video in this room?" he asked. The room looked different than the background in the video.

"Downstairs. I set it up like a studio. I got a digital camera and some lights down there."

"Could we see it?"

Gaspare stared at him, his eyes darkening. Vic waited, his jaw tight. He hit this moment in every interview, the moment when the person being interviewed realized that, as a cop, Vic wasn't going to believe anything he was told without proof. People reacted differently to that moment. Some got huffy or angry, others acquiesced, some were unconcerned. He watched Gaspare bite back a comment. When he spoke his tone was sharp.

"I'll show you."

Gaspare led them under an archway into the kitchen and opened a narrow door just past the arch. He waved toward a flight of steps.

"After you," said Vic.

Gaspare's face tightened again but he headed down the stairs. Vic followed. The basement was a single room with a washer and dryer at the bottom of the steps and the furnace and hot water heater centered on the longer side wall of the house. At the far end of the basement the entire end wall was covered with white board. In front was the warren of half pipes Vic had seen in the video as well as two standing lights. To one side, on a low table, sat three robots that looked similar to the one from Monahan's office.

"Satisfied?" asked Gaspare, and there was no mistaking the sarcastic edge in his voice.

Vic turned and looked at him. "Just like to be thorough," he said evenly. He saw Liz studying the setup. Vic turned for the stairs. "That's very helpful," he said to Gaspare, holding his eyes so Gaspare would follow his movements. "We really appreciate it when people we interview are cooperative." Out of his peripheral vision he saw Liz snap a quick picture of the video studio set-up with her cell phone.

"Yeah, we appreciate it," echoed Liz. The cell phone was gone from her hands. Vic broke his eyes from Gaspare and started up the stairs.

Outside Vic and Liz slid into the car. Liz stuffed her notebook into the small haversack she called a purse. "Unless he sent some bot up the side of the Monahan's office building, through the window and used some knife attachment to stab him to death, I'm not seeing him for this."

"Beats me. Monahan turned him down and chose Leaner, and maybe Leaner stole his ideas."

"So maybe if Leaner was dead I'd look hard at him. There's a good chance Monahan didn't even know the ideas were stolen. And his alibi looks solid. What now? Leaner?"

"Not yet. Let them finish processing all the envelopes. We need our ducks in a row before we talk to him about the money."

"What is it with all these sayings you've got now? Crush or mush, what does that even mean?"

"The PI I know in Sewickley says that sometimes. He was Marines, so maybe it's military. But I was thinking last night. We need to push Clair Standish, Monahan's first wife. Find out if she knew about the changes to the will. I'm thinking we do that while evidence processes the last of the envelopes."

"Okay. And I'll double check that set-up in the basement with the video. Make sure that holds. And we got the janitor tonight when he goes on shift."

"Yeah. The crush is on."

Liz shook her head. "You need to get serious, Vic." She spent the remainder of the drive back to the North Side staring out of the passenger side window.

CHAPTER 13

When they reached their desks Liz left to book the flash drive into their Technology Center, a new department created two years earlier to process electronic evidence. Vic had visited it only once. Despite Crush's pre-construction hype, the grand opening revealed a single long room equipped with grey metal shelving down the center and four workbenches against the walls. Vic guessed the problem immediately. While the room was easy to allocate and inexpensive to equip, finding technicians who understood the technology and thought like cops was almost impossible. In the two years since its opening the department's staff had turned over more often than a pig on a spit. But when Liz returned she was smiling.

"You gotta hear this, Vic," she said, arriving at his desk.

"Yeah?"

"You remember Charlie Luntz? Had Crush's job before he retired?"

"Sure. Good boss. Thirty years in."

"Yeah, they hired his son, Craig Luntz, in the Technology Center. When he saw your name on the evidence form he asked about you. Said his dad told him to look you up."

Vic sat back, surprised at how much he appreciated the thought. "No kidding. Charlie was my first sergeant. He got me through my first few years in uniform."

"Vic, I don't know, you almost sound nostalgic."

He nodded, not meeting her eyes. It wasn't nostalgia. He

hadn't thought about Charlie in years, despite everything he owed him. He was embarrassed. "I'll look him up," said Vic, then glanced at her. "I got a call into Monahan's first wife. I'll let you know when I hear back."

It was lunchtime before Clair Standish called back and they set an appointment for three p.m. Her address put her in Fox Chapel, a suburb of wealthy professionals that was located exactly on the opposite side of Pittsburgh from Sewickley Heights. Feeling better with lunch and two bottles of water in his stomach, Vic drove to the meeting and mused about the skill that let Clair Standish move as far from Sewickley Heights as possible but still retain a selective zip code.

"You got anything?" he asked Liz as the GPS directed him along a two lane road overhung with leafless trees. Short driveways led to large colonials and a few houses with a more modern take to their architecture, but the houses lacked the size and stateliness of the Sewickley Heights mansions. They passed a pair of brick columns that flanked the driveway to a private school, dropped over a hill and crossed a narrow, treeless valley as Liz read from her phone. Several houses sat on a ridge facing them, and the GPS directed them to a steep driveway and a modern-looking ranch house with a stone façade and floor to ceiling windows.

Liz looked up. "Not much. From the divorce records looks like they split seven years ago. Your Mary Monahan, wife number two, said they been married five years, so they didn't overlap in an obvious way. Plus Mary Monahan strikes me as a fast mover, kinda like a shark, so I figure when she saw interest from Monahan she closed the deal. Monahan had two kids with Clair Standish, both boys. They been living with their mother since she moved out." Liz nodded back the way they had come. "Those pillars, that was the entrance to Shadyside Academy, the private school, right? That's where the boys go. How'd Standish sound on the phone?"

"Bad case of Cop-*itis*."

"Jesus. You're starting to talk a whole new language."

"You know how people get the 'stop talking disease' when cops come calling? Just the opposite of the Erica girl who found Monahan's body."

"I guess that's better than boltin' out the back door when they see you, yeah."

Vic slid the car to a stop in front of a double garage, next to a silver Mercedes E-Class. Unlike the Sewickley Heights Monahan home, this driveway was narrow and didn't include a turnaround area. Outside the car, Vic drew air into his lungs and for the first time that day felt connected to the world again.

While they waited for someone to answer the door, Vic peeked through the nearest window. His view was through a sunken living room to an arched kitchen entry.

The door was opened by a woman in her late forties, Vic guessed, her blonde hair swept into a tended shoulder length cut. There was a time when Anne would help him understand female suspects by dissecting their hairstyles, and from those discussions, Vic guessed Mrs. Monahan's hairstyle required an hour of preparation to maintain the 'just thrown together' look. The cut and style had money behind it. He took in the woman's brown eyes, compact figure and clear complexion. She took care of herself, he thought. The neat tailoring of her tan slacks and pink blouse confirmed it.

"Mrs. Standish?" asked Liz. They had agreed that Liz would lead the interview.

"Ms. Standish," the woman replied quickly. "I use my maiden name, now." She glanced at Vic.

He stayed quiet, noting a nervous energy about her. When he didn't say anything, her forehead creased and she gestured them into a large entry, and from there into the sunken living room. As they took the two steps down a man in his forties entered from the kitchen. He was trim, in a blue oxford shirt, muted red tie and grey flannel pants. With his closely cropped hair Vic decided that he didn't need the sign around his neck that said 'lawyer.'

Ms. Standish gestured toward him. "This is my lawyer,

Peter Reiner. I thought it might be good to have him here. So there is no confusion." She spoke hurriedly, watching Vic, as if she expected him to say something.

"That's certainly your prerogative, Ms. Standish," answered Liz.

Vic heard annoyance in Liz's voice, and knew she had picked up how Standish was focusing on him.

They introduced themselves all around and settled on two leather couches that faced each other, Standish on the couch next to Reiner, her knees pressed together and pointed toward Vic. Vic knew that she expected him to conduct the interview, not Liz.

Liz started slowly, passing along her condolences, and then asked some general questions about her relationship with Mr. Monahan and when the divorce proceedings were completed. Ms. Standish faced Vic the entire time, sometimes twisting her head around to answer Liz. She answered the questions briskly but tried to maintain eye contact with Vic. Vic waited as Liz built up to whether the Monahan divorce was acrimonious, but as she closed in on the question Reiner cut in.

"I'm sorry, Detective Timmons, I can't help but wonder about this line of questioning. It seems very open ended. And I certainly don't understand why it matters how a divorce was conducted seven years ago."

Liz considered him for a moment and Vic waited for her to say something tart, but she smiled tightly and said, "We're just trying to understand the victim's life. You never know what might be important."

"Surely you aren't suggesting that Ms. Standish might be involved in Mr. Monahan's death?"

"I don't think I've made any such suggestion. As I said, we're just collecting background information."

Vic knew that Reiner was protecting his client, but this was an informal interview and they had no obvious reason to believe Ms. Standish was involved. He changed position, realizing that something was off about the lawyer, he just couldn't tell what.

"Then I'll ask something more recent," said Liz, her tone tightening. She looked at Ms. Standish, who was staring at Vic. "Ms. Standish, we do need to confirm where you were this last Saturday night, between eight p.m. and one in the morning." As Reiner leaned forward to speak, Liz turned on him quickly. "So we can eliminate her as a suspect."

Some redness appeared on Reiner's face. "So you do consider her a suspect?"

Liz shrugged. "We have no reason to consider her a suspect, and if she can provide us with her whereabouts from Saturday night, and a way to verify that alibi, then we'll only need to ask one final question to complete the interview and eliminate her. Unfortunately, without that alibi we will need to ask more questions. A lot of specific ones."

Reiner sat forward and perched on the edge of the couch. "What is the final question?"

Liz, whose back until now was ramrod straight, leaned back. She waited. Vic smiled inwardly and saw that Ms. Standish had taken a deep and abiding interest in the coffee table. "I think that can wait until we've cleared the alibi," said Liz slowly.

Vic struggled to keep a smile off his lips. He knew that Liz intended to ask whether Ms. Standish knew of any changes to Monahan's will, but she didn't want to give away her hole card just yet.

Reiner shifted his legs and glanced at Ms. Standish. "Can you give us a moment?"

Vic looked at Liz. She was upright again, and sitting so straight her back had to hurt, but she betrayed no emotion.

"It's not a complicated question," said Liz slowly. She made no move to stand up.

Reiner looked around the room as if he hoped someone would pop through a doorway and offer him a solution. Nobody did. He turned to her again, and Vic liked Reiner better for keeping the discussion between Liz and himself. "I'd appreciate it. This meeting was short notice and I need to discuss this with my client."

Liz stared at him without speaking. Standish's face tightened into a mask as the seconds ticked by. Finally Liz rose and looked at Vic. "Detective Lenoski?" She turned and strode gracefully toward the arch that led into the kitchen. Vic stood and followed. As they stepped inside, Reiner and Standish bent their faces toward one another, whispering.

Liz turned and looked at Vic, her eyes wide. "What the hell?" she whispered.

Vic stayed quiet, thinking.

"You see that Standish woman? How she keeps looking at you? She don't take me seriously at all."

"Yeah." And then Vic knew what was off about the lawyer. "You know what, did he say what law firm he worked for?"

"No."

"What was the name of the lawyers that Monahan used?"

Liz frowned, pulled out her notebook and shuffled through the pages. "Kravinsky, Lewis and Associates. Why?"

"That's what was missing. Why didn't he tell us the name of his firm? Or give us his card? Lawyers do that all the time. It's like some competition with them."

"Detective Timmons?" Reiner's voice sifted in from the living room.

Liz held his eyes for a moment and he saw her weigh the significance of the lawyer's omission. She returned to the living room. Vic glanced around the kitchen, took in the granite counters, custom built cabinets and stainless steel appliances and decided that Ms. Standish's alimony was paid on time. He followed Liz.

They took their original seats. Ms. Standish was leaning against the back of the couch, her face tight with anger.

Liz waited. Reiner straightened the folds of his pants and said, "It will be quite simple to prove the alibi, we're glad to do it, but unfortunately that will have to wait until tomorrow."

"That's odd, Mr. Reiner." Liz waited.

"We're glad to cooperate, Detective Timmons, but we

need to check the timing of some things. I realize this could be construed as obstruction, but in actuality, Ms. Standish is doing this on my recommendation."

"I hope you understand," said Standish directly to Vic.

"It's really up to Detective Timmons to decide," Vic replied. The room fell silent. Standish's face reddened but she refused to look in Liz's direction.

Liz slowly wrote something in her notebook, then looked at Reiner, considering him. Vic saw the conflict on her face. She wanted to charge Standish, but they had no other evidence to suggest she was guilty.

Reiner broke the silence. "We can meet tomorrow, at our offices on Grant Street. We can answer all of your questions at that time. Is there a convenient time for you?" He looked directly at Liz, and Vic had the feeling that it was the way Reiner treated her that decided it. She checked her phone and after a moment said, "one o'clock."

Relief flooded Reiner's face. "One o'clock it is."

Vic saw that Liz wasn't going to ask the question he wanted answered, so he asked, "Mr. Reiner. Actually, you never mentioned what law firm you worked for. Perhaps you have a business card?"

Reiner's smile tightened. "Of course. It's Kravinsky, Lewis and Associates."

Vic felt warm. "Then you'll need to help me out, Mr. Reiner. Isn't that the same law firm that Mr. Monahan uses?"

"I believe it is, yes." He added a note of nonchalance to his voice, but it sounded forced to Vic's ear.

"Unusual, isn't it? For the same firm to handle the divorce and represent the two parties afterwards."

"I used someone else for the divorce proceedings," Standish cut in quickly, as if she was glad to be speaking to Vic instead of Liz.

"After the divorce you returned to the same law firm your husband used?" The disbelief dripped off Liz's words, and Vic knew she was not about to let Standish off the hook.

"Yes." Standish kept her eyes locked on Vic, willing Liz away.

"Well, that raises some interesting questions," said Vic carefully.

"Such as?" asked Reiner, but his words were soft, as if he already knew the answer and didn't want it spoken out loud.

Liz cut in. "Well, that would be something for us to discuss tomorrow, when you are *prepared* to prove your alibi."

Everyone fell silent, and Liz's anger sifted across the room.

Reiner looked beaten. He stood up. "Tomorrow, then. And you said there was a final question you wanted Ms. Standish to answer?"

Liz stood up as well. "That can wait until tomorrow."

Liz headed for the front door. Vic stood slowly, nodded to Reiner and Ms. Standish, and followed Liz outside. When he pulled the front door shut Liz was standing beside the car, staring at the sky.

Vic waited by the door, counting in his head.

Still staring at the clouds Liz said, "God, I hate people like that."

"That's okay, they're rattled. How she proves her alibi is going to be interesting." Vic reached the number twenty, leaned to his right and looked inside the house through the nearest window.

Behind him Liz said, "Did you see how she was looking at you the whole time? I do not deserve that disrespect. And screw you. You getting soft? You just take that shit? You let her? You call that being a partner?"

Vic heard her but didn't answer. Inside the living room Standish was leaning toward Reiner, mouth working, stabbing her finger at him, her face twisted in anger. He guessed she was shouting but they were too far away to hear anything. Reiner was sunk into the couch cushions, pale, staring at a spot on the ceiling. He looked as if he had spotted a tracer bullet headed toward him.

Vic turned back to Liz. "What do you want me to say to her? Tell her not to be a racist? You know you can handle someone like that without me." He crossed to the car and slid behind the wheel. As Liz jammed her seatbelt into place he added, "But nice job holding back on our question about whether she knew about any changes to the will. They're so hung up on the alibi that question will catch them off guard."

"Damn right."

Vic felt the anger pulsing from her rigid body. He stayed silent and slid the car though the curves that took them toward Pittsburgh. As they climbed the entry ramp to Route 28 Liz said quietly, "Never thought I would say this, but I'm starting to think I like the new Mrs. Monahan a hell of a lot more than that Monahan number one."

Vic glanced at her and saw she had settled back into her seat.

"See, the new Mrs. Monahan has that winning personality you like."

"No. She got everything guys like. But at least she talks to me like I'm some human goddamned being."

CHAPTER 14

Back at their north side offices Vic updated the murder book, aware of Liz typing on her keyboard as she added her notes from the Standish meeting into the electronic system. Within five minutes Vic heard a swishing sound and Lorna leaned against the edge of his cube. Her green velvet shirt was unbuttoned far enough to demonstrate how easy it was to lose her gold necklace in her cleavage.

"Vic?"

"Lorna." He sat back. "What can I do for you?"

"She smiled, her lipstick a touch too red, her green eyes wide. "I can think of a few things, a guy like you. But right now Crush wants to see you." She turned around and called across the aisle to Liz. "You too, Liz. By the way I think he figured out that you're the only one updating the system. Not the old dinosaur over here."

Vic found himself staring at Lorna's backside, which was tight and shapely and at eye level. Somehow, the way she said 'dinosaur' sounded warm and inviting. Lorna spun around, a smile on her face. "Now that I have your attention, pretty sure he means right now." She launched herself back down the aisle toward Crush's office. Vic rose, and after waiting for Liz to join him, followed her.

Crush was standing behind his desk, his arms out-stretched, level to his shoulders. "What the hell?" he boomed, as Vic and Liz entered. "Explain this goddamn money you found." Keeping his arms straight, he slowly raised both arms until his palms were pressed together above his head.

Vic guessed yoga and it made him feel tired. He blinked once to keep himself civil. "We have three areas we're investigating. The money is just one of them. Apart from that it turns out that Monahan's ex-wife might know about a change in the will that is bad for her, which could be motive. Plus we're checking the alibis of people who pitched Monahan but didn't get funded. They also would have motive."

"Yeah, that's the flash drive you red flagged to the tech team, right?"

"Yes. And the sooner it gets processed the sooner we cut that person loose."

Crush separated his palms and slowly lowered his extended arms until they were even with his shoulders. "Depends how much time they need. But I'm letting the red flag stand." As he talked he shifted his arms in front of his body, keeping them straight at the elbow. "But the money, you gotta explain how we found a couple of fingerprints from Thuds Lombardo on the envelopes." His eyes glittering, he glanced from Vic to Liz and back again. He pressed his palms together, his arms outstretched like a cartoon character on a diving board.

"The fingerprint report just popped up on email a few minutes ago," said Liz. "It mentioned a Vince Lombardo. The name didn't mean anything to me."

Crush jerked his head around and stared at Vic, waiting. When Vic stayed quiet he dropped his arms and leaned over his desk, his hands balled into fists.

"Jesus H. Christ. Mother F me." His voice notched higher. "What the shit? Thuds Lombardo? Vic, you told me yesterday you had this! Have you even read the Bad Guy file?"

"I read it, but it was a few months ago," said Vic. The Bad Guy file was another of Crush's administrative creations. The file listed anyone named in federal case documents as associating with known felons, or as witnesses, suspects or persons of interest. Vic had skimmed it once then ignored it. He didn't see how a witness or a person of interest could be considered a 'Bad

Guy.'

Liz broke in. "I just got the email about the fingerprint and I hadn't mentioned it to Vic yet. Like I said, in the email the name was Vince Lombardo, not Thuds Lombardo. Thuds?"

"So anyway," Vic cut in, tired of the way Crush was treating them like children. "Who is this guy? Nice nickname, by the way." He wondered why Liz was covering for him. He had received the email, he just hadn't opened it yet.

Crush gave Vic his best 'cut the crap' stare, but his eyes were small so it just looked like he was squinting.

"Bandini!" shouted Crush. He looked from one to the other as if that explained everything.

Liz and Vic glanced at one another. "We know Bandini," said Vic. "Are you saying Thuds works for Bandini?"

"Now you start acting like detectives? Right, he goddamned does! And Bandini is Pittsburgh's worst nightmare! Thuds does all his shit work for him. The nasty crap. Bodies hit the ground, he's the one doing it. How do you think he got the nickname Thuds?"

Liz shifted on her feet. "I thought Bandini was legitimate now. I heard the feds looked at him for money laundering but only found some strip clubs and a bunch of restaurants. They're even in his own name, not holding companies."

Crush leaned closer. "You believe that? How do you detect anything at all? Sure he owns a bunch of legitimate businesses. But it's what you don't see that matters. Wanna bet half the drugs in this town come through his organization? Wanna bet he's laundering that cash through those businesses he owns? The guy is dirt." Crush's neck flushed. "He needs to be in jail!"

Vic strained his memory. He remembered meeting Bandini years earlier while he was still in uniform. A short round man with doe-like eyes that seemed completely out of character to the gravel in his voice and the businesses he ran in the 1980s and 90s. Before Pennsylvania legalized gambling, Bandini had run most of Pittsburgh's numbers from an Italian restaurant in the Bloomfield neighborhood, in addition to his loan sharking and protection rackets. But everything he'd heard in the last decade said he was legitimate.

"How old is Bandini now?" asked Liz. Vic knew she was doing the same calculations in her head.

"Sixties." Crush waved his hand vaguely and his eyes searched his desktop. He picked up his coffee mug. It was the only chemical he allowed in his body, he liked to point out.

"So Thuds's fingerprints were on the envelopes?" asked Vic. "We got a jacket on him?"

"Damn right we do." Crush plopped into his seat and peered at his computer screen. Vic and Liz settled into their chairs. A quick flick of his mouse and some typing on his keyboard got Crush's eyes moving. "Three assault charges. All dropped. Person of interest in the disappearance of three different people. Investigations went nowhere, witnesses wouldn't get on the stand. Two years in jail for conspiracy. Feds had him on tape setting up a drug deal."

Liz shifted to the edge of her chair. "But that's got be twenty years ago now."

"Right. He got out in '97 and there's been nothing since. We got an undercover into one of the strip joints about five years ago, a bartender. She heard a lotta rumors saying he beat up dancers who didn't behave or showed up stoned, that kind of thing. But no one's brought charges or actually witnessed anything. In the old days he was Bandini's muscle. Now he runs a lot of the businesses. Still has a concealed carry permit. Tell me why Bandini needs a guy like that if he's legit?"

Vic felt a frown on his forehead. "Old habits? But how did he get a concealed carry if he's a felon?"

Crush sat back, his eyes on Vic. "Now you're detecting. Because the conspiracy charge wasn't a federal charge. It was state. This is the shit bad part. See the feds picked him up on a wiretap setting up a coke delivery from Miami to Pittsburgh. This was the late 80s. Delivery is supposed to be at this warehouse in the Strip District. Feds tell our department it's coming, it's like two weeks out. On the night we go in, all we find is three dead Columbians and a trailer truck with ten kilos of pure cocaine hidden in the load. But apart from that we got nothing. We can't figure out what happened, only answer is that someone leaked the raid. We blamed the feds, they blamed us. But the key is that Bandini never took possession. The dead guys are all lined up in front of the truck, bullets to the back of their heads. Executions. Lombardo musta walked down the line behind them, bang; thud. Bang; thud. Bang; thud. Two weeks later everyone on the street calls Vince by his new nickname: Thuds. You do the math. We sweated Thuds but he had an alibi. He also said there was another phone call after the first that the feds missed, and in that one he told the Columbians he was backing out. So all the feds have is one phone call setting up a deal, a bunch of coke and three dead Columbians. But they got no possession on Thuds, and he has an alibi for the time of the murders and a story about why he wasn't involved. We got nothing that will stand up in court. So the feds lost interest in him and just took credit for the bust. State took over and gave Thuds two years on the conspiracy charge for the recording of the phone call, but it wasn't a felony. And there you go."

"Columbians were okay with that?" Asked Liz.

"This ain't the movies. If the Columbians got paid for the load, they wouldn't care. Three dead guys is better than lost distribution in Pittsburgh and a bunch of feds sniffing up their asses. And Bandini walks clean on all of it. He's never seen the inside of a cell."

"Wonder if the three Columbians thought it was a good trade," said Vic quietly.

"Foot soldiers." Crush looked at them. "And now Thuds's fingerprints show up on a couple of the envelopes you found. So this gets priority. You can worry about the first wife and the losers who didn't get funded later. You read me? Bandini is the guy we get. He's a plague. I want Thuds in here and interviewed. Here. In one of our rooms."

Vic stared at him. It was a lead, but it wasn't something to upend the investigation over. He rose quickly, Liz a second behind, but as they turned for the door Crush yelled at them, "Whoa. Where you guys going? I ain't done."

Vic and Liz turned back to him, waiting.

"You get how important this is? Taking down Bandini and Thuds?"

Vic nodded, knowing Crush could see his lack of enthusiasm and not particularly caring about it.

"Yeah," said Crush. "What I thought. You guys aren't getting it. So I'm adding someone to your team." He looked at the doorway. "Kevin!"

Vic pointedly did not look at Liz. Through the doorway stepped a tall, thin man without a wrinkle on his pale face. His thick blond hair was long and carefully combed against the sides of his head.

Crush swung a hand at the young man. "You guys know Kevin Sligo, right? Out 'a West Virginia University a couple of years ago?"

Vic heard himself saying, "Sure." Liz's agreement was so quiet any cat walking by would have drowned it out.

Crush glanced from Vic to Liz and back again. "Kevin's been doing some cold case research for me. But when we got Bandini on the line we need everyone in for the kill, right?"

Again Vic heard himself say "sure." Kevin was the last of three detectives Crush had hired directly out of college. He'd argued to management that he needed youth and an understanding of the 'modern criminal mind,' and how the new techniques taught in today's college criminology courses outweighed the traditional five years of uniform work.

"Can't wait to work with you guys."

Vic stared at the hand Kevin extended toward him before he realized he needed to shake it. He looked up and was unsettled by how young Kevin looked. His grin was tentative, his hand so warm and damp that Vic couldn't let go of it fast enough.

"Okay," said Crush. "Put Kevin here to work."

Liz slid out of the office and Kevin followed her. Vic

turned to Crush to complain but faced a large raised palm, as if Crush was trying to stop a tank.

"Don't even start, Vic. You've been barely functional this past year. You think I don't know Liz is carrying you? We got the biggest lead on Bandini in a decade. You need help."

"Help would have been Chris or Tanner. Forty years between them."

"You need a new way of thinking about how to investigate." He waved his hand at the door. "Now get. Go on! You ain't catching Bandini sitting here. Get going!"

Vic turned to the door. As he exited Lorna rolled her eyes and waved him over. She leaned forward and Vic held eye contact to avoid looking down her blouse.

"Couple of us are going out for drinks after work," she whispered. "Want to go?" She waved toward Crush's office. "Get you away from that."

Vic dragged his mind back to her, but he knew they had to interview the janitor that night.

"Not tonight, Lorna. Work."

She pouted at him. "It's just a drink, Vic."

He frowned at her. "Is it?" he asked, then headed back to his desk.

When he reached their cubes Liz was sitting at her desk, glaring at her computer as if it listed America's nuclear codes. Kevin was standing in the aisle waiting for him.

"Where should I start?" he asked. He seemed interested in looking anywhere but Vic's eyes.

"Where's your desk?" asked Liz from her cube.

Kevin stepped back so he could see them both. "It was over in cold cases, but Crush told me I should move into the empty cube behind you, Liz." He smiled again, but there was a sense of desperation in it.

"Uh huh," said Liz.

"I tell you what," said Vic. "You heard Crush. We need to focus on the Bandini link. So you can help us eliminate other suspects. Guy named Gaspare gave us a flash drive. Can you go down to Tech and see how they're coming with it? If it holds up then we'll get you on Bandini."

"Great!" He almost jumped he was in such a hurry to start. As soon as he was gone Liz looked at him.

"Are you kidding me?"

"I asked him for Tanner or Chris. He wants Kevin."

"No shit. He's trying to save his ass. The other two guys he hired are gone. One's on permanent disability and the other one got fired for not following procedure. We do not have time to train this guy. And he just got promoted from cold cases to homicide? And you get what's really going on, right? Crush wants someone to tell him what we're doing."

Vic sat down and rubbed his face with his hands. "I know."

"And what's up with you and Lorna? What, she not dressing sexy enough for you?"

"It's not that easy," said Vic quietly.

"Ain't nothing ever easy with you lately. But it's real easy, really."

Vic glanced at her. "Maybe."

"You're thinking about it too much. And it's time you got out. That whole thing about you sitting home with a bottle every night ain't working for you. Or me, days like today."

"Okay. Jesus. I get it. Now, Thuds Lombardo."

"Yeah." Liz sat back and Vic watched her take a couple of deep breaths as she stared at the photos of her son. "Okay. Well. Good job getting rid of Kevin for a while."

"Keep thinking of ways to do that.."

She nodded. "Okay." Vic heard the tension drain from her voice. "You know what, we need nicknames like Thuds Lombardo. Bad guys and spooks get all the cool nicknames."

"Yeah. And it turns out our boss doesn't even know how to curse. Did you hear him? Sounded like a fourth grader who just learned the words."

A small smile touched Liz's lips and she turned back to her computer. But her mention of spooks made Vic think of Levon Grace, the PI in Sewickley. Levon sometimes worked with a private intelligence firm, making him a private spook, but it crossed his mind that Levon also had history with Bandini.

A half thought came to him and Vic straightened in his chair. "We need a way to get to Lombardo. We show up at his house and say we want him in here, he'll just hide behind some Grant Street lawyer who talks in circles for a living. It'll take weeks. We need a way in."

Liz turned from her computer screen and looked at him. "Yeah, easy for Crush to say." She rose and wandered down the aisle, past the other cubes and back. Satisfied they were alone, she pulled her chair over next to him and dropped into it. "You get why Crush is so fired up about Bandini, right?"

Vic nodded. "Sure. Career maker. Collaring a guy with Bandini's rep puts him in line for deputy chief."

"Yeah. And balances out how he never found your daughter."

Vic went tight. It was one of the few times Liz had directly mentioned Dannie. "Yeah. But Thuds's fingerprint is a fact, like how quick he will lawyer up. We need a way to approach him, but we need to know everything we can about those envelopes before we do."

"Did you read the email? I just did. Holy shit. Thuds Lombardo's fingerprints are on a few of the envelopes, and Monahan's are on every single one, but guess whose fingerprints also show up on every envelope as well?"

Vic raised his eyebrows, waiting.

"Leaner. CEO of PipeMine. That rat-faced nervous guy we interviewed a couple of days ago. Same guy with the assault beef on Gaspare."

"Now that's interesting. Monahan invested in him, but it turns out maybe Leaner is giving him back money in envelopes?" Vic felt the half thought start to take form. "So we squeeze our CEO friend Leaner first. Get him to tell us what his fingerprints are doing on the envelopes, then we talk to Lombardo."

Liz grinned. "Exactly. There's three people's fingerprints on the envelopes, which means either Thuds gave the envelope to Leaner, who gave it to Monahan, or Leaner gave it to Thuds who then gave it to Monahan. Leaner is way more likely to explain the chain than Thuds."

"And why the cash was moving to begin with. We'll get one shot at Thuds, that's it. We need to know as much as possible when we do."

Liz nodded. "So we hit Leaner again tomorrow?"

"Yeah. I'll have Lorna subpoena his bank records. Then we can see if there are any ten thousand dollar withdrawals. And we question the janitor tonight. Those locked doors still bother me."

"About that."

Vic waited.

"I forgot until I got back this afternoon. I got a parent teacher meeting today. Can you handle that one?"

He nodded as an idea formed in his mind. "Sure. The janitor is at nine, right? That gives me time to meet someone before him."

"Thanks."

She pushed with her feet and rolled her chair back to her desk. Vic pulled an old address book from the lower drawer. He shuffled through the pages until he found the number he needed and dialed. It only took two rings to get an answer.

"Levon Grace," said the person on the other end.

Vic leaned back in his chair. "Levon Grace. Vic Lenoski. You doing anything? I wanted to stop by and talk. Catch up."

Silence on the line for a moment and then Levon said, "Vic, when I think of you it isn't about shooting the shit. When are you thinking? I got back from Europe yesterday. It's nine o'clock at night my time."

"Good. Then you'll be ready for a nightcap. I can be there by six. That work?"

"If you buy me dinner. You know the Sewickley Hotel? Meet me there. I'll buy drinks. If you turn them down I'll know it's official, not a shoot the shit kind of thing."

"Okay by me. See you then."

He hung up and watched Liz shrug into her short leather coat. He noticed that she was still wearing her weapon.

"You gonna shoot the teacher?"

She swung her bag onto her shoulder. "Only if she talks trash about my son. I'm just hoping I don't have to shoot Kevin." She frowned and took a step toward him. "Vic, you know I was pissed after that interview with Monahan's first wife."

Vic nodded.

Her thumb picked at her purse strap. "You ain't soft, Vic. And you're too goddamn stuck on catching bad guys to care you're white. I was pissed when I said that shit. You were the wrong guy to take it out on."

Vic watched her, knowing that was the most apology he would ever get. "I know. Don't worry about it. I didn't."

She nodded. "Okay."

"Okay. Tomorrow we get Standish's alibi figured out, maybe we get the flash drive figured out and eliminate Gaspare. Tonight I'm meeting that PI I talked about in Sewickley. I want to ask him if he knows the Monahan family. I got myself some free drinks. Then I'm gonna go pistol whip the janitor."

Liz half smiled and started down the aisle, before calling over her shoulder: "I like you got plans for tonight, but you got some crazy hobbies, white boy."

CHAPTER 15

Rush hour meant that Vic reached Sewickley only a few minutes before six. He parked in a triangular shaped parking lot in front of a dance studio and crossed the street to the Sewickley Hotel. As he approached the door Levon Grace materialized from a nearby recessed doorway, his shoulders square, some redness in his deep set eyes.

"Detective," he said, a half smile on his lips. He was carrying a week's scruff of beard, dark along his jaw.

"Mr. Grace." The formality was a running joke between them, from the first time they met, when Vic investigated a murder Levon discovered while working a case. Vic usually disliked PIs, but Levon proved him wrong. They shook hands.

"You looked tired. Can you say where you were in Europe?" They stepped inside the Sewickley Hotel and waited for the hostess.

"Krakow. Then I did a side tour. Long story." They fell silent while the hostess gathered menus. Vic scanned the restaurant and bar automatically, looking for blonde hair. He knew better than to ask Levon more because he'd seen Levon's military record. His two tours in Iraq, Purple Heart and Silver Star told him a lot, but his stint in Marine Intelligence and the classified section of his military record said more. He always let Levon decide how much to tell him, and he guessed that Levon appreciated his discretion.

When the hostess led them to some high top tables near the front window Vic chose a seat facing outside. As they took their seats and gave the hostess their drink orders Vic studied Levon's face. In the orange light his skin carried a yellowish tinge and his brown eyes had a hollowness he hadn't seen before. But something remained about Levon's face that Vic had always liked, something in the bone structure, the way his high forehead and deep set eyes gave him an open and trustworthy look. He wondered which of his parents had gifted it to him, his black mother or the white father he'd never met, or if it was a happy conjunction of the two.

Vic opened the menu. "You still working for that intelligence company?"

"Yeah. This job was for some New York hedge fund manager. We didn't even have to sign a non-disclosure. It was two flights daily over four steel mills in southern Poland. Counting loaded rail cars. The hedge manager figured out there was a gap between steel production and the sale results showing up in their financial reports. Since the stock price moved on the financial reporting, he figured that knowing the production volume before the report meant he could long or short the stock. He did pretty well for a couple of quarters, until people figured out what he was doing, so that ended it for us."

"Jesus, he made enough to have you and some pilot fly around Poland twice a day?"

Levon shook his head in disgust. "For nine months. When he makes a long or short bet, it's like a hundred million dollars a pop. Yeah, he can afford it. I was spotter for the last two months. We had to rotate guys, it was boring as hell. But he made a boat load of money, from what I hear. What he paid us was chump change. What have you been up to?"

Vic shook his head, trying to get his mind around it. "Working a murder, venture capitalist. It's ridiculous how much money some of these guys make. I saw his bank records."

"Monahan death?"

They fell silent as the waitress placed drinks in front of them. They touched glasses and sipped.

Vic nodded. "Yeah."

"Monahan is a Sewickley Heights guy. So this isn't a social call."

Vic liked the way Levon fell silent and waited for him to lead the discussion. He respected Vic's boundaries as much as he respected Levon's. "Not totally. I was wondering if you knew anything about them, but I wanted to ask a favor about something else."

Levon sipped his drink and waited.

"That case you were working when we met. It led you to Dom Bandini. You guys ended up on pretty good terms."

Levon sat back. "I don't know about good terms. What's the old word? *Détente*? That's a better way to say it. Why are you asking?"

Levon's choice of words reminded him that Levon had attended Sewickley Academy, Pittsburgh's preeminent private school. "I need a meet with Thuds Lombardo, Bandini's right hand man. Guy like that, if I knock on his door, he'll lawyer up. I was thinking something more informal. Maybe if you do the introduction he'll sit down. If it gets uncomfortable for him he can walk away, I get that, but I was thinking this approach might get us around the gymnastics."

Levon sipped his whiskey, watching him. "Okay. Do you have something on him? I'm not setting up a meeting if you plan to arrest him. I don't do shit like that."

"I wouldn't ask you to. It's the Monahan case. Okay, this part you don't tell anyone." He waited as Levon closed his menu. "Thud's fingerprint turned up on an envelope in Monahan's possession. I'd like to hear his side of the story on how it got there. I'm guessing he knows his fingerprint is on the envelope, so he'll also know we plan to come calling. A guy like that is way too careful to leave a fingerprint somewhere he doesn't want to. You can tell him I know that and I'm guessing he's got a reasonable explanation why his fingerprints are there. That's why I wanted to try this approach rather than getting the lawyers involved and taking a couple of weeks to sort it all out."

Levon cracked a smile. "I don't know, Vic. Seems very

courtly of you. Not the old hardass I met a couple of years ago."

"I'm trying to improve myself. Anyway, he can always say no to you. Then I'll take the hardass route." He drained his whiskey as the waitress approached and they ordered another round as well as dinner. His eyes followed someone as they flashed past the window. When he looked at Levon he was watching him, and he knew Levon had picked up on why Vic had chosen the seat that overlooked the street.

Levon nodded. "Okay. I can give it a try. It's been more than two years and he may just tell me to forget it."

"Thanks. With that out of the way, maybe I will ask the fishing question."

"Do I know anything about the Monahans?"

"Yeah. Any rumors. You never actually bumped into them, did you?"

Levon sat back, a quizzical look in his eyes. "You don't know, do you?"

Vic stared at him. "What do you mean?"

"Mrs. Monahan and I go way back."

Vic stared at him. Levon broke into a wide smile, the corners of his eyes crinkling. Vic was glad to see his exhaustion evaporate. Levon tapped the rim of his glass. "You hadn't figured this out yet? Wow. Mrs. Monahan's maiden name belongs to her mother, not her father. She took it after her mom and dad divorced."

"Okay."

"Her dad is Dom Bandini."

"Jesus Christ. The eyes. I knew there was something about her eyes. Dom Bandini has those big brown deer eyes, she's got them as well."

"Yeah. Bandini divorced her mother when she was small, so she took her mother's maiden name. Tough to make the link. Plus she changed her first name from Marie to Mary. Marie wasn't going to work in the Heights. Maids are called Marie. Wives are Mary."

"Christ. That and she alibied out early, so we stopped

looking at her."

"She's the whole reason I met Bandini. I never told you this story?"

Vic swallowed some whiskey to help him sort through the information.

Levon sipped his own whiskey and sat back. "Okay. You don't tell anyone this, right?" Now it was his turn to wait until Vic nodded. "So, I get a call from a guy I went to high school with. He's a lawyer. Turns out he wants me to find the daughter of one of his clients. I need the business, so I take the name and start looking. I hadn't connected her to Bandini yet, because my asshole high school buddy left Bandini's name out of it. I finally figure out this girl has an uncle who owns a rental house through some holding company. I stake out the house and sure enough, couple of days later, out she comes. I watch a couple of days more and see she stops at a Starbucks regularly while walking to work. So I set up inside and the next day while she's waiting for her drink I confront her and ask for a sit down, mainly because I don't trust my high school buddy. The whole thing smelled and I didn't like it. Almost got my head knocked off by her cousin, who was watching her and turned out to be a cop, by the way. Anyway, she sits down and we talk. I don't get the whole story until later, but it turns out that when she was a kid her dad had his lawyer put a bunch of his businesses in a trust in her name to hide them from the IRS or whoever. Trust has a rule that she gets ownership when she turns thirty. This lawyer was my high school buddy, and being the asshole he is he forgot to change the trust before she turned thirty. So the day after her birthday she just moved the businesses into a new holding company. Bam, old man Bandini loses a third of his businesses. Then she took off, because she knew her dad would come after her."

"She stole his businesses?"

"Technically, no. By the terms of the trust they came to her legally. Plus, she hated her dad for what he did to her mother, so it all made sense to her. Took some balls, though. So here I come, hired by the dumbass lawyer I know who had forgotten to move the businesses out of the trust."

"Okay."

"So this is where it gets good. When I sit down with her, turns out I'm exactly what she's looking for. She has a plan and needs someone to negotiate with Bandini for her. She's willing to give the companies back to her dad, but he has to do a few things first. So I'm the idiot ends up negotiating with Bandini. That's how I met Thuds."

"What did she want?"

Levon grinned. "You ready for this? Bandini owns like nine or ten strip clubs in Western PA, Ohio and West Virginia, right? What she wants is for dear dad to give all his strippers medical insurance. Dental. Access to programs for drug addiction, retirement plans, the whole thing."

Vic chuckled. "I never heard anything like it."

"Right. Bat shit crazy, in a good way. And it gets better. To start, she agrees to give him half of the revenue back from the businesses she stole, half after eighteen months assuming he's made the changes she's asked for. But not ownership of those businesses. That way he gets his money, but she has a lever to keep him giving the benefits. She's no idiot. Bandini agrees to this, even though it means his profit goes to shit for a while. He's got no choice, really, he needs cash flow. He sets it all up, but after six months he learns something: he's suddenly up to his ass in girls who want to be strippers, because he's the only guy giving benefits. And Bandini, that guy can figure out how to sell sand to camels. He's suddenly got so much high end talent that he opens a modeling agency, then a bunch of websites where girls do webcam shows, and I guarantee if you lift another rock you'll find escort agencies. He built the whole spectrum."

"She gave her dad a whole new business model."

"Right. Unintentional, but she did, and he was smart enough to ride the new horse. No hard feelings."

"And she still actually owns the businesses. What are they?"

"Apart from the strip clubs, some restaurants, a commercial janitorial service, that kind of thing. I'm pretty sure they're all legitimate."

"How about the lawyer?"

"My stupid high school buddy? Doesn't work for Bandini anymore. That screw up was one too far, on top of the whole question of why he put legitimate businesses in the trust to begin with. So, Bandini fires him, and then a couple of months later, Thuds pays him a visit and they discuss how Bandini's businesses need to stay secret. Three months later my buddy gets off crutches, but he can't even play tennis anymore with that new limp of his."

"That part figures."

"Yeah, but he'll never agree to bring charges. Or open his mouth about Bandini's businesses, unless he's got terminal cancer and is looking for a faster way out than hospice."

Vic sat back, smiling. "That's a story."

"Yeah. So Mrs. Monahan? We have lunch every once in a while. She's one of those people who keeps her contact list up to date. I like her. She also kept up on her husband's business investments. She and her husband talked about the businesses he was looking at all the time."

The waitress arrived with their food. As she put the plates in front of them, it crossed Vic's mind that if Drake Monahan talked to his wife about his investments, trusted her judgment and knew the story Levon had just told him, then it explained why he changed the will and prenup to leave her the venture capital business.

Vic watched Levon cutting a pork chop. "Okay, so you'll reach out to Thuds?"

"It would help if I knew what was in the envelopes."

"I guess so, or Thuds won't talk to us. Cash. Looks like some kind of regular payment."

"Yeah, that's interesting. Okay, I'll reach out to Bandini first. Thuds is a very smart guy, most people way underestimate him, but Bandini runs the joint. Thuds won't meet unless Bandini knows about it. But if they agree to meet you can bet they feel they're on solid legal ground."

"Makes sense."

Levon smiled. "Follow the cash."

"Always takes you somewhere."

Suddenly Levon frowned. "Something like that, it's a payoff or money laundering. I thought the feds investigated Bandini a few years ago but couldn't find anything."

"Right. But Monahan ran a legitimate business that invests cash. And now it turns out he was married to the daughter of a guy who maybe needs money laundered. Makes you wonder."

"Yeah." Levon fell silent and Vic knew he was thinking through the possibilities.

Levon studied him. "Those dots are pretty far apart. But I can see why you need to talk to them." He speared an asparagus stalk. "Give me a couple of days. I'll let you know. I'd start with my old high school buddy, but, you know, he doesn't do much now except watch TV and keep checking that his windows and doors are locked."

CHAPTER 16

Two hours later Vic parked outside Drake Monahan's office building. He counted three cars in the lot, a white BMW, a Chevy SUV and an early model Toyota Corolla with faded paint that sat low on its tires, as if the weight of its last 150,000 miles was winning. As he reached the front door he saw a reed thin black man waiting inside next to a garbage can on wheels and a cart that included cleaning materials, a broom and mop. When Vic tried the front door it was locked, so he held his badge up to the window and knocked on the glass. The man stared at him for a few seconds before crossing to the door.

Vic watched him unclip a large ring from his belt and sift through the keys, his fingers gnarled and slow. He selected one and let Vic inside. Vic watched him relock the front door and snap the key ring back onto his belt. He turned and stared at Vic, his head back, his eyes red rimmed and yellow in the corners. His neck was a mass of ridges and stringy muscle.

Vic stuck out his hand. "I'm Detective Vic Lenoski. Good to meet you."

The man took his hand briefly, the feel of it like a dry leaf blowing across Vic's palm. He then widened his stance, his dark green Dickies pants and shirt hanging off him in folds.

"Calvert White," he answered, eyeing Vic down his nose. From his eyes and white flecked hair Vic placed him somewhere in his late sixties.

"Thanks for taking the time."

"Okay, but I gots a schedule. Gotta keep to it."

"Won't take long. You know about Mr. Monahan, right? The guy who was murdered on the fourth floor?"

Calvert nodded. Now that they were standing close to one another Vic smelled the sourness of alcohol, as well as an aggressive pine smell, he guessed from one of the cleaning solvents. He wondered if Calvert could smell the whiskey on his breath from his dinner with Levon.

"Yeah."

"And you cleaned the building Saturday night?"

"Yeah."

"Including the fourth floor?"

"Yeah."

A vague annoyance slid through Vic at Calvert's one word answers. "Okay. And when you cleaned the fourth floor, was Mr. Monahan there?"

"Sure. I seen him lots of times. He's real nice to me. When he hears me he puts his garbage can by his door so I don't gotta go into his office. Always tells me to dust next time he ain't there."

"And he did that on Saturday night?"

"Yeah. But Saturday ain't a dustin' night."

"Was anyone with him?"

"Nah. He's by himself. Lookin' at his computer."

"And you cleaned the whole office?"

"Yeah. I do the garbage cans and bathrooms. But Saturday ain't dustin' night. That be Monday and Thursday night. Saturday is a vacuuming night. So I gotta work through every office. Vacuuming."

"Okay, did you see anyone in the building while you were doing that?"

"Nah. Just Mr. Monahan."

"Did you let anyone inside?"

"Un uh. Ain't allowed to do that."

"And what time did you see Mr. Monahan?"

"Maybe eight. Ah starts on the ground floor at six thirty, work up through the building doin' cans. Vacuuming. Then do bathrooms. Lobby is mopped down last." He gestured to the two carts. "Cain't take two carts around, gotta do one then the other."

Vic nodded. "And you're sure you saw no one that whole time but Mr. Monahan."

"Yeah. I'd a remembered. Only sees Mr. Monahan on Saturday night."

"Was he here often on Saturday nights?"

Calvert frowned and fingered one of the black earphone buds that hung from a wire around his neck.

Vic helped him along. "Was it a lot of times?"

Calvert nodded. "Nah. Maybe once a month. Yeah, pretty regular once a month."

Vic thought about that. "Okay, let me make sure I got this. You come in, start in the ground floor offices and work up the building emptying garbage cans. You vacuum each floor as you go. Then you start at the bottom and work up, cleaning the bathrooms."

"Un uh. Cleaning bathrooms, I starts at the top. Then if I run out of cleaner after a few bathrooms I be closer to the supply closet. That's on the ground floor."

"Yeah, makes sense. And I guess cleaning the bathrooms takes longer than emptying cans?"

"Yeah suh."

"And you listen to music while you do that?" He pointed at the ear buds.

"Yeah. While I do all of it." He pulled out a bulky and outdated portable cassette player. "Jazz, man."

Vic nodded. "How long to clean everything?

"Three hours, maybe four. Depends how bad it is."

Vic was aware of how quiet the lobby seemed, and the way the light was washed out and pale. The space felt empty and sterile, and it bothered him. He reached into his pocket and produced a card.

"Okay, Mr. White. I appreciate your time. If you think of anything else, let me know. I may call you again, and if I do make sure you call us back quicker than last time. The only thing I'm interested in is what happened to Mr. Monahan. Okay?"

"Uh huh." Vic could tell Calvert didn't believe him, but he took the card.

Vic considered him a moment longer and then crossed to the door and waited for Calvert to unlock it. Outside he slid into his car and started the engine, but the idea of going back to his house overwhelmed him. He couldn't do it. Instead he pulled the car into a parking space at the side of the building, flicked off the headlights and killed the engine. Wind pushed against the window. He was suddenly tired and displaced. To pull himself back he stared at the building's loading dock and the side door, forcing his mind to work, noting again how the door had no outside handle. He shifted position, felt inside his jacket pocket and slid out a pint of whiskey he'd bought at the state store a short walk from the Sewickley Hotel. He cracked the seal, took a good swig, capped it and slid it back into his pocket. Slowly, he sequenced the timeline Calvert had given him.

Monahan died between eight and one a.m. Calvert started his job on the ground floor at six thirty, worked his way up the building and saw Monahan around eight. He thought about that. Calvert had said he'd been vacuuming. It had only taken him ninety minutes to vacuum four entire floors? Vic set that fact aside. Calvert then went downstairs, switched cleaning carts, returned to the top floor and worked his way down, cleaning bathrooms. The bathrooms took him perhaps two more hours. Following that logic he had been in the building when Monahan was stabbed, possibly in the bathroom on the fourth floor. But the earphones meant it was unlikely he would have heard anything. More likely, the murder happened while Calvert was on the second or third floor, cleaning the bathrooms.

Vic felt run out. He closed his eyes for a moment, planning to reopen them, but a noise made him jump. He realized that he had nodded off. He saw blonde hair out of the corner of his eye and snapped his head around, only to see Erica Lauder crossing the parking lot, bouncing on the balls of her feet. Her shoulder length blonde hair waved around her ears. He watched her slide into the BMW. Moments later the engine turned over, headlights sprang to life and she wheeled past him, headed along the access road. A hard pressure bore down on him and an image of his daughter danced through his mind. Her running the bases during a T-ball game, the same bounce and lightness to her stride as Erica. He struggled to breathe, forcing his chest to expand, until finally air flowed again. He wiped his lips with the back of his hand and glanced at his dashboard clock. He'd been asleep for almost an hour. Slowly he reached for the keys to start the car, but hesitated.

The loading dock door swung open. Calvert rolled the large garbage can onto the loading dock and kicked a brick into the door jamb to keep the door open. He trundled the bin along the loading dock, his hand steadying the small mountain of white garbage bags stacked above the edge of the can. He wheeled it down the ramp and over to the dumpster, flipped open the dumpster lid and transferred the white bags inside. He then dragged the garbage can back to the door, rolled it inside and removed the brick from the door jamb. The door slammed closed, the circular piece of metal covering the door knob hole winking at him as it caught the light. Vic was suddenly warm. He stared at the door, judging the distance from the door to the dumpster. He guessed at the length of time the door was propped open. Ninety seconds, give or take? He looked along the side of the building at the waist high shrubs. It was possible.

Someone could wait among the shrubs until Calvert propped the door open, then dart inside while he was emptying the garbage bags into the dumpster. It wouldn't even be hard. He reached to start the ignition but his hand dropped to his lap again. Calvert had said that he emptied the garbage cans, then did the bathrooms. Vic wondered if he repeated the dumping procedure after the bathrooms were cleaned. They had garbage cans as well.

He glanced at the dashboard clock. Two hours.

Like you have something better to do? he said to himself

softly, and settled back into the seat of his car.

He slugged more whiskey and drifted off once more as he waited, the kind of light sleep where dreams grip your body and are as real as a slap in the face. He was in a swollen river again, grasping for something. His hands closed around nothing again and again, as if the harder he tried to grab something, the farther it floated away. Finally, with a groan, he jerked awake, his mouth tasting like the bottom of a dumpster. His bladder ached.

He checked the time. Just over two hours since Calvert had first come outside. He scanned the parking lot. The tired Toyota was still there, under a lamppost. He gave himself five minutes before he went to find a bathroom. After five minutes he set a second five minute target. That came and went. He reached for the ignition key, then thought of something. He stepped out of the car, his leg muscles stiff, and crossed to the shrubs against the side of the building. He figured he would give it five minutes, and if Calvert didn't show, he would water the bushes. Problem solved.

Less than two minutes later the door swung open and Calvert again nudged the brick back into the door jamb. Vic caught a gentle jazz riff from Calvert's ear buds as he worked the wheeled garbage can over the jamb and started toward the dumpsters. As soon as Calvert turned his back Vic stepped from the shrubs, crossed to the door and slid inside the office building. He found himself in an emergency exit hallway. He walked to the far door, opened it and stepped into the lobby beside the elevators. Moments later he was inside the elevator headed to the fourth floor. When the doors opened he stepped into the lobby outside Monahan's business offices. He ducked into the newly cleaned bathroom.

He wasn't sure what felt better. Emptying his bladder or knowing how the murderer might have entered the locked building.

Relieved, he opened the door and stuck his head out, searching the fourth floor lobby. The front double doors to Monahan's offices were locked, but a side door was propped open with a small can that contained a fresh garbage bag. He stepped though the door into the office area, finding himself in the corner opposite Monahan's office door. It would be easy for him to walk straight down the hallway and into Monahan's office. He wouldn't be seen until he stepped inside the office. He nodded to himself, walked down the row of cubicles and took a seat in one of them, where he could see the garbage can propping open the door. He waited.

About ten minutes later the garbage can disappeared from the doorway and the door slammed shut. He guessed the garbage can belonged to the receptionist's desk. He understood what Calvert was doing. It was quicker to leave the doors propped open while he worked than take the time to find the right door key every time he went in or out of an office. He waited a few more minutes then headed toward the elevators. As he waited for the elevator to arrive the lights went out, leaving only the emergency lighting.

The loading dock door didn't have a deadbolt, and Vic simply turned the knob and stepped outside. He waited until the door slammed shut, made sure it was locked and crossed to his car. Before he pulled away he checked the parking lot. The old Toyota was gone.

And so am I, thought Vic, fighting back a grin.

CHAPTER 17

When Vic arrived at the office the next morning, Liz was already there, standing by her cube, talking to a slender young man with a mop of unruly blond hair and square, stylish glasses. She nodded toward the young man.

"Vic. This is Craig Luntz from Tech. I was telling you about him yesterday?"

Craig stepped toward Vic, his hand outstretched and eyes bright. "Mr. Lenoski. I mean Detective Lenoski. Pleased to meet you. My dad told me to say hello from him."

Vic found himself smiling and shook the young man's hand. He saw some of the father in Craig's hooked nose and the slight slope to his forehead.

"What's your dad up to these days?"

"Retired. He fishes a lot. He was in the bass fishing contest they held on the rivers last year. Top ten."

Vic nodded. "Tell him I said hello." His eyes drifted to the four or five day growth of beard sprinkled across Craig's chin and cheeks like pepper on cooked egg whites. It crossed his mind that he had never seen Craig's father needing a shave.

Liz cut in, her tone upbeat. "Craig was the one who looked at Gaspare's flash drive."

"Yeah?" Vic noted that Craig had missed a loop when stringing his belt onto his chinos.

"Yep," said Craig, his eyes skimming Vic's cube. "You guys wanted to know when the video was made?"

Vic waited.

Craig seemed put off by the fact that no one encouraged him to keep talking. "Um, okay, I checked the file source. The file was created last Saturday night. Yeah. No problem."

"Do you have a time stamp?" asked Liz.

"Sure. File was opened around seven thirty?"

Vic cut in. "Around? You can't be exact?"

Craig blinked quickly and met his eyes. "Yeah. Sorry. Seven thirty-one p.m."

"So he opened the video file at seven thirty-one. What time did he finish working on it?"

"Well, the file was closed at twelve thirty a.m."

Vic glanced at Liz and saw the blank face she got when she heard bad news.

"Okay," said Vic slowly. "Let me back up. We have this person of interest named Gaspare. We need to know if he was in his house making a video between eight to one on Saturday night. That's the time of death of our vic. Does the file show that?"

"In his house? I don't have any meta data attached to the file to confirm that. But it was open and being worked on in that time frame, no question."

"Okay." Vic stared at Craig. He felt something wasn't adding up.

Liz shifted positions. "Craig, is something bothering you about this file?"

Vic nodded, glad that Liz had also caught it.

Craig glanced down the aisle and then looked from Liz to Vic again. "So here's the thing. The file was created, and I can tell that it was closed at twelve thirty. What I can't tell is if someone was actually working on the file the whole time. Logically he was, because the video is there, and a lot has to happen. Audio has to be laid in, film edited, that kind of thing."

Vic softened his opinion of Craig. He thought about things the right way. "Can you give me percentages? Seventy-thirty he was working on it, or fifty-fifty?"

"Hey, what are you doing up here?"

Vic turned to find Kevin Sligo standing a few feet away, a

briefcase in his hand, his hair perfectly trimmed. Vic wondered if he visited the same barber Crush used so they could hang out together. Kevin's eyes were angry and locked on Craig.

"The flash drive was red flagged," said Craig carefully. "That means it's top priority. The investigating team needs to know the findings as soon as possible."

Vic liked the calmness in Craig's voice, and how he held Kevin's eyes.

Kevin walked by them, threw his briefcase onto his desk and said, "I told you to call me. No one else. You shouldn't even be up here, this is the homicide squad. You're tech support."

"Kevin, it's not a big deal," said Liz. "The drive is red flagged."

"Yeah," added Vic. "Craig's just showing some initiative."

"He didn't do what I told him to do." Kevin's voice dropped and trailed away, as if he realized he couldn't win. Vic also heard a bit of whine in the voice and he wondered if Crush had told Kevin to manage Craig's activities.

"Anyway," said Vic. He looked at Craig. "We were talking percentages. How likely it was that Gaspare was working on the file from eight to twelve thirty. Give or take."

Craig glanced at the ceiling. "I guess if the file's open you can assume that he was working on it. One hundred percent. But there's a better way to check. Next time bring me the computer he was using. That'll confirm it."

"But you're saying one hundred percent he was using the file during that time period," said Liz.

"I can only say the file was open, and given how much work had to happen, it looks that way. I could tell you more if I had the actual computer, not just the file. But, logically, he was working on it."

Everyone fell quiet. Liz looked at Vic and he knew he had to make the call on it. "Okay," he said. "Until we have suspicion that he wasn't that's how we look at it. Anyway, we'd need a warrant to get Gaspare's computer and without more evidence it won't happen." He looked at Craig. "Thanks, we appreciate you coming up here."

"Sure. Great to meet you, Mr. Lenoski. Detective." His cheeks colored slightly. He turned to Liz. "Thanks, Detective Timmons." He gave her the evidence bag with the flash drive and headed down the aisle. Kevin followed him. Vic watched them go.

"What was that all about?" asked Liz, watching as well. She leaned over her desk and noted the custody change on the evidence bag.

Vic shook his head. "Beats me, but I bet Crush told Kevin to get involved in the investigation, so he decided to control whatever Craig was doing. I like that Craig wasn't buying anything Kevin was selling."

"Yeah, looks like he's got some of his dad in him."

"Let's hope. We need more of that around here." He dropped into his chair, leaned back and put his hands behind his head. "Oh and I figured out how the perp got past the locked doors." Liz plopped into her seat, staring at him, still holding the evidence bag with the flash drive.

"Janitor told you?"

"Nope. Figured it out all by myself." He stretched. "Alllll by myself."

Liz threw the evidence bag on her desk. "Alright. Maybe you got one trick left. Tell me."

Grinning, Vic walked her through the story of how the loading dock door was propped open and the janitor wore ear buds. When he was finished Liz said: "You snuck in?"

"Wanted to see if I could get to the fourth floor. Plus I had to take a leak."

"Men and their bodily functions."

"Yeah, but that's not the fun story."

Liz cocked an eyebrow at him.

Vic stretched his arms above his head, enjoying the moment. "The current Mrs. Monahan? She's also the daughter of Geno Bandini. First marriage."

Liz slammed her palm onto her desktop. "Jesus, how'd

you discover that?"

Vic explained his dinner with Levon Grace.

"So this Levon guy is setting up a meeting with Thuds?"

"Let's hope. I figured that was a good way to approach him. And Thuds has to know that if we find the money we'll want to talk to him."

"Maybe it was Thuds who searched the house. He wanted the envelopes back." Liz frowned. "But you know Crush said to bring him in and sweat him."

"Sure. Crush wants everyone to see how hard he's working to get Bandini. But first, let's see if Thuds will talk to us. If he does then it probably wasn't him searching the Monahan's house. And if he won't meet and decides to lawyer up then guess what, we bring him in and Crush is happy. Crush can call him out on it in the media. I say we wait a bit to tell Crush all this."

"Can't argue. You ready to talk to Leaner about his fingerprints on the envelopes? I set it up for eleven. Then we got Monahan's first wife and her lawyer at one downtown."

"Good."

They spent the rest of the morning updating the murder book and online files. With some time on his hands, Vic watched the demo video of Gaspare's robot from start to finish. He was still thinking about it when they left for Leaner's offices. As they pulled up at a red light he glanced at Liz.

"You know. That bot in Gaspare's demo looked a lot like the one that disappeared from Monahan's office."

Liz shrugged. "I didn't see it."

"I believe Gaspare on that. When he said Leaner stole the prototype from him. Wonder if that was it? Hey, who's interviewing Monahan's office staff about it?"

Liz smiled. "I sent Kevin. Keeps him out of our hair. He should finish up today. So far no one knows anything about it. But if the person who took it got in there without witnesses, they could lie no problem. Not sure why someone would want that particular item, though."

"That's kind of the question, isn't it? Like how did the

murderer figure out how to get into Monahan's building. They must have been sitting outside like me."

Vic parked outside Leaner's office building. Inside, they waited ten minutes before Leaner's secretary waved them into his office.

Leaner was exactly as Vic remembered him, his eyes bright and his hands constantly looking for something to do. This time, from the mounds of files and metal components on his desk he found a rubber tread from one of his bots and started folding it over and over again.

"We appreciate you taking the time again," said Vic carefully, letting Leaner see that he was watching his every move.

"Glad to help," said Leaner. Vic didn't believe him for a second. Vic and Liz had discussed how to handle the interview, and Liz took the lead.

"Mr. Leaner, we've had an interesting development in the case and we'd like your reaction to a couple of things."

He nodded so sharply that Vic worried he might hurt himself. Vic carefully placed a manila file on the edge of Leaner's desk, where he could see it. He left it closed. It was an old trick, but he figured that Leaner was nervous enough that it might work. Leaner's eyes locked onto the folder and Vic could have sworn that his hands doubled in speed.

"It's funny how these kinds of investigations go," continued Liz, taking her time. "Sometimes things come up that are important, sometimes they aren't. You just never know. But when something is linked real tight to someone close to the case, you really have to wonder." She stopped. Neither Vic or Liz said anything. They simply stared at Leaner. His eyes jumped from one to the other, to the file and back to them.

"It really is funny how it works," said Vic slowly.

"Ain't it, though?" said Liz. She and Vic looked at each other, taking their time. "Oh, and before we get to the file," she tapped it once with her finger. "You know that we had an item go missing from Mr. Monahan's office. The gift you gave him?"

Leaner tore his eyes from the file and locked on her face.

He actually stopped playing with the tread.

"The prototype?" His voice was hoarse.

"Exactly, the prototype." Liz smiled.

"I don't understand," he said. "Someone stole it?"

"Right out of the office," answered Vic. "Poof. Gone."

"Who?" His voice rose.

"We were hoping you could help us with that." Liz folded her hands in her lap and waited, politely.

"How would I do that? I didn't know it was gone." He glanced at Vic then back at Liz.

"And you know, it looked a lot like a prototype someone stole from David Gaspare." Vic widened his eyes, staring at Leaner, encouraging him to say something.

"Who told you that?" Leaner tossed the tread aside, grabbed a piece of metal and started worrying it with his fingers.

Vic leaned forward. "You understand that we're investigators, Mr. Leaner, so we, well, investigate. And in the course of doing that we came across your criminal record, which includes a couple of charges for assault."

"They were dropped."

Liz jumped in again. "Right, but you were fingerprinted as part of that investigation. So it's interesting that your fingerprints showed up now during the course of our investigation into Mr. Monahan's murder."

"For instance," broke in Vic, "when your fingerprints show up on a bunch of envelopes, envelopes filled with cash, envelopes in Mr. Monahan's possession, we start wondering exactly what the nature of your relationship with Mr. Monahan was." He flipped open the file cover, revealing a photograph of the cash envelopes laid out on the coffee table in Monahan's wine cellar.

Leaner glanced at the photograph and jerked back, his face pale. "We're done," he said quickly, his voice hoarse. "Nothing until my lawyer is present."

Vic felt a rush of excitement and leaned toward him. "Mr.

Leaner, we're just trying to have a conversation here. Your alibi checked out. You were doing something else when Monahan died. But this is an interesting set of circumstances. Mainly because we found other fingerprints on the envelopes."

Leaner crossed his arms over his chest. "Lawyer."

Vic was sure of it now. They were onto something. "You sure you want to play it that way? This means that next time we meet we'll be in an interrogation room in our offices. Are you sure that's what you want?"

"Lawyer!" Leaner shouted. He jumped to his feet, looking from one to the other. Vic and Liz watched him for a few moments, then Vic leaned forward and flipped the file folder closed. Together, he and Liz stood up.

"Just between us," said Vic quietly, "you need to think about what happens next real carefully. We're going to find the truth. You can count on it. So figure out what side you want to be on when we do."

"And you'll want to do that in a hurry," added Liz. She dropped her business card on his desk. "Tomorrow at ten. Bureau of Police on the North Side. Address is on the card. If you don't show, we'll charge you with obstruction." Vic slapped the closed file against his thigh.

"Out," Leaner croaked.

Liz and Vic crossed the shop floor in silence and climbed back into their car.

"Well, that was quick," said Liz.

Vic pulled his seatbelt into place. "Yeah. Gotta love it when you ask a question and someone runs home to their lawyer." He started the car. "And we need Leaner's bank records. Lorna says they're on the way. Because if the money didn't come out of his accounts, we've got some real interesting questions for Thuds and Bandini."

CHAPTER 18

A few minutes before one o'clock, Vic and Liz pushed through a heavy brass door into the headquarters of Kravinsky, Lewis and Associates to meet Ms. Standish and her lawyer, Peter Reiner. The lobby was inside a twenty story, squat structure just off Pittsburgh's Sixth Avenue, one of many buildings built in the late 1800s and early 1900s that, for years, dominated Pittsburgh's skyline. Vic liked that particular generation of buildings. They were all stoutly built of granite or sandstone, some of the foundation blocks the size of small cars. He'd decided long ago that the men who chose to build them were as much about not getting knocked down as getting ahead. Pittsburgh's newest generation of skyscrapers were sleek towers of glass and metal that shouted to be looked at, as if the men who chose to build them wanted to stand out, to be looked at and admired. The lobbies of those new towers were collections of cold granite and tired retail stores, the opposite of the arched ceilings, decorative crown moldings and ceiling mosaics of the older buildings. The difference was enough that Vic believed that an attitude of not getting knocked down as you moved ahead led to a richer interior life than simply bragging about how far you had come.

It took them what seemed like a couple of minutes to cross the lobby. At the reception desk a woman immaculately dressed in a buttoned business jacket with a pearl brooch on her left lapel watched them come. Her brown hair was swept back in a way that looked professional and neat while falling just short of severe. Vic introduced them and gave her Peter Reiner's name. She nodded and dialed her phone. Vic glanced at the glass walled conference rooms on either side of the lobby. When the receptionist finished her call she waved them toward several groupings of arm chairs and love seats. They moved a few steps away from the desk, but remained standing.

"Get Standish pissed," said Vic softly to Liz. "When I looked in the window before we left yesterday, she was unloading on Reiner. She has a temper."

"I got a million ways to piss off people like that. They hate waiting on a black woman."

The elevator doors behind the receptionist opened and Clair Standish and Peter Reiner crossed to them, accompanied by a white haired man well into his sixties. Clair looked as fresh as the day before. Reiner's shoulders were slumped and his shirt partially untucked. The elderly man introduced himself to Vic as Don Lorrie and said something about being one of the partners of the law firm.

When Lorrie shook hands with Liz she held his eyes. "I'm sorry, what is your role here? We know Ms. Standish and Mr. Reiner, but we don't know you."

"I'm sorry, I should have been clearer. I'm a partner here, and the law firm's managing director." As he spoke his perfectly fitted suit almost shimmered. Reiner pointed to one of the conference rooms and headed toward it, walking as if he was about to enter a cell. Liz and Standish followed, but Vic held back, watching Lorrie lean over and speak to the receptionist. She immediately turned to her computer keyboard, swiped her mouse and began clicking through a series of windows.

When they were all seated in the conference room Lorrie looked around. "And which of you is the lead detective?"

Vic instantly didn't like him. "I am," he said curtly.

"Well then," said Lorrie, turning to him. "Let's get started, shall we?"

Vic held his eyes for a moment, then pointedly looked at Liz and said, "Have at it."

When everyone's heads swiveled to Liz, Vic pulled his phone from his pocket and swiped through a couple of screens.

"Thank you," answered Liz. She made a show of checking her notebook and preparing herself. Vic could tell from her eyes that she had caught Lorrie's attempt to marginalize her.

"OK." She raised her eyes to Clair Standish. "Yesterday, Ms. Standish, I asked you to provide proof of your alibi for Saturday night from seven thirty to twelve. You were unable to do so."

"You're mischaracterizing it," said Reiner quickly. "She said she would today, which is why we're here. So we can provide that alibi. So…"

Liz cut him off. "Actually, Ms. Standish did not say that. You said it. And we need to hear from her what her alibi might be."

"I'm sorry," said Lorrie, "you're being a bit aggressive, aren't you?"

Liz turned to him. "Mr. Lorrie, we have asked Ms. Standish multiple times to prove her whereabouts at the time of her ex-husband's murder. So far she has refused to do so and has delayed our attempts to find out. We're at the point where we have to decide whether she simply doesn't have any proof or she's purposely obstructing a murder investigation. With all that implies."

"Wait." Clair Standish shifted in her seat. "I do have one. Last Saturday night I was with Peter Reiner." She nodded to the lawyer beside her.

"So you are saying that your lawyer will confirm your alibi." The sarcasm dripped from Liz's words.

"Again, Ms. Timmons," said Lorrie quickly. "Your tone concerns me. It is almost hostile." He turned to Vic. "As the lead detective do you condone this kind of behavior and how it edges on harassment?"

Vic took a slow breath. "Mr. Lorrie, in my view, you're the one escalating this situation. We've asked a standard and simple question that is part of any murder investigation. Mr. Reiner here stonewalled us yesterday. We could have arrested Ms.

Standish then, because refusing to answer our questions is obstruction. You know that. And now I'm concerned that you're looking for ways to interrupt our line of questioning. Not to mention your vague threat about harassment, which I guess you hope will get us to back off."

"I see it differently. Perhaps I'll have to take it up with your commander. It's Tomkins Davis, isn't it? Crush?"

Vic held eye contact. "See, there you go again. I'm afraid it's you who is interfering with our questioning, Mr. Lorrie."

"That isn't my view of it."

Vic controlled his anger, lifted his hand and placed his phone on the table. "Well then, good thing I've been recording this so if push comes to shove the district attorney can judge for himself."

"You recorded this without our consent?" His face remained calm but Vic saw a ticking start just above his collar at the jugular.

"Which by law I can do during the course of a major investigation. But tell me honestly, Mr. Lorrie. Aren't you also recording this conversation? Without our consent?" Vic swung his arm at the walls of the conference room.

Lorrie sat back, his cheeks tight and eyes hard.

Seeing his body language, Vic leaned forward. "There's good precedent for me to do this, but very little that gives a lawyer the right." He tapped his index finger on the table. "If any."

For about fifteen seconds no one spoke, then Lorrie rose and stepped into the doorway. He called across the lobby to the receptionist. "Susan. Turn off the recording in this room."

"And delete what you have," added Vic.

Lorrie hesitated, then added, "And delete what is already recorded."

Everyone watched Susan nod and set to work on her computer. Lorrie returned to his seat. Vic pointed to his phone, where the flat line scrolled on, waiting to record more of the conversation. Lorrie leaned toward it slightly.

"You can understand why we would want to protect our

client."

Vic relaxed. "That assumes she needs to be protected. But if she can better confirm that she was with Mr. Reiner than just Mr. Reiner giving us his word on it, then she really doesn't need your protection, does she? So let's start again."

Lorrie nodded and they both turned to Liz. She gave a brief nod but Vic knew her well enough to know she was suppressing a smile. She looked at Ms. Standish. "As Detective Lenoski said, do you have any way to confirm your alibi?"

Ms. Standish was uncomfortable for a moment, then quietly and matter-of-factly said, "We had dinner at a restaurant in Lawrenceville. Piccolo Forno. We finished about nine and then went to the downtown Hyatt. We rented a room."

The only sound was Liz's pencil as she wrote in her notebook. She turned a page, wrote a bit more and then asked, "Were you in a room or a suite?"

A flush rose to Standish's face and Vic squelched a smile. "A room."

"King sized bed?"

"I don't see how that matters."

"And when did you check out?"

"About one a.m."

Again Liz took her time writing down the response. Finally she looked at Reiner. "And you can confirm all of that?"

He nodded. Vic pointed at his phone and Reiner said, "Yes. I have the credit card receipt for the hotel and I'm sure they have video of the lobby."

"Ah, so you paid for this...rendezvous?" Liz wrote in her notebook with more care and concern than a mother tending a baby. Ms. Standish turned her head and stared through the glass into the entry hall, her eyes seething. "Okay," said Liz. "Well, we'll need to see the receipt and I'll send someone to collect the CCTV footage. Hopefully it will show you leaving when you said you did." She stared at Standish until she turned her head and met her eyes. "And I'm wondering, how did you feel when you found out that your ex-husband, Mr. Monahan, changed his will and prenup to leave his venture capital business to his current wife?"

Ms. Standish flushed. "I was, ah, concerned," she stuttered. She clamped her lips tight, and Vic knew that she hadn't meant to fall into the trap so easily.

Lorrie stiffened and turned his head, very slowly, to look at Reiner. Lorrie hadn't known about this part, Vic realized.

Liz leaned forward. "And how did you find out about it?"

"Mr. Reiner told me."

A flush climbed Lorrie's neck from his collar and the anger was plain on his face. Reiner stared stone-faced through the glass. Silence unspooled across the room.

Liz lifted her pen from her notebook. "When was that?"

Ms. Standish stared at a spot above Liz's head. "Late last week."

"Just a few days before your ex-husband was murdered. And did it make you angry?"

"Of course it did." She stabbed her index finger on to the tabletop. "That business was for my sons to inherit. His sons as well, I'll remind you. Do you know how hard it is to lose weight after a couple of pregnancies? Instead he decided to pass it along to that slut he called a wife. I actually have to question if he knew what he was doing. If she had somehow maneuvered him into it. Leave a good business to a bimbo in her thirties with no business experience? It seems very suspicious to me."

"Okay, and where were you this past Monday morning between eight and twelve?"

Vic waited, admiring the turn in the questioning, knowing that Liz was asking for an alibi for the time when someone had broken into the Monahan's house. She was a step ahead of him. He hadn't considered the possibility that Standish might have searched the house looking to destroy copies of the annotated will and prenup. He saw Lorrie searching Liz's face, a look of interest on his face. He was trying to understand the reason for the question.

Ms. Standish frowned, then said slowly. "I had my yoga

class. That was eight thirty to ten. Afterwards I ran an errand or two and then went home. Why?"

Vic leaned forward: "Someone broke into the Monahan home that morning. And Mr. Reiner, how about you during those hours?"

He looked startled. "I was at work in our offices. Plenty of people saw me."

Liz broke in. "And if you could explain, Mr. Reiner, how you knew that Mr. Monahan was in the process of making changes to his will? You aren't Mr. Monahan's lawyer, if I recall."

Vic liked the way Liz see-sawed back and forth with her questions, keeping Reiner and Standish off balance. He watched Reiner glance at Don Lorrie, who gave him as much support as a statue. Vic guessed his indifference was a statement about Reiner's future career with the law firm.

Reiner gathered himself. "I guess I overheard a conversation between Mr. Monahan's lawyer and his paralegal. He was warning her to be on the lookout for an envelope with a copy of the will that included his changes."

"You guess?" Liz shot back.

"I did hear."

"Were the paralegal and Mr. Monahan's lawyer aware you overheard them?"

"No."

Lorrie shifted in his chair. Ms. Standish looked straight ahead, ignoring everyone, her lips tight.

Liz held Reiner's eyes. "And when was this?"

"Last Wednesday. Right after lunch."

"And when did you tell Ms. Standish about it? Keep in mind that we can subpoena your telephone and messaging history."

"About an hour later."

Lorrie suddenly swiped at something imaginary on the table. "Obviously," he said to no one in particular, then looked at Vic, "this is new information for me. But that kind of ethics violation requires an internal investigation." He glanced at

Reiner. "I want it on the record that we take this breach of client confidentially very seriously and will take drastic steps to ensure it doesn't happen again."

Liz took her time writing that down in her notebook. Vic guessed that Reiner's career was coming apart like a cartwheeling Formula One racer.

Liz looked at him, a question in the arch of her eyebrows. He shook his head, so Liz added, "very good, Ms. Standish and Mr. Reiner. We'll be in touch. Obviously we will be confirming all of your statements." She rose and everyone followed suit. Vic picked up his phone, turned off the recorder and dropped it into his pocket. As Liz pushed her chair back under the table, Lorrie circled the table and held his hand out to Vic.

As they shook he said, "I want you to know that our investigation into this starts immediately. I hope you understand that we take the privacy of our clients very seriously. If we find anything more, I will let you know." He dug into his pocket, produced a business card and held out to Vic. "I'm sure you are aware that if a lapse of this kind became public it would have grave repercussions for our reputation."

"The thought crossed my mind," Vic replied. "Let's hope it doesn't come to that."

Lorrie nodded. "Thank you."

Vic turned and followed Liz into the cathedral of a lobby. They remained quiet until they reached the street.

Liz broke the silence, speaking over the gentle roar of a bus grinding up the hill. "You taking bets on how long Reiner keeps his job after this?"

"I only take the bets I can win. Like Leaner's bank records. I'm still hoping to see those before we interrogate him tomorrow."

"Yeah, and that's a bet I would take."

Vic's phone vibrated with an incoming text. He glanced at it as they entered the parking garage.

"And Levon Grace did his magic. He got us Thuds tomorrow afternoon. Thirty minutes only."

"How come I feel he's going to be asking as many questions as we are?"

Vic smiled. "Because you're a goddam good detective, Liz Timmons. And you know shit."

CHAPTER 19

That afternoon Vic called the DAs office and spoke to a paralegal. She dragged two different Assistant DAs onto the call. Almost an hour later Vic was still hunched over his phone, kneading his forehead with his fingers, his lips clamped shut so he wouldn't yell at them to make up their minds. When they finally reached a consensus he slammed the phone into its cradle and called across the aisle to Liz.

"Hey, lawyers gave us the green light. They think the changes to Monahan's will and prenup stand up. It's some bull-shit about announced intent. I guess because Monahan warned his lawyer the changes were coming, and then initialed and dated all the changes after that warning, they've got a time se-quence and intent. Ms. Standish can challenge but they figure she'll lose. Best she can hope to do is get Mary Monahan to settle out of court."

Liz grinned, the corners of her eyes crinkling. "You think Monahan will pay her off? She's a Bandini. She'll eat Standish for lunch. Standish ain't gonna know what hit her."

"Yeah, that's what I thought. And I'm still waiting for Leaner's bank records."

Liz rolled her eyes. "Good luck with that."

"Does make me wonder if Mary Monahan knew her hus-band changed the will."

"You gonna go ask her?"

"Yeah. I think I have to. You want to go?"

Liz shook her head. "Not if you're going out there now. I

want to finish updating the system. We got a lot going on. Plus I have to pick my son up after school today."

Vic fell silent for a moment. "How's he doing at school?" He was unsure how far to tread into the conversation.

"He's settling in. The first couple of years were tough. Yesterday the teacher said he's doing real well. My uncle steadied him out. He needed that after his dad died."

Vic saw that she seemed relaxed about the conversation. "I wasn't sure what happened to his dad. Figured I'd let you tell me."

Liz shrugged and her mouth tightened. "You never asked, Vic. Not that I can blame you, after what you went through with Dannie."

Vic fought down the urge to tell her that what happened with Dannie wasn't something he had gone through, that he still went through it every day. "So what happened?" he asked carefully.

Liz shrugged. "Hurricane Katrina happened." She glanced down the aisle to see if anyone was listening to them. "Mitch was his name, he was a beat cop like me. When we knew Katrina was coming we sent Javal inland to my aunt. Katrina hit and everything went bad. No cell service, land lines down, even the police comms were down. Us cops, we just did what was in front of us. Everyone remembers the cops shooting those people on Danziger Bridge, but they forget how many cops died in those first few days. All I know is that a bunch of people came forward later and said Mitch and his partner had rescued them. I guess they got hold of a boat somehow. But when we got comms and started to sort everything out, Mitch and his partner were gone. Best we could figure is they capsized, or someone killed them for the boat, but who knows." Her voice faltered and she looked at her computer monitor, then took a deep breath. "Anyway, after that I needed to keep my mind off it. So I studied and took the detective exam. The department was short of people and they were promoting fast. I stuck it out for a couple of years but being there was too much, so I brought Javal here." She looked at him. "And then they partnered me with your sorry ass."

"That's because I'm such a nice guy."

She smiled bitterly. "Yeah, well, that ain't the word most people use. I still can't figure out what Lorna sees in you."

"She likes dinosaurs. She said that."

"You're a dinosaur as much as I'm Dom Bandini. I worry about you, Vic. Livin' in that empty house. All you're going through. Some mornings you're so pale and stinking of booze I gotta wonder if you even stopped drinking before you came to work."

Vic was suddenly warm and couldn't meet her eyes. "Helps me sleep." Somehow he hadn't realized it had gotten that bad.

"Stops you thinking, is more like it. And Vic, thinking is what you do best. Apart from that whole 'I'm gonna punch the shit out of you' vibe. So, like I said, I worry about you. I don't have answers for the things gone from our lives. But hiding works no better than spending all your time trying to find them. I believe that. You gotta find a different place to live your life from now on."

The warmth passed but a small ache sat in Vic's chest. "Yeah," he said finally. He rose and swung into his jacket. He couldn't look at her. "I'm going to see Mary Monahan. On the way back I'll check for Leaner's bank records." He walked down the aisle, his eyes burning. Liz said nothing. Outside the day was cold and the grey sky felt as hard and low as the brim of a baseball cap. He sat in the car for a time before he could bring himself to turn the ignition.

He drove Route 65 toward Sewickley, trying not to think about how obvious his drinking must be. Instead he focused on what Liz had told him about Mitch and Javal. He found he was glad for Javal. At least he had something. His father had saved lives, he was a hero. It wasn't the same as touching his warm skin and feeling his father's breath on him. But it was something. It was a reason. You could build a life from that.

A white BMW was parked in front of the Monahan house.

Vic recognized it but couldn't remember whose it was. As he stepped out of the car he forced himself back into the moment, tightening his jaw and rolling his shoulder muscles. He glanced once more at the BMW as he waited for someone to answer the front door. He felt his heartbeat slow, and noticed how the wind moved the bare branches of the trees. It calmed him somehow.

Mary Monahan opened the door and a half smile slipped across her lips.

"Detective Lenoski." She glanced behind him. "Detective Timmons won't be joining us?"

"I just had a few questions. She felt she could trust me not to mess it up."

"Well, let's not prove her wrong." She swung the door wide open and stepped aside. Vic entered and waited until she closed the door.

"We're in the kitchen," she said, turning and leading him down the hall. She moved easily, her slacks tight against her buttocks. When they stepped into the kitchen, Erica Lauder hopped off a stool at the island, her blonde hair swinging below her ears. Vic connected her to the white BMW, remembering how two nights before he had watched her trot across the parking lot outside Monahan's offices. She held out her hand. "Detective Lenoski, if I remember?"

"Ms. Lauder." Vic glanced at the kitchen island. Spread about were files next to a laptop, a spreadsheet visible on the screen. Two half full coffee mugs sat on the island in front of two of the stools.

They stood in awkward silence for a moment before Mary Monahan spoke. "Coffee, Detective Lenoski? I really need to call you Vic."

He nodded. "Coffee would be good. Black. Vic is fine." He nodded to the files and laptop. "I guess I'm a little surprised to find the two of you together."

They both laughed easily, as if they were old friends, and then looked at one another to see who should respond. Mary Monahan nodded for Erica to explain.

"It isn't complicated," said Erica softly. "Our COO, John Silver, had a conversation with Mr. Monahan before he passed." She raised her voice to its normal level. "Mr. Monahan told him about his plan to leave the business to Mrs. Monahan. And then I guess the county lawyers passed copies of the will you found to Mrs. Monahan's lawyer, who let Mr. Silver know. So Mr. Silver asked me to start updating Mrs. Monahan about what we're doing."

"I know it isn't official, yet," called Mary Monahan from the coffee machine, "but when my lawyer called and told me, I telephoned Mr. Silver and told him I'd like to get started."

"Which was a great idea," responded Erica enthusiastically. "We have a lot of decisions to make in the next couple of months. We don't want to miss any opportunities."

Mary Monahan glanced at Erica with a smile, then slid a mug under a nozzle on the coffee machine and busied herself pressing buttons.

As the coffeemaker gurgled Erica asked, "Any progress on the investigation?"

Vic nodded and answered loud enough for Mary to hear over the noise. "Actually, yes. Several interesting developments. It's why I'm here."

Mary glanced at him with interest. "Anything you can tell us?"

"Actually, there is one thing I wanted to ask Erica."

She nodded.

"I talked to the janitor and spent some time in your offices while he was working. Did you ever notice that he propped open the office doors with garbage cans?"

Her forehead wrinkled. "I guess I did know that, now that you say it. Not the front door, but the side door near the bathrooms. Maybe he didn't want to waste time finding the right key every time he went into an office?"

"He leaves them all propped open. Just a couple of hours, but it explains how someone got inside without a key."

"And do we know who got inside?" Mrs. Monahan moved

the coffee mug from the coffeemaker and placed it on the island in front of him.

"We have a couple of leads. But Mrs. Monahan, I have a few questions we should discuss in private."

She looked at Erica. "We're about finished, aren't we?" She leaned over and slid one of the files away from the others. "Although I'll hang onto this one. I want to give it a closer look."

"Sure thing." Erica turned to the island, collected the files, snapped the laptop lid closed and stuffed everything into a soft sided briefcase. "Thanks Mrs. Monahan. I'll let Mr. Silver know what we covered."

"Thanks, Erica. Can you see yourself out?"

"I can." She smiled broadly, nodded at Vic and disappeared down the hall.

They listened to her footsteps, followed by the thump of the front door. Vic sipped his coffee.

"Well," said Mrs. Monahan. She leaned a hip against the island. "I owe you a thank you, clearly, for finding the will and prenup. I still plan to move out of this house but I certainly have a different view of things now."

He nodded. "Part of the job. You know we didn't find your fingerprints on the documents anywhere. But I still have to ask if you knew about the changes. Did you?"

"No." The gaze from her large brown eyes was steady. "In retrospect I see it. We talked about his investments a lot. It started because I wanted something to talk to him about. He would talk about the businesses and different industries, so I started doing research, and we ended up talking about it all the time. I found I liked it. A couple of times lately he said I should be in the business, but I was surprised when I heard from the lawyers. I wasn't expecting that."

"Okay, but you know we found an interesting connection on those cash envelopes."

She cocked her head, waiting. He sipped his coffee. "We found the fingerprint of a Vince Lombardo on them. Thuds Lombardo, to people who know him well."

A frown ghosted across her forehead but her eyes stayed clear and locked onto his.

"I'd bet you know the guy," said Vic carefully.

"You've been doing your homework."

"Just my job."

"It's funny, I had a feeling the first time I saw you that you don't distract easily. So far I've been glad about that. Is that about to change?"

"Why don't you tell me about it, then we'll decide if anything changes."

She nodded at his coffee. "Sugar or cream? This may take a while."

"Black is fine."

She settled herself onto one of the stools and pointed at another.

"I like to stand," said Vic. "Too much time sitting today."

"Okay." She looked out a window above the sink. In the distance tree branches waved gracefully in the wind. For a moment the kitchen felt overly large and quiet. "So I'm guessing you know that I'm Dom Bandini's daughter. From his first wife. My loving father is on his fourth now."

"Yeah. We track who Dom marries. And who he divorces."

She nodded again, still turned to the window. "And you know all about Thuds, I'm sure."

"Thuds we pay very close attention to."

"I have to admit, I don't know how or why his fingerprint would be on one of the envelopes. Was it one or several?" She turned to him.

"Enough that it isn't a coincidence."

Her dark eyes turned thoughtful. "Doesn't sound like Thuds. He's careful. Almost meticulous."

Vic shifted position. "I thought the same thing. It made me think that it didn't matter to him if someone found his fingerprint. That he didn't think a crime was involved. But tell me about him."

She studied him as if she was trying to tell whose side he

was on. For the first time, Vic noticed that something in the cast of the bones of her face suggested sadness. With her large eyes and precocious body it was an odd combination that made her seem beautiful and vulnerable at the same time. He wondered if her haughtiness was a defense mechanism.

"Well," she said softly, "when I was growing up in my dad's house we called Thuds Uncle. He was the best of the guys closest to my Dad. He remembered our birthdays, he'd bring us gifts. Even after the divorce. And he's a thinker. He was the one who always told me not to let little things bug me and to take the long view. Later, when I heard some of the things people said he did, I had a hard time believing it."

Vic stayed quiet, letting her reminisce. The wind pressed against the window.

She stirred. "The night my dad came home and told my mother he was divorcing her, he brought Thuds with him. Like he was scared my Mom might attack him, because back then Thuds watched my Dad's back. He came home and called us all into the kitchen and told us. My mother fainted. She had no idea. And Thuds, I watched him. I don't think he knew what my dad was planning to say. It was in his face. He was mad and embarrassed at the same time. He stared at the floor a lot. It was the only time I ever saw him when he seemed unsure what to do."

"And I guess some time after that Maria became Mary?"

She smiled. "You *have* done your homework. Yes. I never liked Maria. But that was after college. My father still calls me Maria. I think to annoy me."

"I guess," said Vic slowly, "that leads to my next question. When did you see Thuds last?"

A faint smile crossed her lips. "About a year ago. It was strange. He just showed up here one day. Out of the blue. We had coffee in the kitchen like you and I right now. He just wanted to know how I was doing."

"And before that?"

"I'm guessing you know the story of the trust?"

"I heard a version of it. I'd like to hear yours." Vic settled onto one of the stools.

She shrugged. "My father's lawyer made a mistake and forgot to rewrite a trust before I turned thirty. The trust held some of my father's businesses, all in my name. I guess he'd done it as a tax dodge and I wasn't supposed to know about it. But the day after my thirtieth birthday I executed the trust, as I legally could, and took the companies." She looked at him, her eyes sharp. "I liked doing it."

"And you got health care and benefits for your father's strippers."

"I did. But that backfired. Once word got out about the benefits so many women applied that he opened up more businesses, thank you very much. He ended up exploiting more women in more ways, although at least they have health care and retirement now."

"You know, I heard that story, but I have one question that didn't make sense to me the first time I heard it, or now. How did you find out the trust existed?"

"Right. You don't miss much, do you Vic?" She slid off the stool, circled the island and removed a bottle of vodka from the freezer. Held it up to him. "It's almost five."

He shook his head and waited while she prepared a vodka tonic. He noticed that all the components—the vodka, tonic and lime—were in the refrigerator, the small cutting board and knife for the lime in the closest drawer. She took her time slicing the lime. When the drink was finished she came back around the island and slid onto the stool. She took a slow sip.

Vic waited.

"My birthday was on a Sunday. I was living in an apartment in Shadyside back then, and things were getting serious with Drake and the chance of me being Mrs. Monahan was in the air. Thuds showed up at my door the day before my birthday. He had a bunch of flowers, I like daisies, and that's what he had. He'd remembered. Even had one of those burnt almond tortes from Prantl's. He asked how I was and then gave me an envelope with a copy of the trust inside. He said I would find it interesting, and that their lawyer had forgotten about it."

"He asked you to take control of the companies?"

"No. He just told me about it and gave me the copy. That was it. Then he walked off into the evening."

"So you decided what to do on your own?"

"I read it, and, honestly? I saw a way to hurt my dad. I was into it. So I sat there half the night eating the cake, drinking," she pointed at her glass, "and sketched it all out. I didn't really want the companies, but I decided that giving the benefits to the strippers would anger him and hurt his bottom line, which is all he cares about. I called a young guy I knew, a lawyer, and told him what do first thing Monday morning. But I made one mistake." She sipped her vodka. "I knew my dad would come after me, so I called my uncle and asked him to hide me. He did, but then I realized I needed to negotiate with my dad. It was the only way I could get him to offer the benefits and work out a schedule to give the companies back. I needed a neutral party. Fortunately, my dad hired someone to find me, and it turned out the guy was smart. And honest." She smiled to herself and sipped her drink. "What are the chances? Anyway, he handled the negotiations and we got it done. Then, maybe six weeks later, Drake proposed."

"Did your new fiancée know you owned a bunch of businesses?"

"And a strip club, but I gave that back to my dad. I didn't want it. No. When Drake and I started to get serious he mentioned a prenup, so when it showed up I just made sure it worked both ways and that I was as protected as he was. I'd actually thought about returning the businesses to my dad but the prenup made me decide to hold onto them."

"Did your new husband know who your dad was?"

She nodded and sipped her drink. "I had to explain why I didn't want my dad at our wedding. I told him about the businesses after we'd been married a couple of years. He thought the whole story was hilarious. He loved it."

Vic rearranged himself on his stool. "Why do you think

Thuds told you about the trust?"

She shook her head slowly. "I've asked myself that. I don't know. My dad is very good at spotting opportunities and creating new businesses, but he's terrible at running them. Thuds does that. And Thuds is a very loyal guy so this was out of character. I do think Thuds hates how my dad swaps his wives for younger models all the time. So maybe he still felt bad about being at the family meeting when my dad announced the divorce, but, really, with him I'd look for a business reason. Maybe he wanted a new lawyer and he needed a way to demonstrate how bad the old one was. I just don't know."

"Okay." Vic drank the last of his coffee. It was cold and left a metallic taste on his tongue. She drained her vodka, the ice cubes rattling.

"You know, Vic, you've asked a lot of questions. But there's one question you didn't ask. It seems out of character for you. A missing question. And that makes me wonder."

Vic waited. He felt she had earned the right to ask him a question, if not several.

"You never asked the name of the man my father hired to find me. The honest guy who wasn't scared by my dad or Thuds. Now why would that be?"

"I can't think of every single question I need to ask."

She smiled. "No, Vic, I don't think you asked because you actually know who it is. And I know Levon Grace wouldn't tell you my story unless he trusted you. So, my question is how do you know each other? I've told you a lot, it's time you tell me a few things."

Vic shrugged. "Levon and I get along. I met him a couple of years ago. He was working a case and one of the people he was investigating turned up dead. He found the body. I got the case. I never liked PIs, but he's different. He's got a code that he lives by and he's honest. Turned out I could work with him."

"I don't know, Vic, you sound dangerously close to actually liking him."

"There's a lot of old school in him. Says what he means,

does what he says. Afterwards we've stayed in touch. We have a drink sometimes, same way you have lunch with him once in a while."

"Looks like I'll need to make him sign a confidentiality agreement."

"Like you said, he knows when to keep his mouth shut, despite how it looks right now. He's solid, don't blame him for this."

She was silent for a moment, absently swirling the ice cubes in her glass. "And perhaps you were hoping he could help you meet Thuds?"

Vic tilted his head and knew immediately that he had given away the truth by his reaction, so he didn't bother to hide it. "Yeah. That was my idea. Maybe I should have come to you."

She shook her head. "I haven't decided if I like you enough for that yet, Vic." She slid off the stool and circled to the refrigerator again. "You sure you don't want a drink? You look like the drinking kind."

"I've still got some work and driving to do. Which I need to get to."

She reached into the freezer for the vodka bottle. "Okay, Vic, and one other thing." She turned and looked at him. "I think at this point, since I'm calling you Vic, you can call me Mary."

"Okay."

"And another thing." She waggled the vodka bottle at him. "Say hello to Thuds for me."

"I will." He turned to go.

"And Vic?"

He kept rotating so he faced her. She was holding the bottle by the neck, down at her side.

"Watch yourself with Thuds. He's unpredictable. It's his strength. If you think he's coming from the right, I guarantee you he'll come from the left. And when you expect him to back off, that's when he comes at you hardest. Keep that in mind. But if he decides he trusts you, you'll have a serious friend. And that's a good and rare thing."

^^^

An hour later Vic swiped his ID card at the outside door to his offices and entered the deserted lobby. The front door thumped closed behind him. He swiped his way through the door into the interior offices and walked the carpeted hallway, the building oddly quiet and dark, thanks to a cost cutting move by Crush that dimmed most of the lights at six. Vic felt like he was sleep-walking. He turned down the aisle to his cube. A light shone from a desk at the end of the row, but when Vic checked it turned out that someone had left on an under cabinet light. He returned to his cube and hung up his jacket.

He dragged his computer to life and parsed his emails. The most recent was from the legal department. He opened it and found an attached file of Leaner's banking records. He sat back, surprised. Bank records required a subpoena and coordination with the financial institution. The process usually took several days, but somehow the records had shown up in less than twenty-four hours.

He clicked on the file and discovered why the records had arrived so quickly. Usually an index and summary were attached, but in this instance it was simply a data dump of various statements and spreadsheets. He rubbed his eyes. The size of the task ahead made him tired.

"Those the bank records?"

Vic almost jumped upright. He turned to find Crush standing beside his cube, bouncing gently on the balls of his feet.

"Yeah. Leaner's. We'll have him here in the morning. When we asked him why his fingerprints were on the money he lawyered up."

"I heard. I asked Liz for an update while you were out. When she told me you needed the records I called Legal and told them they gotta move them right now."

"That's great," said Vic softly. What Crush didn't understand was that by jumping into the process he had made his job harder. To make the records available quickly the bank had simply done a data dump and skipped the indexing that simplified the search.

Crash thumped his right fist into his open palm with a meaty thud. "But Leaner is peanuts. What about Thuds and Bandini? When are you bringing them in?"

Vic realized that Liz hadn't told Crush about the meeting he'd set up with Thuds. "We're working on it. We'll know by the end of day tomorrow. I wanted to get as much information as possible out of Leaner first."

Crush thumped his fist into his open palm again. "Keep that moving. Commander and I were on the phone to the mayor. He wants action on this. He's pumped that we got Bandini in the crosshairs. When you get Thuds in here let me know. I want to watch that interview. And if he doesn't come clean, we'll do a press release afterwards, talk about Bandini's businesses. Put some pressure on him. We got a lot of ways to go on this."

"Okay, but Leaner had more fingerprints on the envelopes than Thuds. We need to connect the dots."

Crush leaned toward him. "You got Thuds's fingerprints on cash payoffs to a dead guy. Just a matter of roping him in now."

"Got it." Vic tried not to close his eyes in frustration.

"Great. Let me know. And tell me if I can move anything along for you. Glad to help on the bank records. Good teamwork." He hesitated, then added, "Good to see you putting in extra time on this, Vic. I said I needed your A game. Good to see it." He pivoted and strode toward his office.

Vic dug his fingers into his eyes and massaged, thankful for the quiet of the offices. Finally he removed his fingers. Stars popped in front of his eyes for a moment as he focused on the computer file. He dragged over a pad of paper and a pen and began to scroll through the documents.

When he finally opened the door to his house it was almost eleven o'clock. He stopped in the kitchen, draped his jacket over the back of the one remaining chairs and put a pizza box on the table. He poured himself four fingers of Jim Beam, walked into the living room and dropped into the armchair. He slurped down half the whiskey and flipped on the television. He switched from channel to channel to avoid the commercials. The pizza seemed a long way away, but he didn't care. Leaner's financial documents had told him everything he needed to know.

When he finally got up to refresh his whiskey the pizza was cold. It hardly seemed worth the trouble.

Later he jerked awake, the television mumbling about a mop he should buy. He staggered upright, the empty glass in his hand, and lurched into the kitchen. He put the pizza in the refrigerator, drank off another finger of whiskey and stumbled upstairs to bed.

CHAPTER 20

The next morning Vic was on his second cup of coffee when Lorna appeared at his desk. Somehow her light yellow blouse and dark green pleated skirt reminded him of an overripe avocado. His stomach turned.

"Vic," she breathed. Her eyelashes held clumped bits of black that he guessed might turn into shrapnel with a good blink.

"Your interview is here. Mr. Leaner and his lawyer. Do you want them in one of the interrogation rooms?" She blinked, and Vic forced himself not to dive out of the way.

"Yep, you pick. Just take the table out, okay? I only want four chairs in there. And you know how to arrange the chairs." He glanced at Liz and she nodded agreement.

"Two of the chairs backed near the wall? I'll put them in B, okay?"

"Sure."

As she headed away, her perfume lingered like a small thundercloud.

"You ready for this?" he asked Liz. Their plan was for Liz to interview Leaner while Vic handled the Thuds Lombardo meeting.

"Sure. Goal is to find out where the money came from and why he passed it to Monahan."

"Right, like I said earlier, his financial records show no regular cash withdrawals of ten thousand dollars a month or anything that would come close to it. So we've got that and his fingerprints on the envelopes."

Liz sat back and folded her arms. "Yeah. Thanks for explaining. Again."

"Sorry. And I appreciate you not telling Crush about meeting Thuds this afternoon."

"You kidding me? Asshole would call out SWAT and the news media to cover us. Last thing we need."

"Yeah. And with Leaner, he's a nervous guy. A good push'll get him talking."

"Not the first time I been fishing, Vic." She rose and headed toward the interview rooms. Vic watched her go, then rose and followed her. Instead of entering the interview room he ducked into the video room at the end of the hall, a semi-dark space filled with monitors that displayed the video feeds from the interview areas. He nodded to the technician, closed the door and sat in front of the monitor for room B. The screen showed Leaner and his lawyer sitting on the chairs near the wall. The lawyer was a middle aged man, well fed, wearing his best Brooks Brothers pin stripe. His face had been scrubbed so well it shined.

Vic watched Liz introduce herself and start the introduction questions. A year earlier, fresh from a three day conference, Liz suggested a new, two-part approach to formal interviews. As Liz worked though the introduction questions about Leaner's family history, education and past addresses, Vic saw the fidgeting in Leaner's hands slow and his eye contact with Liz strengthen. After about ten minutes Vic had a good read on how Leaner acted when he was comfortable and unstressed.

Twenty minutes later Liz left the interview room and joined Vic in the observation room. Vic tapped the lawyer's head on the monitor. "Have you seen him before?"

She shook her head. "No. You heard he's not a criminal lawyer?"

"That was a surprise. Contract law."

"Something different."

Vic sat back. "Man, Leaner's basically a nervous guy, but he settled down with your questions."

"Yeah, it's all in his hands and eyes. He looks around and moves his hands, but the rest of him stays still."

"Even his feet stay still, I saw that," added Vic. "Be interesting to see his reaction when you start asking serious questions."

Liz nodded. "That's why I like this approach. After the first session it's easy to see when they get nervous. I'm going to get a cup of coffee. You got the file with the photographs?"

"Yep."

"When I get back."

Twenty minutes later Vic followed her into the interview room. After introducing himself to the lawyer Vic pulled his chair away from the others so he could see Leaner's entire body. Liz reminded Leaner and his lawyer that the conversation was being recorded.

"Wouldn't have it any other way," said the lawyer. He crossed his legs and uncrossed them. Vic liked the way just the lack of a table in the room unsettled people. Even the smug ones.

"Now, Mr. Leaner," said Liz, once she had named him and the case number for the record. "I wanted to go back to something we talked about yesterday. You may be unaware of this, but inside the home of a murder victim, Mr. Drake Monahan, we found a collection of bank envelopes containing a large amount of cash. Many of the envelopes contained exactly ten thousand dollars. Your fingerprints appeared on every single one of the envelopes."

Liz fell silent, letting the statement sink in. Vic watched Leaner, but apart from some minor movements of his hands, he appeared calm.

"Is there a point you are trying to get to?" asked the lawyer.

Liz ignored him but hitched her chair a bit closer to Leaner, her knees a few inches from his. "Let me say that again. Your fingerprints appeared on every single envelope."

"They look like this," said Vic. From the file he produced

a photograph of the envelopes lying on the coffee table in Monahan's wine cellar.

Leaner barely glanced at them. Liz scooched her chair another inch closer. "Do you recognize the envelopes?"

Leaner nodded, then spat out a "Yeah."

Liz didn't respond for a moment, but when she started talking the pace of her words was slower. "Mr. Leaner, so there is no confusion, you just stated you recognize the envelopes. So, can you explain why they were in Mr. Monahan's possession?"

Leaner shuffled his chair back from Liz and exchanged a glance with his lawyer. "I gave them to him. They were part of a contract agreement we had. Every month I gave him an envelope with ten thousand in it."

"By him you mean Mr. Drake Monahan, the deceased."

"Yeah."

Vic saw Liz's shoulders relax just a bit. "And can you explain why you made that monthly payment?"

"Sure. We had a deal."

"A contract," interjected the lawyer.

"Can I see a copy of this contract?" asked Liz.

"It's a verbal contract," the lawyer countered. "Just as binding as a written one."

"Okay, can you explain the content of this verbal contract? What were the terms?"

His chair creaked as the lawyer leaned forward. "Certainly. Mr. Monahan and Mr. Leaner had a verbal contract in which Mr. Leaner would pay him ten thousand dollars every month until a total of three hundred thousand was reached."

Vic understood why Leaner had brought a contract lawyer, but what surprised him was how calm Leaner stayed. Even his hands were still.

Liz shifted her chair a bit forward, following Leaner's retreat. She ignored the lawyer. "Look, we're just trying to get to the truth, so you'll have to do better than that. What were the conditions of this contract?"

Vic stared at Leaner's face. Not only was he calm, he actually glowed a little, as if he was proud of something.

When he stayed silent Liz tilted her head. "So, let me get this straight. You're saying that Mr. Monahan told the other investors that he was investing two million, but in reality it was only one point seven million?"

"Of course not," broke in the lawyer. "Mr. Monahan stated he would invest two million, and as all the bank records indicate, he invested two million. The other investors can be confident that Mr. Monahan met all of his commitments."

"But he was in the process of getting three hundred thousand returned to him. In cash. On the side. As payoffs."

The lawyer's eyes tightened. "I don't like your tone or what you are implying, Detective Timmons. And note we object strongly to your use of the word 'payoffs.' Mr. Leaner and Mr. Monahan are perfectly within their legal rights to initiate a verbal contract of their own design. You are assuming that Mr. Leaner and Mr. Monahan agreed to this contract prior to Mr. Monahan's two million investment. Was that the case, Mr. Leaner?"

"No. We made that contractual agreement after he had invested his money and after he became a member of our board."

Vic recognized the smooth lead and response. Liz rotated her head as if she wanted to loosen her neck muscles and Vic knew she'd caught it as well.

"Okay." Liz drew out the word and tilted closer to Leaner. "But why did you make this contract, supposing it even is one? To me it just looks like payoffs. I mean, what did you get in return?"

"Contracts can be made for any number of reasons," said the lawyer.

"Great point," Liz replied. "And what were the reasons attached to this contract?"

"I'm not sure that's relevant, Detective."

Vic cut in. "I believe it is. We only have your word that you made the deal to repay Monahan *after* he invested the two million. We need to know the conditions linked to the payments to confirm it had nothing to do with the original investment."

"Exactly," said Liz. "And I'm sure there's a perfectly good reason. We would just like to know that reason. Or reasons."

Vic glanced at Leaner's hands but they still showed little movement, and Leaner was holding Liz's eye.

The lawyer broke in again. "It was a private contract. The terms were only between Mr. Leaner and Mr. Monahan."

"Is that really true?" asked Liz, gazing into Leaner's eyes. "I mean the terms have to affect others." She smiled at Leaner and Vic had the feeling that something somewhere died at that moment. "I guess we'll just talk to your other investors and your board and see if they know anything about it. Perhaps Mr. Monahan mentioned it to one of them."

Leaner's hands clenched, he broke eye contact and looked over Liz's shoulder at the wall. "I thought these rooms had big mirrors in them?"

Liz shuffled her chair closer to him. "I think it's time you told me why you were making these monthly *payoffs*."

Vic watched Leaner struggle to look at Liz. His right hand clenched his left so hard the knuckles were white.

"And we feel so strongly about it," said Liz, and Vic saw her glance at Leaner's hands, "that we will interview all of your investors and board members. I can't imagine that would be a problem for you. I'm sure your other investors will be fine with your *word* that you made this contract after they agreed to match Mr. Monahan's two million dollar investment."

"In fact we may be required to interview them," added Vic. "I mean, suppose one of them learned about the payoffs and was so angry he or she murdered Mr. Monahan? We would have to follow that lead." He knew it was a weak reason, but gambled that Leaner was now nervous enough to believe it.

"I don't like what you are suggesting, Detective." Even Vic heard the waver in the lawyers' voice.

"Wait." Leaner shifted his body in his seat. "Okay, okay. There was a condition. It was pretty simple. Monahan agreed not to invest in my competitor, PipeSafe."

Liz straightened. "You agreed to pay Mr. Monahan three hundred thousand dollars *not* to invest in Mr. Gaspare's business, PipeSafe?"

"Yes."

The lawyer raised pleading eyes to the ceiling camera as if he hoped someone might bang on the door and shout that the digital recorder had malfunctioned.

Liz was sharp with her follow up. "PipeSafe, your former employer."

"Yes."

"And, to do that, you used cash that did not come from your personal or business accounts. There is no record of it. It was magical money, really. Money that you just had lying around."

Vic saw the lawyer stiffen. He looked at Leaner as if he wanted to know the answer as well.

"No," said Leaner, looking at the floor.

"No what?"

The lawyer leaned forward. "You subpoenaed my client's bank records?"

Liz talked out of the side of her mouth to him. "We do that in murder investigations. You'd know that if you were a criminal lawyer." She waited a beat, still watching Leaner. "Time to come clean, Mr. Leaner. Where did the cash come from? Or do we need to go and ask your investors about that as well?"

Leaner pushed his chair back but it hit the wall. In his eyes was the look of someone who knew they had nowhere to go.

"No," Leaner whispered.

"So what's it going to be, Mr. Leaner?" Liz shifted her chair closer to him.

Leaner's eyes darted about the room as if he was trying to track a flying bat. "There's no need to talk to my other investors. I already had the cash."

"Seriously, you had that kind of cash sitting in your

house? Where, under your mattress?"

"Detective, you are badgering my client."

Liz ignored him. "Mr. Leaner, this is your one shot to come clean. I told you at the start, we just want to know the truth, and you need to decide which side you're on, because we will discover it one way or another. You're making good progress, here. Hey, you're a businessman, you saw a way to take out your competitor and you took it. Smart business move." She reached out and touched him lightly on the knee, like they were conspirators. "But you need to make sure you're on the right side when this is done, because someone else is involved with that money, and he's a bad guy. I'm talking about Dom Bandini."

Leaner jerked upright, his eyes wide. "Dom Bandini? What? The gangster?" He glanced at this lawyer, his eyes wide.

"We found other fingerprints on the envelopes, and they lead to Dom Bandini."

"No, the envelopes came from HBK Enterprises. I don't know Dom Bandini."

Liz sat back and the lawyer frowned at the ceiling. Vic could see it was the first time he'd heard about Bandini's involvement.

"Okay," said Liz carefully. "Humor me. Let's say it was HBK Enterprises. How did they get involved?"

Suddenly Leaner couldn't talk fast enough, the words spilling out. "They invested when I first set up my company. I needed cash flow, they provided it. Forty grand a month for a year. More than I needed. They paid in cash, so I simply kept some of it. About two hundred thousand dollars. I was going to start pulling Monahan's payment out of my business accounts next month."

Vic remembered Gaspare's words from their first interview, when he said he didn't know how Leaner stayed in business before Monahan rode in with his two million dollar investment. The two facts came together like a coat buttoning.

"Walk me through it," said Liz.

Leaner gulped a breath. "Okay. When I started out, my

cash flow sucked. I needed sales. I met this guy from HBK, Lombardo was his name, but I only met him then and one other time. After that it was some young guy, Mike Turcelli. He brought me the money every month. They gave me forty thousand dollars a month in cash for about a year. But I got lucky, and about six months in I landed a couple of clients, which helped cash flow, so I started keeping the cash as a reserve."

"And what did Lombardo get?"

"Stock. They're listed on our investment documents, HBK Enterprises. When we got funding from Monahan and the others, they ended up with about half a million shares. That's worth about one point five million now."

"So their half million in cash is now worth legitimately one and a half million?"

"Give or take."

Vic watched Liz rub the palm of her hand along the top of her thigh. He knew she was angry at how Thuds could make that much money. He cut in, "How did you meet this Mr. Lombardo?"

Leaner looked at Vic with relief in his eyes. "Investor conference. It was put together by the High Tech Council of Pittsburgh. We applied to present and got fifteen minutes on stage to pitch a bunch of investors. There were like fifteen other companies and maybe fifty investors. Afterwards this blonde girl from Monahan's talked to me, plus this Lombardo guy. Lombardo asked me to dinner. Then they invested, and after that I dealt with Mike Turcelli. Haven't seen or talked to Lombardo since."

"Who was the blonde girl from Monahan's?"

"Erica someone or other. I remember because she was a pain in the ass and when I pitched Monahan I saw her again. She didn't like me. She knew about Gaspare and PipeSafe and kept asking me to compare my products. She knew I'd worked there. I think Gaspare had been talking shit about me."

Leaner looked quickly from Vic to Liz and back again, his eyes desperate.

The lawyer turned to Vic. "How does Dom Bandini fit into

this? He's the gangster, isn't he?"

"I'll ask the questions here," said Liz, and turned back to Leaner. "Why cash? Didn't that seem odd to you?"

He nodded hard. "Kind of, but they filled out all the investor documents. They met all the legal requirements. My counsel at the time had no trouble with it. There's nothing says they can't use cash."

"Okay, then I just have one last question before we take a break. Why did you steal the prototype from Mr. Monahan's office?"

Leaner's foot started to jiggle and his hands clutched together in his lap. "I didn't steal it! I told you that before."

Liz leaned closer. "First, did you give a prototype of your product to Mr. Monahan?"

"Yes."

"Okay," said Liz. "Let me get this straight. You paid off Mr. Monahan not to invest in PipeSafe and gave him a PipeSafe prototype as a trophy of the company you both ran into the ground."

The lawyer leaned toward her. "Now, Detective, that's a very negative way of interpreting the facts."

"We both worked on it," Leaner almost shouted. His face mottled red.

"I didn't ask you that. I asked if that prototype was developed while you were employed by Mr. Gaspare at PipeSafe."

Leaner glanced at his lawyer, who carefully looked away.

Leaner threw an arm up in disgust. "Yes."

"Okay," said Liz. "Putting aside the question of how you ended up in possession of it. What was so attractive about that prototype that you gave it to Mr. Monahan?"

"He gave me two million dollars. And I put a lot of work into that prototype." Leaner shifted hard in his seat. "I added a video feed, it's what makes my company go. I'm working on the next generation of it now."

"So why did you go into his office and take it back after he was murdered?"

"I didn't," he shouted, and fleck of spit arched across the room, just missing Liz.

She sat back, staring at him, then said quietly that she was suspending the interview. Vic followed her out of the room. They walked back to the viewing room in silence. Inside Vic smiled at her.

"Threatening him with talking to his investors? Wow. But honestly, I'm starting to think that he didn't steal the prototype. But why did that set him off more than the money?"

Liz made a sound that sounded like a strangled laugh. "God. One point five million. And it might be legitimate. If Bandini is doing that kind of crap no wonder he's gone legit. Loan-sharking ain't gonna get you that kind of cash."

"We need to figure out if HBK belongs to them. And where the money it invested comes from."

"They got investigated by the Feds a couple of years ago. Bet it's legit?"

Vic shook his head. "Not a bet I'd take."

"Exactly."

They lapsed into silence. From inside the room Leaner said loudly, "What is taking them so long?" He stood up and started to pace.

Liz turned to Vic. "Anything else?"

Vic shook his head. "Not that I can think of right now. Turn him loose."

"Yeah, if he tells me more I might get sick. One point five million dollars."

"We got Thuds Lombardo this afternoon. Let's see if he'll confirm it. And I'm gonna try and track down this Turcelli guy and call the Feds. See if they know anything about HBK Enterprises."

"Please tell me they don't and that it pisses them off."

"You need to talk to Kevin and see where he is looking for that damn prototype. Because something big time is going on with that."

CHAPTER 21

Vic and Liz were silent as they drove to the Bloomfield neighborhood restaurant where Thuds Lombardo had asked to meet. As they crossed the Fort Duquesne Bridge, Pittsburgh's skyline hidden by the overhead deck, Liz looked at him.

"Okay, so? You track this Turcelli guy down?"

He shook his head. "Not yet. I didn't have time. I got hung up with the feds."

"What did they say?"

"I thought you didn't want to know."

Liz closed her eyes. "Vic."

"Okay, yeah, I tracked down an FBI guy who was on the investigation team. He knew about HBK. Bandini uses it to invest in local companies, it's got about three million dollars in it. Money came from Bandini's legitimate businesses, they followed the accounting trail and tracked the source of it all. Why they used cash with Leaner he has no idea, but as Leaner said, it isn't illegal. Maybe old habits die hard with Thuds, I don't know."

She shook her head. "Man, that was all bad money once."

"Maybe, but the HBK money is legit. And Crush will not be happy."

"That's why I get up every day. To make Crush happy."

Vic turned left onto Penn Avenue and began the bumpy drive to Bloomfield. In time Liz glanced at him. "You ready for this?"

He shook his head. "I don't like to say it, but if Leaner told the truth, then Thuds will have no trouble confirming it, and then we're done. The money is legit and everything is public record. It sucks, but that's it. Thuds has a perfectly legal reason why his fingerprint was on the envelopes."

They drove the rest of the way in silence. Vic found a space halfway down the block from the restaurant and parked. A few stores down from the entrance, Levon Grace stepped out of a coffee shop and waited for them in the center of the wide sidewalk, his shoulders back and square.

"Levon," Vic called. "You decided to come for the show?"

Levon's eyes settled on Liz and Vic sensed her tighten. Vic gestured toward Liz. "My partner, Liz Timmons."

He watched them shake hands. For a second he thought they might not let go of each other, but they did.

"Sorry you have to put up with this grouch," said Levon to Liz.

"Everybody has something to redeem them." Liz's eyes searched Levon's face. "I'm hoping someday to find what Vic has."

Levon grinned. "Could end up being your life's work."

"Felt that way for a while now."

Levon's eyes lingered on Liz for a moment before he turned to Vic. "OK. Thuds is inside. Don't know about Bandini. That'll be up to him. Remember he said thirty minutes. He'll hold you to it."

"I remember." Vic glanced at Liz. She was studying Levon's face and he sensed that Levon was aware of it. "You ever hear of a guy called Mike Turcelli working with them?"

Levon shook his head. "No, I just know those guys. When I first met them Thuds had a blond guy who hung out with him, he always wore one of those shiny high school jackets from the eighties. Still had a mullet. His nickname was Sweets. If you see him, call for backup. He's a shoot first and let God figure it out kind of guy." Levon looked at Liz. "Pleased to meet you, by the way."

"Yeah. The same. I heard about you. Vic talks sometimes."

"Not if he can help it."

Liz smiled and there was a warmth in it Vic hadn't seen before.

Levon stepped aside and waved his arm down the street toward the restaurant. "After you guys."

Vic led the way into the restaurant. Thuds was sitting alone at a table near the rear, facing the door. Directly behind him was the glass enclosure for the restaurant's grill, but Vic noted that his table was also beside the hallway that led to the kitchen and the back exit. Thuds spotted them and stood. He was tall and rangy, slim as an I-beam and looked just as hard. His face was lined and cragged under short grey hair, the tendons of his neck like steel cables. He wore a blue herringbone jacket over a black t-shirt and blue jeans. On the table in front of his chair was a short glass and an open bottle of imported mineral water.

When Vic reached him he stuck out a large hand, his brown eyes steady. Vic shook it, aware of the roughness of Lombardo's palms. He introduced Liz and waited as they shook hands. As they settled into their seats Vic noticed Levon perch himself on a stool halfway down the long bar.

"I appreciate you taking the time," said Vic, turning back to Thuds.

"I'm okay with you if it comes from Levon. I can give you thirty minutes." Thuds voice was deep and direct.

Vic nodded. A waitress approached the table but Thuds waved her away with a quick movement of his hand.

"I guess no lunch," said Vic, watching him, trying to read how far he could push him.

"Thirty minutes."

"Okay. Not sure what Levon told you, but Drake Monahan was murdered. I'm sure you heard. We're the investigators. So we're investigating." He paused for a beat, looking for Thuds to smile or recognize the humor. Nothing. "Along the way we found some envelopes with cash in them. Your fingerprints were on a few of them." He leaned back. "We're hoping you could tell us how they got there."

"When'd you find the envelopes?"

"Doesn't matter. We ran the tests, your fingerprints came up. You're in the system, you know." Again Vic waited, but Thuds didn't see the humor in his statement.

"No shit." Thuds sat back and when his jacket moved Vic glimpsed a holstered automatic under his arm. He stayed silent.

Vic gave it a few moments, then said, "Okay, let's do it this way. I'll use my formal questioning. Can you explain why your fingerprints are on the cash envelopes we found in the possession of a murder victim?"

Thuds poured some mineral water into his glass and took a sip. When he put the glass down he said: "I don't actually know."

"So let me help you." Vic gathered his thoughts, guessing that Thuds was fishing to find out what he knew.

"This morning we interviewed the CEO of PipeMine. Last name of Leaner. You know him, or so he says."

He waited a breath, but Thuds stayed absolutely still.

"You invested in his company a couple of years ago via HBK Enterprises. All legit, from what we can see. The feds agree."

Thuds gave just the slightest of nods.

"Oddly, that investment was in cash. Paid monthly. So says Leaner."

Vic paused again. Thuds glanced at the door as someone entered, then looked back at Vic. "Yeah. He wanted cash on a monthly basis. That was the deal."

"You didn't think that was unusual?" asked Liz.

Thuds turned sharp brown eyes on her for a moment and then shifted his gaze to Vic. "Nothing illegal in paying cash, last I heard."

Vic nodded. "Unusual but not illegal in the investment world. Okay, were the payments made in bank envelopes?"

Thuds gave the slightest of nods, almost as if giving away

information was against his better judgment.

"So perhaps some of that cash made it to Drake Monahan? Any idea how that might have happened?"

"You'd have to ask Leaner."

"Did you touch any of the envelopes that went to Leaner?"

Thuds tapped the table with the tips of his fingers on his right hand. "It's possible."

Vic felt a slow anger uncurl inside him. He leaned forward. "Mr. Lombardo. Here's the deal. I asked Levon to set up this meeting because, from what I can make out, everything you guys did with Leaner was legit. I figured we could sit down, have a discussion, keep it friendly, and maybe my partner and I could learn some things. We do that then we don't have to drag you downtown, do everything on the record and get a shitload of Grant Street lawyers involved, which takes weeks and costs all of us time and money. We got simple questions, I think you got simple answers. I figured thirty minutes would be all we need, rather than the whole days and weeks thing with your lawyers. So we got about fifteen minutes left, I'm guessing. You want this to last fifteen minutes or go a shitload longer?"

Thuds watched him for a few seconds, then raised his arm. The waitress appeared beside him. Thuds asked, "You guys want a drink of anything?"

"Diet Coke," said Liz.

Vic pointed at the bottle of mineral water. The waitress faded away. Thuds took a slow breath. "You guys are making progress."

"That's what we do."

"Okay, yeah." Again he checked the door as someone entered. "Sometimes we invest in new companies. I found Leaner at some High Tech Council presentation. What he presented made sense to me, so I had dinner with the guy. I was not crazy about him personally. Too much of a bullshit artist, some gaps in his story, but his product was interesting. We have some money in the natural gas industry around here. The fracking companies? And those guys have refineries, holding tanks, pipelines. After I have dinner with Leaner I talk to them and they say, yeah, they need bots and pigs to clean and monitor their pipelines. I saw a market. We offered Leaner one year of financing. He wanted cash, which I took as a bad sign, but I've worked that way before. About six months into it he lands his first client, who I helped him get. It was one of the frackers I know. I put 'em together. From there he got cash flow pretty quick. Yeah, at that point he may not have needed all of the cash we gave him, but we had a contract. I can show you a copy. How the hell one of those envelopes got to Monahan I don't know."

The waitress appeared and placed cocktail napkins in front of Vic and Liz and topped them with their drinks. After she slipped away Vic sipped his mineral water. He liked the taste.

"Okay," Vic said, "You helped me just now so I'll help with that part. You probably know Monahan invested in Leaner as well. Two million dollars."

Thuds nodded.

"Turns out Leaner cut some deal with Monahan to repay some of his investment. He says it was something else but I'm not sure I believe him. They're trying to say it was legal, and maybe it is, but that was the deal. I think Leaner wanted Monahan's name as an investor so he could attract other investors. Three hundred thousand dollars was the going price."

Thuds' eyes darkened. "That's the kind of bullshit I would expect from Leaner. That's why I didn't like him from the start. So he was using our cash to pay off Monahan?"

"So he says."

Thuds sat back. "Okay. I follow that. He wanted to keep the Monahan payments off the books. Or his investors would crucify him. I sure would have."

"Exactly." Vic sipped his mineral water again. "Anything else you can add? Any involvement by Bandini's daughter, I mean Mary Monahan, in all this?"

Thuds' eyes snapped onto him. If it was possible the tendons along his jaw tightened. "She's got nothing to do with this."

Vic watched him. "If you say so."

Thuds studied him and Vic could see his brain working. "I'll tell you again. She wouldn't know about any of this. She definitely doesn't know what I'm going to tell you now."

Vic nodded, aware of Liz nodding as well.

"You need to know that Leaner's business is missing some shit. Like a bot that actually works. I said I got friends in the fracking business around here, and I got them to use Leaner's bots, right? Turns out they work for shit. So I had a guy do some checking up. Turns out Leaner worked for another guy who actually developed the bots."

"David Gaspare?" cut in Liz.

"Yeah, something like that. Anyway, Leaner is losing his shit fast. My investment is probably a write-off. I give his business six months. So here's my math. Monahan was smart. I bet he figured out Leaner's business was shit and wanted to blow the whistle on him and warn the other investors. Board members have fiduciary responsibility for crap like that, and we can be personally liable for shit if the company goes belly up. I bet Leaner's solution was to pay off Monahan to stay quiet while he fixed his business. So Leaner was buying himself time to fix the bots before Monahan blew the whistle."

Everyone was silent. Vic's mind was working.

Thuds leaned forward again. "And I'm telling you, Monahan's wife knows nothing about this. She's out of it. Okay. That's thirty minutes."

Vic sat back. "See? Thirty minutes, no lawyers, just a conversation. It works."

Thuds stood up and waited for Vic and Liz to do the same. He stuck out his hand. As he and Vic shook he said, "Maybe it works between you and me, but how about your boss, Crush Davis? This gonna work for him?"

Vic dropped Thud's rough hand and held his eyes. "I can't speak for him, he's got a career to worry about and you're a career maker for a cop like that. I just want to figure out who stabbed Monahan. So this worked for me. I'll try and keep it that way."

"I guess we'll see."

He watched Thuds and Liz shake hands. As they shook, a short, round man slipped lightly out of the hallway and joined them. He had dark hair and Vic recognized his large brown eyes.

"Mr. Bandini," he said carefully. Beside him, Liz straightened. Bandini held out his hand and they shook. He shook hands with Liz then turned back to Vic and looked him up and down.

"Vic Lenoski, right?" Bandini asked.

"It is."

"Yeah." He gesticulated to the four of them. "I like this. Old school. Cops these days sit in their cars staring at computers. They don't show up and look you in the eye. You remember a sergeant named Wroblewski?" He pointed to his nose. "Busted here?"

"Yeah. Saw him on Sunday. He's one of those guys doesn't know how to retire."

"You see him next time, tell him I say hello. I know him from the old days. He took down those East End drug selling assholes. Did everyone a favor. You couldn't work with those guys."

"I remember."

Bandini looked Vic up and down again. "Yeah, and I remember that during the raids a rookie took a .45 slug off the shoulder. Still got his guy. Chased him across three fenced back yards leaking blood the whole way. Tackled the guy."

"You got a long memory, Mr. Bandini." Vic felt an itch from the scar on his shoulder and ignored it.

"Long memory is how you get ahead," said Thuds. "You gotta play the long game."

"Yeah," replied Vic, meeting his eyes. "I heard that before."

Bandini glanced at Liz, nodded, then said carefully to Vic, "I heard about your daughter. I'm sorry about that. Must be hard as hell."

Vic struggled to keep his face impassive. "I met one of your daughters recently. She goes by Mrs. Monahan now."

"Maria? Yeah. She calls herself Mary. I guess Maria wasn't

white bread enough for her neighborhood. I feel bad for her. Early to be a widow."

"Looks like she's gonna be running her husband's company now."

Bandini blinked his large eyes carefully. "I guess I heard that. Okay, good to see ya." He turned and nodded at Levon and as quickly disappeared down the hallway to the back of the restaurant.

"You need me again," said Thuds, "let Levon know. Maybe for you guys I can find another thirty minutes." He nodded at them and followed Bandini down the hall.

"Jesus Christ," said Liz as they watched Thuds disappear down the hallway. "Leaner had motive to want Monahan dead."

"Yeah, if Leaner bought six months from Monahan with cash, Monahan dead might buy him another six months. Or longer. Until Thuds calls him on it."

Levon walked up. "You guys good?"

"Yeah," said Vic. "That helped. Thuds said if we want to talk again to do it through you."

Levon cracked a smile. "Okay, good sign. Maybe I don't have to sleep with my sig under my pillow tonight." He looked at Liz. "Good to meet you."

"You said that."

"Yeah. I'll need to come up with something more."

"I got time." The smallest of smiles ghosted across her lips.

Vic looked from one to the other, feeling like a third wheel.

CHAPTER 22

As they drove back to the North Side, Liz asked a string of questions about Levon. He walked her through his birth in Sewickley, the missing father, Levon's high priced education and two tours in Iraq. How he free-lanced for a private intelligence agency. When the conversation lagged she looked at him, and Vic could tell her mind had moved back to the case.

Liz stretched her neck. "Leaner. Like you said, if what Thuds said is true and he needs more time to save his business, that gives him motive."

"Yeah. He'd want Monahan out of the way. Otherwise Monahan tells the Board about the product problems. And remember the oil on the knife blade? Leaner has a tool shop outside his office. Maybe he made whatever stabbed Monahan. No record of the knife purchase that way."

Liz nodded. "I forgot about the oil stains. So he's our number one?"

"With a bullet." Vic steered the car into the parking lot behind their offices. "I say tomorrow we run his alibi again. See if we can crack it."

Vic parked but Liz made no move to get out. "I ain't hearing it in your voice, Vic." She watched him.

Vic knew what she meant. "I guess I'm eighty percent right now. Let's look at his alibi. Maybe I'll feel better after that. But right now he's our number one suspect. No question."

"I'd like to get the guy just for being such a sleaze ball."

"No law against that, unfortunately."

"And explain something to me. You took a bullet during a drug bust? How is it I never heard that story?"

Vic stared through the windshield. "It wasn't that bad. Grazed the top of my shoulder. Four inches to the right and you'd be working with different partner. I was pumping so much adrenaline I didn't notice until after I'd caught the guy." He looked at her. "So there's not that much to talk about."

Liz shook her head. "Guys. You coming in?"

"Something I gotta do first. Then I'll type up interview notes and take a run at finding Turcelli."

As Liz crossed to the front door, Kevin Sligo popped out as if he had been waiting for her. Vic gritted his teeth, annoyed, knowing Sligo wanted an update he could pass to Crush, but he was sure Liz wouldn't mention Thuds. He steered the car toward Lawrenceville. Fifteen minutes later he wound along an access road inside Allegheny Cemetery. He parked in an area of newer graves, left the car and crossed to his daughter's headstone. Somehow, Bandini mentioning his daughter had made him want to visit.

A small vase lay on its side at the base of the stone, dead flowers scattered nearby. Vic gathered them up and placed the vase on the base of the headstone, tucked around the side. He guessed his wife had visited, perhaps several weeks prior. He stared at his daughter's name etched on the stone, feeling the oddness he always felt when he visited. Like every other marker in the cemetery it listed someone who was no longer there, but in his daughter's case, even her remains weren't there. It was a memory of a memory and he could never get comfortable with it. Finally he patted the top of the stone and headed back to the car, still holding the dead flowers.

He headed toward the North Side but couldn't bring himself to return to work. He had no desire to bump into Sligo, or Crush for that matter. And something Bandini had said was stuck in his mind, something about the way he picked his words. Instead he stopped at The Barking Shark, a North Side bar frequented by police officers. It was Wroblewski's second office.

It was still early and only three men were scattered along the long bar, three more at a table. He picked a stool one down from a half full draft and an empty shot glass someone had left unattended. He ordered his own draft and a shot of whiskey. As he sipped Wroblewski settled himself onto the stool in front of the unattended drinks.

"Wroblewski," said Vic.

Wroblewski pointed his broken nose in Vic's direction and grinned crookedly.

Vic raised his beer and they both sipped. "So you know, I ran into someone today, told me to say hi to you."

"Yeah?"

"Dom Bandini."

The bartender, without being asked, replenished Wroblewski's shot glass. He sipped carefully and turned to Vic.

"That old fart still alive?"

"Yeah. Had a sit down with Thuds this afternoon. Bandini showed up at the end. Still got those big brown deer eyes."

"Yeah. Not what you'd expect for a guy like that."

Vic studied Wroblewski. "You knew him, back in the day, right?"

Wroblewski drank some beer. "Yeah. When I worked undercover. Hard not to in those days. I was put into his organization, but I think he smelled me out right away, or he had a guy inside our department who told him I was a cop."

"I'd bet on the inside guy."

"That fox, I'd bet the same way."

Vic remembered Bandini's comment. "You know, I was always amazed how fast you got inside that East End gang. The ones you busted? And Bandini said something today, made me wonder."

Wroblewski turned on his stool and faced him. His eyes were red rimmed but sharp. "Is that a fact? About what?"

"I always wondered. Usually takes six or seven months

to get a gang to take you on. Even then it might not work. But that gang you busted, Bandini said no one could work with that gang. Makes me think he wanted them out of the way as well." Vic watched Wroblewski for any anger, but he seemed unconcerned, almost amused. "I could give a shit, by the way, but I just wondered about it."

Wroblewski shrugged. "Yeah, well, you gotta dance with the devil if you want to get to heaven. So yeah. Bandini gave me an introduction to one of the guys running the gang. They figured if Bandini recommended me then I was clean. That's how I got in so fast. I didn't have to earn my way in."

Vic held up his beer as a toast. "Good move."

"I get what you're really asking me. And so we're square, no, back then I hadn't figured out that Bandini was using me. He told me he wanted me to work for him in that gang, report back to him, and I thought what a great way to get good with Bandini. So I took the introduction and went in. A year after we rolled up the gang, Bandini was dealing all over their city. That's when I figured out he'd worked me. A twofer. He got me out of his gang and I rolled up a competitor for him." Wroblewski drank down the rest of the whiskey. "Seems he's mostly legit now."

"Right. He figured out the crooks who make the real money hang out on Wall Street. So they got into that. But today I saw Thuds had a gun under his coat. You gotta wonder."

Suddenly Vic caught the smell of something, like flowers past their prime.

"Oh God. Should have known I'd find you dinosaurs in here."

Vic turned to see Lorna standing behind the empty stool between them.

"This stool taken?" She asked.

"Hell no, Lorna," said Wroblewski. He patted the stool between them. "Hop on up."

"Thank god," she said, brushing her breasts against Vic as she squeezed onto the stool. She settled her purse on the bar top, a large soft sided bag that gaped open. Inside Vic saw a cell phone and a pack of Virginia Slims. He was surprised; he had never seen Lorna smoke.

Wroblewski waved at the bartender and ordered something for Lorna, but she put her hand on Vic's forearm.

"Crush was looking for you this afternoon. He wants an update on Thuds. Wants to know when you plan to bring him in. He wants to see you tomorrow morning."

Vic nodded, suddenly tired. "He didn't email me."

She leaned closer to him. "He was talking to that Kevin Sligo in his office. He told Kevin to find out what you're doing."

He nodded. He knew Crush would be angry that he'd already talked to Thuds and saw no reason to bring him in. "Thanks, Lorna," he said quietly, avoiding her eyes.

The bartender placed a colored drink in front of Lorna and she pointed at Wroblewski and Vic's glasses, so he set them up again with whiskey shots and beers.

Vic drank and before long noticed that Lorna had swung around on her stool so her back was to Wroblewski and she faced him. Her breasts were just a few inches from his arm. The noise in the bar grew louder and he felt warm. He nodded as Lorna spoke to him, taking in what she said but not really understanding it, his mind returning to Leaner. He kept trying to believe that Leaner was paying Monahan to stay quiet, but that bothered him. And then a thought formed. Monahan had invested two million dollars with Leaner and was getting back three hundred thousand. But if the business went belly up, he would lose one point seven million. He didn't see how that made sense. It would be worth more to Monahan to force Leaner to wind down the business right away. Sell the assets.

"Vic!"

He blinked and found Lorna's face just a few inches from his own. His nose filled with the flat smell of face powder.

"You're a million miles away! Did you hear what I said?"

He tried a defensive smile, hoping that she might let him off easy. "Sorry. I was thinking about a case."

She pulled back a bit. "Well, that's okay, but I was starting to think you didn't like me."

Vic swigged the last of his beer. "How could anyone dislike you, Lorna?" He smiled as if he meant it. "Sorry, I have to get to the office and close down some things. Write up some notes."

"Vic, you need to cut loose a little." She leaned closer, her breasts settling onto his arm. "Have some fun."

"Yeah, I'm a guy born for fun," said Vic, sliding off the stool on the opposite side from her. He tossed a twenty on the bar and slapped Wroblewski on the back. "Take it easy."

Wroblewski craned his neck around to look at him. "Watch yourself with Thuds and Bandini," he said to Vic, his eyes bloodshot above his bent nose. "They always got something going."

"You know that." Vic stopped and slid closer to him. "You ever heard of a guy named Turcelli, works with them? They were using him as a bag man on one of their deals."

Wroblewski's forehead wrinkled and he nodded, his chin against his shoulder. "Yeah. Mike Turcelli. You watch out for him. Wind-up toy. Just the kind of guy Thuds likes. Too stupid to think for himself, but you feed him a load of crap and cut him loose and he'll take down anyone. He did four in Somerset for assault, you can look him up. Pretty sure he worked over a lawyer Bandini employed a few years back, but the lawyer won't talk. He puts that kind of fear into you."

"Thanks."

A smile cracked Wroblewski's lips. "You take care, Vic. I'll tell the devil you got the next dance."

CHAPTER 23

V ic slid behind the wheel of his car and sat for a few moments, breathing slowly. He was too drunk to drive, he knew, but he didn't care. It was barely four blocks to his office. With exaggerated care he turned on the ignition and pulled out. Five minutes later he settled into his cube in the half deserted offices.

It took him half an hour to type up his notes from the meeting with Thuds and print them out. He placed them face down on his desk to reread in the morning. He checked the online case system and saw that Liz had already appended her notes from the interview with Leaner. He scrawled a quick reminder to himself to think through all the possibilities around Monahan's decision to take the three hundred grand in payoffs from Leaner, and opened his top right drawer to put the note away. He stopped, staring at the thick files and rubber bands that held all of the notes and documents related to Dannie's disappearance. Carefully, he placed his other palm over the top file, as if he was checking the heat of burners on a stove top. Nothing. He raised his hand, dropped the note onto the folder and closed the drawer.

On his computer he searched the system for Mike Turcelli, and just as Wroblewski had told him, found his rap sheet. The years in Somerset was just the cap on a long career of petty crime, mostly robbery, including a dishonorable discharge from the Marines. Vic sat back and stared at the computer screen, then clicked on the link to Turcelli's military record. The dishonorable discharge was rendered in bureaucracy speak, but Vic could read between the lines. While returning from a combat patrol, Turcelli had beaten up his commanding officer. He stared at the sentences, trying to understand more, because the record showed the dishonorable discharge but didn't list any time in military jail. He knew Marines didn't beat up their commanding officers and only receive a dishonorable discharge. He guessed there were mitigating circumstances, something along the lines of his commanding officer doing something wrong that led to the beating, and the dishonorable discharge was a compromise. He skimmed Turcelli's certifications list, his eyes halting on one item. Turcelli was a black belt in Marine Corps Martial Arts. Vic sat back, aware of the buzzing of the fluorescent lights and the vague smell of carpet cleaner. The Marines martial arts system included edged weapons training, so Turcelli was an expert at killing with a knife. He made a note of that fact and added it to the other in the top drawer.

He was sober enough now to drive home. On his way he thought about Liz's reaction to meeting Levon Grace. He decided he could have some fun with that.

At home he sucked down a double Jim Beam and searched his refrigerator for food. He found the unopened Chinese takeout container from two nights earlier, pried open the lid and stared at the listless vegetables speckled with grease. As he pressed the lid back into place his doorbell rang.

Vic navigated his way to the front door, feeling the rejuvenating effect of the Jim Beam. He pulled open the door.

"Ta-dah!" Lorna stood on his front porch, holding up a bag of takeout food.

"Lorna?" He was confused.

"I brought you dinner. Dinosaurs like you need sustenance." Her eyes shone. She wasn't wearing a jacket, and in the coolness of the evening her nipples struggled against her blouse. Lorna seemed proud about it. She stared at him. "Well, ask me in."

He stepped aside. "How do you know where I live?"

As he closed the door he saw Lorna scan the living room, taking in the single chair and the television perched on the packing boxes. She spun around and looked at him. "Geez, Vic, aren't you a detective? I work for Crush. I see all the personnel files. Home addresses are a snap." She snapped the fingers of her free hand to make her point.

"Ah, okay." He was uncomfortable with her in the house. The walls pressed in on him.

She held up the plastic bag of takeout. "I wasn't sure what you liked. So I got Indian and Thai."

He started to say that he had already eaten as the first step to easing her out of the house, but what came out of his mouth was "Is there any of that bread stuff with the Indian food?"

"Naan? You bet. Where's the kitchen? I could so use a drink."

Vic found himself pointing at the doorway and hating himself for it. She launched herself in that direction, calling over her shoulder, "I don't know who decorated your place, Vic, but you did *not* get your money's worth."

Vic followed her into the kitchen, listening as she giggled at her own joke. He didn't know how far drunk she was but he'd bet she'd had more than a few. He found a clean glass in the cupboard and offered her Jim Beam. She shook her head.

"I figured you weren't used to entertaining, what with Anne not living here anymore." Somehow she said the last part of the sentence pointedly. Vic knew that police spouses met frequently, and he realized that Anne must have stopped going to the get togethers. With a smile and a flourish, Lorna pulled a bottle of vodka from the same bag as the food, and followed that with a two cans of Red Bull. She wagged one of the cans at him. "And you are going to need some energy tonight."

Somehow he believed her.

Vic stuck to Jim Beam as he ate, all doubles, while Lorna sipped down two vodkas. As they finished the edges of the night softened and the house walls moved away from him. At some point Lorna was sitting on his lap, slurping another vodka and Red Bull, as he finished another slug of Jim Beam. He heard himself laughing, the sound of it strange, and then his hand was inside her blouse, finding whole handfuls of her. Then they were in bed together, and he was overwhelmed with her heat, as if he had moved close to a blazing hearth after a week of crossing the tundra. It radiated through him, drawing him out of himself, his whole body aching with the heat and tightness of it all.

He was shaking and sweaty when he woke. He glanced at his phone on the bedside table. It was past three. The bedroom was at the front of the house and overlooked the street. Lorna's breathing was regular and peaceful, and in the orange light from the streetlight her hair appeared redder than he remembered. He rubbed his face and wiped the dampness from his forehead, grimacing at the churning in his stomach. He rose and drank water from the bathroom tap. When he returned to the bedroom he stared at Lorna's shape in his bed, her wide hips tenting the sheets. It emptied him as he suddenly realized how much he missed the shape of his wife sleeping in their bed, the way the sheets formed to her slight frame.

When his phone's alarm woke him again at six thirty he showered and dressed, leaving Lorna to sleep. His mouth was dry, despite drinking shower water. His head didn't hurt, but he felt dislocated, as if he'd taken a knee to the temple. At the bottom of the stairs he turned into the living room to find Anne, his wife, standing in the center of the room, a small frown on her face. Vic stepped backwards involuntarily at the sight of her.

"Sorry to stop by so early. But I wanted to catch you before work. I kept my key."

Vic tried desperately to focus. "Sure."

"Kind of a mess," she said, looking around, more to herself than to him. Somehow her faded blue jeans and a yellow cotton crew neck sweater seemed right for the house. He had the feeling she'd lost weight.

"I like how you're doing your hair now," Vic heard himself saying. "It's longer and that sweep."

She looked down and self consciously touched her hair.

"Anyway," added Vic. "I've been meaning to clean up. Maybe buy a bit more furniture."

She looked at him, her brown eyes serious. "The hours you work? I doubt it."

He shrugged, not having an answer, thinking of Lorna upstairs and hating himself for having her in the house.

"Anyway." Anne shifted one step closer to him. "I wanted to talk to you about Dannie's anniversary." Her eyes clouded. "My sister took control of things last time you came over. You weren't in the right frame of mind, but I think you meant well. And I didn't handle it well when you talked about her grave."

"You were right. I don't know why I said that."

She was silent for a beat, not disagreeing with him, but also not wanting to pile on about it, he guessed. "So what do you want to do?" he asked.

She pursed her lips to speak but the stairs creaked and a moment later Lorna stepped into the living room, wrapped in an old bathrobe of Anne's that was too small for her. Anne stiffened, her eyes wide.

"Anne!" said Lorna. "What a nice surprise!" She glanced at Vic and touched his arm. "You didn't tell me Anne was stopping by."

"I didn't know." It came out as a whisper.

"It wasn't planned," said Anne, her words overlapping Vic's.

As Vic watched, Anne seemed to shrink. She retreated a step.

"Can I make you tea or coffee?" asked Lorna.

"No, I was just going." The words sounded strangled. Anne glanced at Vic, her eyes sad. "We can talk later." She faded backwards toward the door, as if she was disappearing, and then she was just gone, the screen door slamming. It was the first time he had ever heard her slam a door. He knew it wasn't from anger, just her hurry to get away.

He and Lorna stood in silence for a moment and then

Lorna said, "That was kind of awkward. I knew you guys were separated, but does she come over much?"

"No," said Vic softly. "That was the first time." *And also the last*, he thought. He couldn't take his eyes from the place where she had been standing. It was as if something was supposed to be there, but wasn't.

Lorna giggled. "I need a bigger robe. Anne is so petite."

She opened the front of her robe, rearranging it, and Vic knew that the flash of her naked breasts was on purpose. He ignored her and turned toward the kitchen. His cell phone rang. He crossed to the counter and pressed the accept button.

"You awake?" Liz's voice sounded tight.

"I am now."

"Then get out here. Chris Leaner's house."

"We don't have enough to charge him. We have to break his alibi."

"Not any more. And so much for him being our lead suspect. He's dead. Stabbed. I'll text you the address."

"How'd you find out so fast?"

"I know the first cop on the scene. He called me, so it didn't work through Crush like usual."

"Okay. Jesus." Vic closed his eyes and opened them, trying to focus.

"And you're gonna like this part."

"What's that?"

"Same cop got a partial plate on a black Caddy SUV leaving the scene."

"Okay."

"It's registered to a Vincent Lombardo."

"Thuds."

"Oh yeah. Crush is gonna cream his pants."

CHAPTER 24

As Vic drove he kept drinking in large gulps of air, the picture of Anne backing out the front door riveted into his consciousness. He stopped at Dunkin Donuts for coffee, hoping that would shake the image loose and hot wire his brain. He followed residential streets into the South Side. Leaner's home address was a row house overlooking the Monongahela River and the railway lines that ran along the southern shore. As he parked alongside the crime scene tape the grill of the coroners' van filled his rear view mirror. Knowing he couldn't carry the coffee inside the crime scene, he slugged back a mouthful, scorching his tongue and the roof of his mouth. He climbed out of the car, poured what was left into the gutter and waited as Freddy slid out of the van's passenger seat and collected the large square box he used to transport his equipment.

"Not a good way to start the day," called Freddy as he joined him.

"You have no idea." Vic pressed his tongue to the roof of his mouth, trying to ease the pain. They ducked under the crime scene tape and walked to the front door, where Vic nodded to the officer guarding the scene. As he and Freddy struggled into booties and gloves, a train churned past, so loud he could feel it.

"Detective Timmons called me. She says this is related to Sunday's murder? Perhaps?" shouted Freddy over the clattering of the train.

"Dead guy was our lead suspect from Sunday's murder."

"Just because he is dead he is no longer?"

Vic didn't answer because Freddy was right, and it was a level of complication his brain wasn't ready to process. As they stepped into the front hall, Liz appeared out of a room to the right that contained a lot of white furniture and chrome.

Liz looked him up and down, a frown tightening her face. "In the kitchen," she said, her words angry. Without waiting she headed down a narrow hall toward the back of the house, her booties shushing on the hardwood floor. Vic followed, working his tongue around his mouth. Every few steps he heard a thump and a string of German curses as Freddy's equipment box hit one of the walls.

The hallway opened into a large, modern kitchen of stainless steel and sleek white cabinets. The room was so large that Vic guessed someone had combined several smaller rooms by knocking down the walls. Liz was standing on the far side of a large island. She pointed at a stainless steel range top and double oven that looked like it belonged in a restaurant.

Vic walked around the island. Leaner was crumpled at the base of the stove, his back against the oven doors, one leg thrown out and a pool of dried blood around him on the hardwood floor.

Freddy pushed past. "I will give you my professional opinion," he boomed, his voice filling the kitchen. He banged down his large box, looked from Vic to Liz and back to Vic, then pointed at the body. "He's cooked."

Liz looked at the ceiling in exasperation. "Jesus, really?"

Seeing her reaction, Freddy grinned and snapped open the latches on the lid of his box. "You do not want to enjoy your job?"

Liz glared at him. "I interviewed this man yesterday."

Vic shook his head slowly, his count of stab wounds at fourteen, including three horizontal stabs above the belt line. "Same MO as Monahan." He looked at Liz, trying to get his tongue working. "You said the cop who found the body saw an SUV pulling away?"

Liz studied him for a moment and Vic knew she was deciding whether to stay angry with him. "Yeah," she said finally, her tone normal. "As he came down the street it blew by him going the other way. It was why he only got a partial plate. He had to stop and get out of his car to read it."

"Good work." He closed his eyes and tried to focus. His tongue still burned. He could hear Freddy rummaging through instruments in his box. "But the blood is dry. This happened last night some time." He felt his mind straining to process what was in front of him and he opened his eyes. "Freddy, soon as you have it. Give us a time window when this happened."

"And Crush is on his way," said Liz, a note of warning in her voice.

"You called him?"

"Had to, we're out of protocol. At least he won't show up stinking of booze."

Freddy waved a long metal instrument with a point on the end. "Hey, Vic, if I punch your liver with this, I find out how long your liver has left?"

Vic pointed at Leaner's body. "There's nothing wrong with my liver. Time of death, Freddy."

Freddy shrugged and started toward the body on the balls of his feet, looking for a way to get near without stepping in blood.

"How and when exactly did this get called in?" Asked Vic.

"Six forty-seven this morning. Anonymous. First responder happened to be on Carson Street a few blocks away, it's how he got here so fast."

Freddy found a way to kneel next to the body and inserted the instrument into Leaner's side and waited, timing it with his watch. Liz turned through an archway into the room with the white furniture and chrome side tables and crossed to a wall thermostat. When Freddy withdrew the instrument from Leaner's side Liz called out to him.

"Sixty-eight degrees Fahrenheit."

Freddy nodded and checked a piece of paper taped to the inside lid of his equipment box. "Dead since last night," he said as Liz rejoined them.

Vic was having trouble sorting out the time sequence and was glad when Liz cut in. "Maybe around midnight? That explains the sweat pants and t-shirt. He was getting ready for bed."

"What have we got?" Crush's voice thundered through the kitchen. Vic stepped aside so Crush could see Leaner.

"Stabbed!" said Crush.

"Right you are," answered Vic, trying to keep the sarcasm out of his voice.

"What else we got?"

Vic nodded at Leaner's body. "We just figured out that he died last night. From what he's wearing maybe closer to midnight. No murder weapon we can see, but we need to search the house yet and, who knows, it might be underneath him. Tech guys are on their way. And we got a partial plate on a black SUV leaving the scene."

Crush thumped a fist into the palm of his other hand. "Owner?"

Vic was aware of Liz watching him. "Yeah. Liz ran it through. We only got three letters so it's not confirmed, but we have a partial match to a black caddy SUV owned by Thuds Lombardo."

"Damn!" Crush thumped the flat of his hand on the countertop and Liz winced. Crush was wearing booties but hadn't bothered with latex gloves. "We got him! When do you have Thuds in our offices to interview him?"

Vic felt his body tense but his mind was oddly loose, and he just didn't care. "Actually, we did it yesterday. Met him at a restaurant in Bloomfield."

Crush's face froze and he peered at Vic. "What the shit did you do? I told you to bring him in. That was an order. I want him on tape. Not some half bullshit conversation that everyone remembers differently." He looked around. "And where's Kevin? I told you to have him shadow you." He edged toward Vic as he talked until he was standing a few inches away. Vic smelled some kind of woodsy aftershave. "You ignored a direct order?"

Crush's voice turned hoarse.

"There wasn't enough to bring Thuds in," said Liz.

Crush pointed at her, his arm fully extended, his eyes never leaving Vic. "You shut up." He leaned closer. "Well?"

Vic felt himself leaning back. "It would have taken two weeks of lawyers pounding tables to get him into an interview room. Thuds is too smart to leave his print on an envelope if he was doing something illegal."

Crush reared back. "Crooks are crooks because they're stupid. I told you to bring him in for an interview."

"My way was faster. I got a sit down in two days and he's willing to meet us again."

Sweat beaded Crush's forehead. "You got his fingerprint on an envelope in the possession of a murder victim. And you got my order to bring him in. And now you got him fleeing the scene of a crime."

"We have his *car* leaving the scene of a crime. Maybe. And Leaner died last night, not this morning, when the car was seen leaving the scene." Vic looked away. He sensed Crush lean in closer and felt his breath on his cheek. He held his breath, wondering if Crush had picked up the smell of his breath.

"You understand insubordination, Detective Lenoski? I gave you an order. Now get Kevin here. I want him attached to your hip." He spun and left the kitchen, leaving the three of them in silence.

"I will mark where he hit the counter," said Freddy, into Crush's wake.

Vic shook his head. "No. Just process the room as you find it. If his print shows up let him explain it." He turned to Liz. "Don't get caught up in this. Stay out of it. I'm the one he's after."

Liz's face clouded. "Screw that. He's an asshole. We got good information out of Thuds. That was the right way to handle that interview."

Vic met Liz's gaze. "Thanks, but be careful, okay?" He tried to wet his lips and failed. "Look the place over?"

She nodded. "I'll call Kevin."

Vic shook his head. "No. I'll do it. Or I'll get that handed to me as well." He turned and crossed the kitchen to the archway that led into the dining room.

"There's a study at the front of the house," said Liz. "I'll take upstairs."

Vic called his agreement and checked the cupboards and drawers in the dining room breakfront. He found a few linens and a smatter of service plates and cutlery, but nothing of interest. He exited into the hall and swung around into the office at the front of the house. The study held a desk, chair and a couple of armchairs facing a wall-mounted flat screen television. He sat down in one of the armchairs, pulled out his phone and dialed Kevin's number. When he answered Vic knew from the background noise that he was driving.

"It's Vic. Okay, so, Leaner was murdered last night about midnight. Same MO as Monahan. We're investigating the scene if you want to stop down."

Kevin was silent for a few moments. "Yeah," he said finally. His voice was high as if he was angry. "Crush called. He said you'd call. That was like fifteen minutes ago."

Vic closed his eyes. "You on your way?"

"Yeah."

"So you know the address. See you when you get here." He touched the disconnect button, dropped his hand and sat in the chair with his eyes closed for a few moments. In the darkness, he gradually realized something was out of place. He opened his eyes and listened. The rumble of the train was gone. It had finally passed through. In the quiet he heard Freddy reciting his findings from the inspection of Leaner's body into a portable recorder and the good-natured banter of the crime scene techs as they lugged their equipment through the front door. Above him the ceiling creaked as Liz moved around. He stood up, slid his phone into his pocket and motioned to the nearest tech.

"Photos of the room," he said quietly. "Then I want to tear this place apart."

The tech nodded and dragged a camera from one of his

carry boxes. Vic waited as he moved about, the camera clicks like a latch falling again and again, locking something away. When he finished, Vic moved to the desk, sat down and began to empty drawers, leafing through the papers he found.

Kevin arrived about fifteen minutes later, and after surveying the study disappeared to talk to Freddy. Liz appeared ten minutes after that.

"Nothing much," she said as she entered the study. "How about you?"

Vic shook his head. "Main thing is what isn't here."

Liz cocked her head to the side, her eyebrows arched. He pointed to an empty space on the desktop and a single charger wire lying at its edge. "Laptop. Perp must have taken it."

"Or it's in his office."

"We'll know that soon enough." He leaned back in the chair and shouted, "Kevin!" Liz looked away quickly so the crime technician wouldn't see her smile.

Kevin appeared in the doorway. Vic noted that his red tie was perfectly matched to his light blue shirt and grey wool pants. "Kevin, here's the deal. This is important. Leaner's laptop is missing. We're guessing he left it in his office. Can you run down there, pick it up and get it over to tech? We really need to see what's on it. The appointment book may identify the perp."

Kevin's eyes widened slightly even as he tried to appear nonchalant. "I'm on it," he said, spun and disappeared out the front door.

Liz laughed softly. "You know damn well that laptop is nowhere near his offices. Everyone brings them home with them."

"Kevin needs to learn that." Vic looked at her. "But you never know, do you?"

She nodded her head, but the smile stayed put.

Vic rubbed his eyes. "Did you find anything at all?"

"Not really. I don't think he has a girlfriend. One toothbrush, no women's clothes or any drawers kept for someone else. Box of condoms is unopened. Not a very imaginative dresser, but I guess no law against that."

Vic nodded. "Only interesting thing I found is this." He pointed to a large evidence bag laid out on the floor with a series of others. "That big one with the folded papers inside? All mechanical drawings from PipeSafe, David Gaspare's company. Remember Gaspare said Leaner stole them? There they are."

"Check Gaspare again?"

"Yeah. I want to confirm those are the stolen documents. Not sure it helps much, but I guess it's worth doing."

"Maybe also see if he has an alibi for last night." In the distance a faint rumbling sound asserted itself. Vic shook his head. "Damn trains. I don't know how he lived here. They go by every few minutes and they are long."

"Once you get used to it you hardly notice them. My parents' place was near a railway."

Vic stood. He felt stiff all over and while he wasn't as exhausted, the tiredness still lingered in his joints and behind his eyes. "We need the laptop. Maybe he kept everything on the cloud and we can get to that."

In the kitchen he found Freddy snapping the locks on his equipment box, shaking his head and talking to himself under his breath. He stopped when he saw Vic and straightened up. "I just finished, so your timing is good. Okay. I get you full report in two days. But I can say this. Cause of death is stabbing, stab pattern is very close to how your last victim was attacked. Und the stabs were made by a very wide blade, like last time. So likely the same attacker. Very few defensive wounds, maybe he knew his attacker."

Vic glanced at Liz and she nodded. "No forced entry. He let the person in or they had a key. Just like damn Sunday."

Freddy broke in. "No oil on the blade this time, but it looks as if there is dirt. I will confirm."

Vic nodded. "Yeah, and I saw the same orientation with the stabs, the left side of the body."

Freddy nodded. "Yes. Right handed killer. But I put all this in the reports. *Und* now you know what I say?"

Vic and Liz stayed quiet, knowing what Freddy wanted them to say. To keep things moving Vic finally spoke up, "All of this is speculation until it's confirmed and in the final report."

Freddy smiled. "See? Crush should know how easy you are to train. Like a monkey."

Vic turned to Liz. "Gaspare? I want to make sure those mechanical drawings belong to him, and like you said, check his alibi. And he's five minutes from here."

"Yeah. I got my car here. I'll follow you."

"I'll sign out the mechanical drawings from the tech guys."

They followed Freddy down the hall, watching him bump his large plastic equipment box on the wall several times, cursing each time he did. Vic collected the mechanical drawings and signed for them. Outside, he breathed deeply, closing his eyes for a moment. The burn in his mouth was now a gentle ache, but his eyes felt disconnected from his face and he didn't know what to do with the churn of anger that was growing over the way Crush had yelled at him. He leaned against the top of his car and tried to summon some saliva and spit last night's bad taste out of his mouth, but nothing came.

He watched Liz slide into an old Ford Escort and execute a three point turn before stopping farther down the road to wait for him. He started his car and did the same, the rumble of the latest train permeating the car. Vic shook his head, finished his turnaround and passed Liz, headed toward the row of bars and restaurants that lined South Side's main street.

As Vic drove he searched for a convenience store where he could buy a bottle of water, but spotted nothing before he had to take the left turn leading into the South Side Flats. Each time he checked on Liz she was a consistent twenty feet behind him, her running lights on. Two minutes later they parked against the curb outside Gaspare's house.

Vic climbed out holding the plastic evidence bag of mechanical drawings and waited for Liz to joined him. She was talking on her phone as she did.

"Sounds good," she said, as she approached, then pressed the disconnect button. There was contentedness in the smile of her full lips and the way she carried herself.

"What was that all about?" Asked Vic.

"Personal," she answered, and slid the phone into her purse. The smile vanished when she looked at Gaspare's house. "He cleaned up." She started up the walk and Vic followed, noting how the dead leaves were gone from the porch and the metal chairs pushed together and covered with plastic. But what stuck in his mind was that he couldn't remember a time when Liz had ever told him that a call was 'personal.' Or seen her smile quite like that.

Liz waited for him, standing to one side of the front door. He rang the bell, aware of how wet and cold the wind felt. He noticed that the trowel was missing from the plant pot.

When the door opened, Gaspare was wearing grey flannel slacks, a starched blue shirt and pale red tie. The outfit reminded Vic of Kevin's. Gaspare's hair was combed and his face shorn of beard and stubble. Without the dark facial hair he looked paler than Vic remembered, and there was also a sharpness in his eyes that was new.

"Yes?" Gaspare frowned at them.

"Mr. Gaspare," Vic said carefully, trying to catch up to all the changes since their last visit, "you remember Detective Timmons and I. I was wondering if you could help us with a couple of things. Starting with this." He held up the plastic bag holding the mechanical drawings.

Gaspare peered through the clear plastic and his frown lightened. "Okay. Sure. But you guys need to be quick. I have a meeting in forty minutes and I have to go."

"It won't take long," called Liz as she followed them into the house.

Gaspare led them through the living room and into the dining area he used as his office. While the living room looked the same as their last visit, the dining room was spotless. Vic glanced through the door into the kitchen. It was also tidy, and for some reason this change from their last visit made him cautious.

"Well?" Gaspare looked at them, his eyes darting from one to the other.

"Okay," said Vic. "We came across these mechanical drawings at a crime scene. I just wanted to make sure they're yours, or belonged to your company originally." He placed the large plastic bag with the mechanical drawings on the table. Gaspare bent over and stared at them. He didn't touch the bag.

"Yeah. Those are the ones Leaner stole."

"Thought they might be. I was just wondering, when did you last see Chris Leaner?"

"You kidding me?" Gaspare stared at him. "That dick? Not since I kicked him out the front door of my business a few years ago. The guy is slime. Can I have these back? Where'd you get them? What crime scene?"

Liz interjected, "So you haven't seen him in at least a couple of years?"

"Shit no. And if I did, I'd go the other way. I want nothing to do with that guy."

"Okay," Vic shifted position. "We were also wondering what you were doing last night, between ten and one a.m.?"

Gaspare stared from one to the other. "What the hell is going on?"

Vic waited a moment, then said, "We were hoping you could answer the question."

Gaspare straightened. "Why? Why would I need to do that?"

Vic felt himself getting annoyed. "It's a simple question."

"No shit. But I want to know why I have to answer it. What's going on?"

Vic breathed through his mouth and leaned toward him. "Okay. I don't understand your attitude, but so you know, Mr. Leaner of PipeMine was murdered last night. We're trying to establish the alibis of people who knew him."

"Or might hold a grudge toward him," added Liz, and Vic

knew that she had also picked up on Gaspare's anger.

"Oh." Gaspare backed up a step, his eyes downcast and thoughtful, but just as quickly anger shifted over his face. "You think I killed him? Jesus. What is wrong with you people?"

Vic automatically widened his stance and straightened his shoulders. "We don't know who killed him, and that's why we're checking alibis. We found the drawings in his home office. We wanted to confirm they belonged to your company. If they did then we could arrange to have them returned to you."

Gaspare's eyes darted from Vic to Liz and back again. Just as quickly his anger was gone. "Actually, I don't need them anymore. There were flaws in that generation of design. I've fixed them now, they're obsolete. You can keep them."

"Okay." Vic shifted position, searching for another approach. "Looks like you got a business meeting. Maybe good news to get your company going again?"

Gaspare watched him. "Yeah. I'm always looking for ways to get my business off the ground. Wouldn't you?"

"Okay," cut in Liz. Vic recognized the tone she used when she was sick of listening to men argue. "Mr. Gaspare. Last night between eight and one. Where were you?"

He frowned and hesitated, then said, "Here."

"And was anyone with you, or is there anyone who can confirm that?"

"No."

Everyone stood looking at one another.

The same anger Vic had felt with Crush rose up into his throat. "You need to do a bit better than that. For a guy who said he has to be somewhere, you sure are acting like you got all day."

"Yeah?" Gaspare's voice rose. "And what about me? I'm getting sick of this. I gave you an alibi the first time. Now you're back, offering me some bullshit mechanical drawings so I'll play nice. Let me tell you about those drawings. I knew Leaner stole one of my prototypes and then I caught him snooping around the flat files where we kept the drawings. After hours. So I made a couple of alterations to some drawings and left them out on my desk. I wanted to see what would happen. Sure enough, the dumb shit stole them. What he didn't know is that the changes I made screwed up the bot when it was inside a pipe. I changed the calculation on the torque needed to make the bot reverse. So the dumb shit steals the drawings and starts his own company, using my crap designs to build his bots. And now his bots get stuck in pipes. So yeah, I see an opportunity. I know how to fix the bots so they reverse and don't get stuck. I've talked to a couple of his clients and right now they think I'm goddamn superman. I got a meeting with another one of his clients today. So I want to get there."

Liz cut in. "So your alibi is that you were here alone last night?"

Vic was glad Liz stuck to the alibi. He was still digesting Gaspare's story of how he tricked Leaner into stealing doctored drawings.

"Yeah." Gaspare folded his arms. "And think about it. Why would I kill him? I just told you why I wouldn't. I'm stealing his business out from under him. Right now, in real time. I'm meeting with this new chick who's running Monahan's business and I can tell you she doesn't understand shit."

Vic cocked his head. "Mary Monahan?"

"Yeah. With Leaner gone her only choice for that company's CEO is me. But do you get it? I wanted Leaner alive when I took over his company. I wanted him alive so I could spit in his eye. Tell him exactly what I'd done. Watch him shit himself."

"Yeah. You're a real superman, alright," said Vic slowly.

"Screw you. He stole my ideas. And he was too damn stupid to see the design flaw. He got everything he deserved."

"Even killed?"

"Like I said. I wanted him alive so I could enjoy watching him spend the next twenty years thinking about how I screwed him."

They all fell silent until Gaspare broke the silence. "Anyway, if it'll get you guys out of here any faster, last night I was doing an updated presentation about the bots. I'm gonna show it to his client today. Demonstrate how I fixed the design flaw and that my bots will reverse the right way. You can have a copy."

"What is it?" asked Liz.

"A video."

"Same as the last one you gave us?"

"No, this one demonstrates the way the bots reverse. Are you listening? Shows how they back up around corners. They don't get stuck anymore."

Gaspare's attitude prickled the back of Vic's neck. "Yeah," he said. "We'd like to see it."

Gaspare disappeared into the kitchen. A few moments later he returned and tossed a small piece of plastic at Vic. "Thumb drive," he said. "Like the last one. I made the video last night. Finished about one."

Vic glanced at the drive. Impressed on the sides was what looked like a stylized robot tread, next to the word TrakBots, Inc. It was a new logo and company name, he realized. And then, despite how dislocated he felt, he remembered the conversation with Craig Luntz from the Tech Center.

"Actually," he said slowly, "you gave us a flash drive last time. I was wondering if we could borrow the computer you used to edit the video? I think it would do a better job of eliminating you as a person of interest. Then we don't have to bother you again."

Gaspare said nothing, just stared at him. Vic could see something moving behind his eyes, as if he was trying to think something through.

"That's my laptop," he said finally. "I use it every day. How long do you need it for?"

Vic shrugged. "Two days at the most, I would think."

"I'm sure that you could check your email from another computer without too much trouble," said Liz. "I saw two laptops when we were here last time."

"Don't you need a subpoena for my laptop?"

"Not if you volunteer to lend it to us. And like I said, we

only need it for a couple of days. If we have to go the subpoena route then our Tech guys always figure they have legal cover and they'll be in no hurry to return it."

"Might take a couple of months that way," added Liz.

Gaspare's forehead clouded. "Fuck." He disappeared into the kitchen again and returned, carrying a laptop. He handed it to Vic and Liz searched her bag for a receipt. As she wrote it out Gaspare said, "I need that back as soon as possible."

"No problem, we'll red flag it so it gets looked at first. Any passwords we need to know?"

Gaspare told her and Liz wrote them down.

"Thank you, Mr. Gaspare," said Liz. She handed him the receipt.

"Yeah, thanks," said Vic, and he could hear how tired he sounded. "We'll be in touch."

"Better be tomorrow. I need that laptop back," Gaspare replied.

Outside, he and Liz walked to their cars in silence. They stopped on the sidewalk, Vic aware of how heavy the laptop felt in his hand.

"Anything in there bother you?" asked Liz.

"In which way? I can count about five things that were off."

"How fast he came up with that flash drive. It was like he had it ready for us."

Vic turned and stared at the house, then into the gap separating the neighbors house. Through it he could see a narrow slice of the Monongahela River, slate grey under low clouds that threatened rain. On the far side of the river cars and trucks slid along the parkway, each barely larger than the head of a pin.

"Okay," said Vic. "Make that six ways. But you want to bet the file proves he was making the video when Leaner was killed? And I'll tell you something else. Mary Monahan is going to eat him for a snack."

"She will. He won't know what hit him. And I bet the file shows he was editing a video when Leaner was killed." She turned for her car, and as she opened the door, added, "and I'm not sure that means a god damned thing. See you at the office."

"I have to make a stop on the way," he called to her. She nodded and slid into her car. Vic watched her pull away and then looked at Gaspare's house. It was cleaned up, but it still seemed grimy somehow. And then his eye caught Gaspare standing near the living room window, watching him. He climbed into the seat, placed the laptop in the foot well in front of the passenger seat and started the car.

CHAPTER 25

Twenty minutes later Vic pulled into his driveway, guessing that Lorna was headed to work. He knew Crush liked her to start her workdays early. Inside the quiet house he noticed he was moving in the same restrained way he did at crime scenes. He stopped, disgusted with himself, and surveyed the living room. It looked untouched. In the kitchen, bottles stood on one corner of the card table, packed together, the long neck of Lorna's vodka bottle towering over the squat whiskey and scotch ones. Angrily he plucked it out, unscrewed the cap and emptied the contents down the drain. The smell reminded him of medical solvents. He tossed the empty bottle into the recycling container.

Upstairs, the tangy smell of sex competed with the flat smell of face powder on the sheets. He dumped the pillows out of the pillowcases, tore the sheets from the bed and carried them downstairs, his head turned to avoid the smell. In the kitchen he dug a garbage bag out from under the sink and stuffed the linens inside. The plastic bag went into the garbage can in the garage. Breathing heavily, he returned to the kitchen and stood for a few moments.

It wasn't enough.

He crossed to the front door, opened it and latched open the screen door, letting the damp smell from outside invade the room. He went back upstairs. In the bathroom he grabbed the robe Lorna had borrowed, stripped the towels from the racks and dropped them in a pile at the top of the stairs. In the bedroom he opened the window as wide as possible then yanked at the mattress pad, working it off the bed so roughly that the mattress ended up askew. On his way downstairs he scooped up the robe and towels and carried this second load to the garage and added it to the garbage bag. Breathing heavily, he returned to the living room and stood in the open door, the air surging into the room like a salve.

He waited a full ten minutes before he could bring himself to close the front door and the bedroom window. Finally he locked up the house and returned to his car, dreading what he had to do next.

The drive to Anne's mother's house only took fifteen minutes. It was as if every red light conspired to turn green as he arrived, purely to hurry him along. As he walked to the front door it felt as if he was walking against a heavy wind.

He rang the bell.

Anne's sister answered. She opened the front door and stood with her hand on the screen door latch staring through the glass, her face set, the lines around her mouth as fixed as stone.

"I'd like to speak to Anne," said Vic, surprised at the anger in his voice.

She didn't blink. "Why would Anne ever talk to you again?"

"I don't know. Why don't you ask her? See what she wants to do. Look, I know you're her older sister, but Anne can make up her own mind. If she says no, I'll respect that and leave. But she and I need to talk."

For a moment Anne's sister could have been a statue. Even her eyes took on the odd statue-like combination of emptiness and distant focus. Vic waited, aware of a tiredness in his shoulders. The ache on his tongue and the roof of his mouth had subsided, but lingered like the ghosts of past mistakes.

Anne's sister suddenly stepped backwards and closed the front door. The way the house creaked in the wind, it was as if it was waiting as well.

The front door opened and Anne stepped up to the screen door glass. Like her sister, she made no move to open the door. She waited with her arms crossed. Vic searched her eyes and what he saw snatched the breath out of him. She looked as if her insides had been turned over, leaving the most vulnerable part of her open to the air. The look was so raw that he hurt just to see it. He tried to swallow and was unable.

"I don't know what to say," he said finally. It sounded as if someone else was speaking and he was watching it happen. "I just gave in somehow and let it happen. It was the first and only time. I'm going to make sure of that now. I'd say I'm sorry, but I know you're not ready to hear or believe that. I just want you to know I'm going to fix this."

He found he had nothing else to say. Anne's blue eyes deepened and turned flat and he wanted to believe it meant something, but he suspected it was just a shift in the outside light as clouds scudded across the sky.

"I don't know how you fix that, Vic." Her voice was resigned. It wasn't a statement that asked for a reply, but Vic searched himself to find one.

"I let myself go. Completely. You know why. I can't get any lower. I can't fix it like it was before. Before she was gone, I mean. Dannie. I just can't do that. But you and I, I want us in a better place than we are now. Wherever that ends up being. Just give me that one chance."

Anne blinked and looked past him at the sky. After a moment her eyes settled on his. "There's always lower, Vic. I learned that today. When you think it can't be worse, it absolutely can. You need to understand that."

Carefully, as if she was scared of breaking something, she backed away and closed the door. Vic listened to the deadbolt thump home.

Carefully he placed the fingertips of his right hand on the glass, right where Anne's face had been. He stood like that for a moment and then dropped his hand, turned and began the long walk back to his car. Above him the clouds thinned and the day brightened, hurting his eyes.

He was barely aware of himself driving to his offices or entering his cube. It wasn't until he placed Gaspare's laptop on his desk that he reconnected to his surroundings.

"You okay?" called Liz from across the aisle.

He placed his service firearm in the desk drawer. "About as well as can be expected," he answered. He hesitated before he closed the drawer, staring at Dannie's file underneath his weapon, the surface stained by gun oil. Finally he pushed the drawer closed, and it was as if he was pushing something inside himself.

"I'm writing up our notes from the scene," said Liz. "Should have it ready in about an hour."

"Sounds good." He held up an empty three ring binder from his desk drawer without looking at her.

"Thanks," said Liz, understanding what he planned to do. They lapsed into silence and Vic tried to concentrate. But the buzz of the fluorescent lights, the distant conversations and ringing telephones settled around him like a fence, and he felt he had no way out.

CHAPTER 26

At some point later, Vic noticed Gaspare's laptop and picked up the phone, checked the directory and dialed.

"Tech," came a voice at the other end of the line. The man sounded so young that Vic's words caught in his throat.

"Yeah," he finally managed to eke out. "I've got a laptop here." Something clicked in his mind. "Is this Craig?"

"Yes, Detective Lenoski?"

"It is. Good." Vic wondered how he had blindly remembered Craig's name. "You remember you looked at that flash drive for Detective Timmons and I? We got another from the same guy, also an alibi. But this time we got the laptop. Last time you said that would be better. Can you pick it up and take a look? Same story, the file is his alibi. He says he was making it at the time the latest victim was killed."

"I remember. Some bot moving through a pipe. Sure thing, sir. I'll stop up for it."

Vic thanked him and as he hung up Kevin appeared next to his cube. He held out his palms. "I went to Leaner's business to look for his laptop. It wasn't there. His secretary says he takes it home with him every night." He couldn't hide the annoyance in his voice, and Vic knew he understood they'd sent him on a fool's errand.

"That's good, Kevin," he said quickly, trying to find cover. "That helps. If the laptop was missing from his house, then most likely the perp took it with him. Now we know that. Did you get a description of the type of laptop?"

Kevin stared at him suspiciously, as if trying to understand if Vic wanted to trick him again. Finally he said, "I did."

Vic saw Liz sit back with a tight smile. Kevin checked a small notebook. "PC, made by LG, brushed silver case. Has a couple of stickers on the case, one of them is from the band Smile Empty Soul."

"Good job," called Liz.

"Yeah," Vic said quickly, piling on. "Most people get too task oriented. When they can't do what they were asked to do they shut down. They wouldn't think to get the description of the laptop."

Kevin nodded and Vic was surprised to see a tinge of red along his cheekbones. Kevin stayed next to his cube, and Vic realized he was waiting for another task.

"Okay," he said, searching his brain. "Did you have any luck finding out what happened to that prototype that disappeared from Monahan's office?"

He shook his head. "People remembered it, but no one said they took it."

Vic nodded, wondering about that, until he remembered Kevin was still standing next to his desk. He looked at him. "Um, yeah. Now. Detective Timmons and I visited a possible suspect after we left the murder scene. Guy named Gaspare. Check the Monahan murder book and you'll see his relationship to the deceased. He gave us a video as an alibi. It's on this laptop and I called Craig in Tech and he's coming to collect it. Can you dog that work with Tech? We need to be sure the file was created when Gaspare says it was."

Kevin grinned. "Sure thing."

Vic lifted the laptop to give it to him and went cold. "Crap."

Liz called across the aisle to him. "What?"

"Chain of custody," said Vic. "I forgot to bag the laptop and log it in."

Kevin stepped back to give them room to talk, a small frown on his face.

Liz stood up and crossed the aisle to him. "I should have said something at Gaspare's. I didn't think of it. Bag it now?"

"Yeah, but it will never stand up in court. I drove off with it and ran a couple of errands. It sat in my car while I was in my house. Lawyer would eat us alive."

"Check it and if we find something we'll take it back to Gaspare with a subpoena, have him verify the contents and the laptop and then we can bring it back in, handle it the right way."

"Yeah." Vic turned to Kevin. "Bag it into evidence, but mark the time and place as now and here. Never fudge that shit. The mistake is the mistake. You got it?"

Kevin nodded, his head bouncing between Liz and Vic. "Sure, I got it."

"So go."

Liz turned back to her cube as Kevin headed toward the Tech Center, the laptop held out in front of him like an offering.

Vic stared at his computer screen, angry at himself, and clicked open his email program. He skimmed his messages and sat back.

"Liz," he called across the aisle. "Crush wants to see us. He said any time. Get it over with?"

She nodded, and together they headed toward his office, Vic less worried about Crush than about having to see Lorna.

"Vic!" called Lorna as they approached her desk. Somehow her hair was impeccable and Vic's brain flashed to Lorna on her hands and knees in front of him, her hair still perfect as they ground against each other.

"Lorna, yeah, Crush wanted to see us?"

"He said." She leaned close, and despite some darkness under her eyes she seemed as well put together as always. Vic guessed that she must have stopped at home before she came into the office. To avoid talking to her, Vic veered into the doorway of Crush's office. Crush was on the phone but he waved and pointed at the empty chairs. Liz and Vic each took a seat.

"Yeah," Crush said into the phone. "I got them both right here. I'll tell them, and then we move. This is gonna be good. I'll give the press office a heads up." He thumped the telephone into its cradle and looked back and forth from Vic to Liz. "OK, that was the chief. Just want you guys up to speed. We're sending in a team to arrest Thuds. Bring him in on suspicion. We got that partial plate that puts him on the scene of Leaner's murder."

"Isn't it our job to pick him up?" Vic didn't care about the anger in his voice.

Crush straightened in his chair, his chest muscles straining the fabric of his shirt. "No. Not after you played that game and met him already. You were insubordinate, but I'm gonna let that go right now. We have more reason to bring him in now. And since you screwed it up the first time, you both stand down now. Except Kevin. I want him to go in with the team, learn what a big time bust feels like."

"It's just suspicion," said Liz. "We don't have the evidence to bust him."

"Not yet. But we'll leak to the press that Bandini is involved in two murders, put some pressure on him. I bet he comes in and does a deal to give up Thuds so his businesses don't go down the tube."

Vic knew he should stay silent but he couldn't help himself. "Crush. Those guys are not going to give each other up. They've been together forty years. They'll fight you every step. At least keep the press off so we don't look like assholes when you have to let him go."

Crush slammed a fist onto his desk. "What the hell did you call me? You call me Commander! This is why you're on that side of my desk. You have no clue how to work a case like this. We need to show the public we're all over this and use the press to make Bandini cave. Guys like that want to live in the dark. Drag 'em into the sunlight and they piss themselves. Works every time."

Liz cut in, her voice tense. "Do you really need a team to snatch him?"

"Goddam right. Guy like that. Safety in numbers." Crush sat back, a satisfied look on his face, and locked his hands behind his head. His shirt strained around his armpits and shoulders.

Vic stood up, his heart beating hard, but he had a thought. Modulating his voice he asked, "And who interviews Thuds?"

"I'll figure out someone."

"Liz can do it. She's good at it and she knows the case."

Crush gave Liz a slow look, a half smile on his face. "Yeah, well, we'll see." He unlocked one of his hands and motioned them out of the office. Liz left the office like a shot, her shoulders so straight and sharp they could have cut glass.

Vic followed, so angry that he stopped just outside the office, unable to feel his feet touching the floor. Liz was nowhere to be seen.

"Vic?"

He blinked at the sound and his eyesight swam back to normal. Lorna was leaning forward, staring at him, her eyes wide. Without thinking, Vic asked, "Can we talk for a minute? Maybe outside."

"Sure." Lorna gave him a broad smile, glanced at the doorway to Crush's office then rose, dragging her large handbag with her. Vic pivoted and headed down the hall, not waiting for her to join him. She caught up to him as they crossed the lobby to the outside doors.

"Vic, what is going on? You look like you want to hit someone."

Vic shook his head, unwilling to explain what Crush had done. Instead he held open the outside door so she could lead the way. He followed, and motioned her over to the small awning protecting the building's smoking area.

As they reached it he said, "Lorna, last night was great but that's all it was. I don't want a relationship."

She blinked and stepped back. The harsh sunlight revealed a tiny half-moon sliver of brown above the green of her eyes, and he realized she was wearing green tinted contact lenses. Somehow he had never noticed that before. It focused him, and he realized how harsh his words must have sounded. It wasn't what he intended.

"No!" Lorna stepped forward again. "You can't do that. I wanted to go out with you because you don't seem like a guy who just wants a night of fun." Her cheeks flushed.

Vic took a quick breath to calm himself. "I didn't even want one night of fun. I was drunk and it got out of hand. I can't excuse that but I'm not going to act like it didn't happen. But I do want it to stop. Now. The only person I want to have a relationship with is Anne."

She stamped her foot. "Good luck with that. So why did you come on to me at the Barking Shark?"

Vic blinked, searching his memory. "I didn't. What are you talking about?"

"You'd better think harder. I got your message. I showed up and you had your fun and now you want me out of your life?"

"I was drunk. Jesus, Lorna, you're a good looking woman. You were right there and you were willing. But I screwed up. I shouldn't have been drunk."

She slapped him so hard his ears rang. He watched her quick march through the doors into the lobby. Vic stood rooted to the spot, rubbing his jaw. The ringing in his ears wouldn't go away, but somehow the ache on his tongue and the roof of his mouth was gone. He pivoted slowly and looked across the parking lot toward the river. From where he stood he couldn't see it, but for some reason he knew it was there and it calmed him. Someone shuffled up beside him. He looked and saw Sergeant Wroblewski standing a few feet away, lighting a cigarette. Vic stayed silent. The sergeant loosed a cloud of cigarette smoke that whipped over Vic as it escaped into the wind.

"Saw Lorna when I was coming out," he said, also looking in the direction of the river neither of them could see. "She looked pissed."

"Fair thing to say."

"Yeah, I saw what she was doing last night with you and wanted to warn you, but you left without her so I figured it didn't matter. So you know, since her divorce she's been making the rounds of guys with twenty years. Working down the batting order. How many years you got in?"

"Twenty-two."

"Uh-huh."

Vic raised his eyes to the hill on the far side of the river. Something wormed into his stomach. When he spoke it came out flat. "She's looking for a guy with a pension."

The sergeant turned his head and examined him with red-rimmed eyes. "About right."

Something crumbled inside him and he wanted to laugh, but the ringing in his ears drained away and the dull ache in his mouth returned, joined by a slow throbbing on his cheek. He guessed Lorna was wearing a ring. At the same time he wanted to do something. Anything.

"Figures." He glanced at the sergeant and headed inside, Wroblewski's yellow-toothed smile imprinted on his mind.

When he reached his cube, he glanced at Liz. She was typing, her head down, her fingers stabbing the keyboard. Kevin wasn't back yet. Vic sat at his desk, thinking about Crush, steeped in his own anger. And then he knew what to do. He flipped through his address book until he found the number he needed and committed it to memory. A few minutes later, when Liz stepped away from her desk, he slipped into Kevin's cube and dialed the number from Kevin's phone.

"Levon Grace," said the careful voice on the other end.

Vic cupped his hand around the phone mouthpiece and spoke softly. "Levon, it's Vic. Do me a favor. Call Thuds and tell him Crush and his boys are coming for him. Today. Warn him they're gonna come in hard dragging the press behind them. He needs to be ready, and for Christ's sake tell him don't put up a fight. They're itching for a reason."

Silence for a moment and then Levon breathed out slowly. "I guess you've got your reasons for this."

"Tell him we got a partial plate from his Caddy leaving the scene of Leaner's murder. It's suspicion. But Crush wants a show."

Just the slightest trace of static rolled over the line.

"You got it."
The line went dead.

CHAPTER 27

Vic spent the remainder of the morning rereading the Monahan murder book. He studied the autopsy results, then his notes from the meeting with Thuds, looking for anything he might have missed. By lunch time he had re-read every report and started a new set of notes. Liz's shadow crossed his desktop.

"I need to get out of here. Lunch?"

"Yeah." He stood, slid into his sports coat and together they walked to his car.

"Where to?" called Vic over the roof of his car.

"Someplace nowhere near here."

"I hear you." They both climbed in and Vic drove toward Oakland. Twenty minutes later they were seated at a Mexican restaurant near the university, waiting for their orders. The restaurant was deserted except for a group of students hunched over a table stuffing burritos into their mouths.

"Are you as pissed as I am?" asked Liz, after a few moments.

"Yep. The asshole isn't listening to us. He just wants the glory of bringing in Thuds and Bandini."

"Yeah, you heard they brought in Thuds about half an hour ago? One of the SWAT guys texted me. He said Thuds and his lawyer were sitting in his living room with the front door wide open, like he knew they were coming. Didn't argue at all. Crush got in his face, trying to get some footage for the press. Thuds just ignored him. I guess Crush was wearing full uniform and walking around with a bullhorn."

"Good TV."

"Bullshit casework, though. What the hell happened to your face?" She stared at the cheek Lorna had slapped, her eyes evaluating.

"Cut myself shaving?"

"You are such an asshole. You know we're on the same side, right?"

A waitress brought their baskets of tacos and returned to the counter. Liz took a bite, chewed for a moment then asked, "Before this turns into a serious bitch session, any chance Crush is right? Thuds might be the guy?"

Vic shook his head. "Leaner's murder was last night, he was spotted there this morning. I doubt he sat in the house all night." He washed down his taco with water, the taste oddly refreshing.

Liz examined her second taco. "You need to think about something. Thuds never gave us an alibi for the Monahan murder *and* he has something to gain from Monahan's death. It lets him protect his investment in Leaner's company. Plus he's pissed at Leaner because he made him look bad in front of his fracking business buddies. And, Leaner sold him on something that didn't work."

"So you're saying if he knew Monahan was being paid to delay fixing the problem with Leaner's company, he'd want to get Monahan out of the way, then he got rid of Leaner because he made him look bad?"

Liz nodded. "Maybe. So we can be pissed about Crush dragging in Thuds, but there's one scenario where he's guilty."

Vic sipped his water. He still had two tacos to go but didn't have the stomach for them. "And that means Bandini is in on it. But I still don't buy it."

"Why not?"

"Does he really need to kill Monahan? He's legit now. He could just send a lawyer to confront him and Monahan would have to back off."

"This is Thuds we're talking about. Remember three Columbians dead in a warehouse?"

"Yeah, but he was desperate then. He needed them dead to avoid serious jail time for him and Bandini. And Thuds, he is a guy who runs risk analysis for breathing. All those years loansharking, making sure whatever he and Bandini did they avoided jail? Bankers talk about managing risk, but I guarantee they can't hold a candle to those two. Also, if he invests in companies, I bet he's lost money before. They won't all pan out. He's used to that. And killing Leaner just because he made him look bad? Same thing, I'm not buying it. The frackers, they're businessmen. They know sometimes their vendors don't come through and in the end they were the ones who decided to bring in Leaner, not Thuds. It's just business to them. They might give Thuds some shit about it, but that's all."

Liz frowned and broke off a piece of her taco. "So what's left?" she asked around a mouthful of food.

"Well, there is one thing related to Thuds, now that I'm thinking about it. The bag man for him, Mike Turcelli? I forgot to tell you. Last night I tracked him down. Guess what, dishonorable discharge for beating up his commander, and he's a black belt in Marine Corps Martial Arts."

Liz swallowed and her eyes sharpened. "He knows how to use a knife."

"Trained to use it, and a history of violence. And he delivered the payments to Leaner. They know each other. Leaner would let him into his house no problem."

Liz sat back. "Makes more sense. Thuds wouldn't do the deed himself, not at this point in his life."

"Yeah, but we need a motive. Plus it makes no sense that Turcelli would stab Leaner at midnight, then go back to the scene with Thuds in the morning. And then call it in. If they thought they forgot something at the scene, I could see them going back, but still, why call it in?"

"Wait, when you told me about Mary Monahan and how Thuds told her about her dad's trust, you said it wasn't clear why Thuds told her about it. I mean if Bandini found out, he would be pissed."

"Right. Thuds showed up and gave her the trust documents listing Bandini's businesses."

"So maybe something's going on between Bandini and Thuds? Maybe Thuds was set up this morning."

"You mean like Bandini used Turcelli to take out Leaner, knowing Thuds was going to visit this morning?"

"Yeah."

Vic sat back, thinking about it. "Maybe, but that gets deep. Murders aren't usually complicated like that. So I keep thinking that we missed something. I reread the Monahan book this morning looking for a new connection between Monahan and Leaner. I tried taking it down to two bullet points. I got this: perp had to be close to Monahan and Leaner, perp benefits from Monahan and Leaner being dead..."

"Or wanted Monahan and Leaner dead. Revenge."

"Maybe, I thought about that. But revenge crimes aren't always planned well. This was the opposite, apart from the act itself. Perp only gets angry while he's in the act."

"So say the stab wounds."

"Right. But everything else is well planned. How he got in. Catching the victims alone late at night. Keeping the crime scenes clean. Closing the office door on the way out. Maybe there's an end game. Someone wants something and killing Monahan and Leaner is the way to get it. We just don't know what the end game is."

Liz squeezed hot sauce onto her last taco. "But are the murders really linked? And does it have to be the same motive for both murders?"

Vic eyed her. "Well, the victims knew each other and the MO is the same, but no, now that you mention it. Maybe that's what's confusing. Maybe one is part of a plan and the other a murder for some other reason. Linked, we know that, but Leaner wasn't as premeditated."

Liz crunched through the shell of her taco and wiped

some shell fragments from her lips into her mouth. Her eyes drifted to the front window and the street outside. Vic had seen the look before. She chewed, but it seemed irrelevant to her. After a moment she swallowed and said, "I get all that. Yeah. But now we got a real problem."

Vic felt his jaw tighten. "Yeah. We don't get to interview Thuds, and whoever does won't be looking for the right things. We really need to know why the hell Thuds was visiting Leaner this morning, and if he and Bandini are getting along."

"Plus whether Turcelli works for both of them. We know all that and maybe we start to see a case against Thuds."

They stared at one another. Vic threw his paper napkin onto the table. "We need to get back there."

Liz nodded. "Yeah. I'm sick of feeling sorry for myself."

CHAPTER 28

Pulling into the parking lot at headquarters, Vic maneuvered around four TV news vans, their tops bristling with satellite dishes and antennas.

"That didn't take long," said Liz, her voice sour. When they turned down the aisle to their cubicles, the first person Vic saw was Kevin, leaning against a cube wall and talking to the detective whose desk was at the end of the row.

"Kevin," Vic called. He tossed his jacket onto his desk chair and placed his weapon in his top desk drawer. Kevin detached from the wall and walked over to him, his eyes bright. "Where are they interviewing Thuds?"

"I finished," said Kevin, bouncing on his toes.

Something turned in Vic's stomach. Liz swiveled in her chair so her back was to them. Vic forced himself to speak evenly. "So what did you learn?"

"He said he was there. Stopped by to talk to Leaner early this morning and found the body and called it in. We're waiting for his phone records now to confirm it."

"Did he tell you why he was there this morning?" Liz still had her back to them. Vic knew that she didn't want Kevin to see the expression on her face.

"Yeah. And he gave us his alibi for last night. He was with some lawyer in Sewickley. Talking business, he said. That went until one thirty or something. Then he went home, got like five hours sleep and went to see Leaner. Found him like that."

"How'd he get in?"

"Front door was unlocked."

Liz slowly swiveled back around and Vic met her eyes.

"Right," said Vic carefully. "And did you press him on his alibi for the night Monahan was killed? How did you link that?"

Kevin frowned. "When Thuds told me he was at Leaner's this morning, Crush pulled me out and called a press conference to say we have a person of interest. I think he's going to talk about Thuds and Bandini and use that pressure to get them to confess."

"That'll never work," said Liz quickly. Vic could tell from the way she cut off her last word that she regretted saying anything. She knew that Kevin would relay the remark to Crush.

"I tell you what," said Vic quickly. "Could we watch the tape of the interview?"

"You mean the digital recording?" Kevin leaned his head back slightly, looking down his nose at Vic.

"Whichever, I just want to actually hear what he said."

He shrugged. "I don't see why not. I uploaded it to the case file. You know how to make that work, right?" His question dripped with sarcasm.

Vic tightened but felt Liz's hand on his arm. "My desk," she said quietly. "I want to see it too."

"In the Monahan record, right?" Again Vic forced his voice to sound normal.

Kevin rocked on his heels. "No, Leaner's. Monahan investigation is yours. Leaner is mine. Crush gave it to me."

Liz tugged him toward her desk, Vic breathing through his mouth to calm himself. They arranged themselves in front of Liz's screen and she clicked through a series of windows until she reached the table of contents screen for the Leaner investigation. Without saying anything, Liz swirled her mouse pointer over the field identifying the lead investigator, calling Vic's attention to it. It showed only Kevin's name. Vic went warm all over, but stayed silent.

Liz clicked through a link. Moments later a new window appeared that showed an interview room. Thuds sat at the only table, his long legs wide, his hands in front of him, his knuckles large and fingers interlocked. Next to him sat a white haired lawyer known for defending high profile cases.

"So. We got Mr. Calm and his white haired attack dog," said Liz quietly.

Vic stared at their facial expressions and body posture. "They've already figured out this is low risk."

Liz fast forwarded until Kevin appeared on screen, his movements jerky. Liz slowed down the playback to normal speed. They both listened, their eyes locked on Thuds, looking for body movements and tells.

Kevin launched right into the key questions, his voice higher than usual.

"Nervous," Liz whispered.

"Yeah, in the room with a guy like Thuds for his first interview, with Crush watching. But I like your technique better."

Liz turned up the volume. Kevin's questions sounded canned. He repeated them quickly and rarely asked for a clarification or more information, but he didn't really need to, Vic realized. Thuds gave clear and detailed answers. The lawyer stayed quiet. It wasn't until near the end, when Kevin asked Thuds why he was visiting Leaner, that Vic put his hand on Liz's arm and told her to stop.

"Replay that. Did you see what Thuds did there?"

Liz rewound to the start of the question and they watched the exchange again.

"See how he looks up," said Vic. "He's looking at the camera. "He's sending a message. Play it again."

Liz toggled through the controls and they listened again. After Kevin asked the question Thuds was silent for a few moments, then raised his head to the camera and said clearly, "I went over there to tell Leaner he was fired. That we had a Board meeting set up and I had recommended someone for CEO of his company. That it was going to happen. I had even talked to the guy we want for the job and he was ready. It was going to happen fast. Leaner was out."

Almost immediately someone knocked on the interview room door and Kevin halted the interview and left the room. The recording ran about another minute, but neither Thuds or his lawyer said anything. Thuds stared at the camera the entire time.

When the video ended, Liz sat back.

Vic shook his head. "He knows the reason he was visiting Leaner is important. He's making that point. And if Leaner was fired, there was no need for Thuds to kill him." Vic scratched his head. "Want to take a guess who's taking over as CEO?"

Liz frowned. "Gaspare? That fits. Explains why he was all cleaned up this morning and why he talked like he owned Mary Monahan. He break any law on what he did with the mechanical drawings?"

"We'd never find a jury who would go after him on that. They'd probably give him a medal for screwing Leaner over."

"So is Thuds trying to tell us more?"

Vic leaned forward and squeezed his arms across his chest, working through the interview in his brain. "He said he arrived at Leaner's and the front door was unlocked."

"Yeah."

"He then described the body pretty much the right way. And then he got out of there, called it in when he got in his car."

Vic leaned into the aisle and spotted Kevin talking to one of the other detectives. He was gesticulating with his hands, reliving the interview with Thuds.

"Kevin," he called. "Did you ask Thuds about Leaner's laptop?"

Kevin separated himself from the cube wall and stepped closer. "I was planning to, but Crush called me out of the interview. Told me we had enough. Like I said, when Thuds admitted he went to Leaner's house, Crush figured that Leaner argued with Thuds, they got into a fight and Thuds stabbed him."

"But Leaner was killed last night, not this morning."

"Yeah. Crush figured Thuds went over twice. Last night when they had the argument, then again this morning to clean up the scene, make sure he didn't leave anything."

"Right. Thuds is that sloppy. That'll never hold up." He glanced at Liz and saw disgust on her face. He looked at Kevin. "Did you ask Thuds if he was alone when he went to Leaner's? Was a guy called Mike Turcelli with him?"

Kevin frowned. "Who's he?"

"He's the muscle and bagman for Thuds. He delivered the money from Thuds to Leaner. He's got a record and he's a trained knife fighter. Marines."

Kevin stepped to the edge of Liz's cube. "You never told me that."

"It's in the murder book."

"You're only supposed to use the on-line system."

Vic stared at the tiny window high on the end wall. Sure enough a grey cloud was all he could see of the sky. "Where's Thuds now?"

"They took him over to county."

"Is he charged?"

"Tomorrow morning, I think. His lawyer was sitting in the living room with him when we picked him up. He's pushing to get Thuds charged so there can be a bail hearing."

"Makes sense." He brought his eyes back to Kevin. "And you know what the lawyer's story is going to be, right?"

Kevin raised an eyebrow.

"Lawyer will call a press conference and tell everyone that we arrested a Good Samaritan. That Thuds did his civic duty, called the police to report the murder, and we arrested him for his trouble."

"But he ran from the scene."

"Did anyone tell him to stay? It's not a law that I know of."

Kevin flushed. "But it makes him look guilty."

"*Looking* isn't the same thing as *being*," said Liz quietly. "You can't put a guy in jail for *looking* guilty. Unless his skin looks like mine."

Vic heard the hard trodden anger in her voice. Kevin looked uncomfortable. A moment later he launched himself in the direction of Crush's office.

"What now?" asked Liz.

"Confirm Thud's story about Leaner being fired. I think that's what he wants us to do, there must be something to that. And double check that Gaspare is their choice for CEO."

"Call the Board members?"

Vic shook his head slowly. "I got a better idea. Let's go talk to Mary Monahan. She runs Monahan's company now, or at least has her fingers in it, and I bet Thuds talked to her." He got up from the chair, crossed to his cube and found his contact information for Mary Monahan.

CHAPTER 29

An hour later Vic and Liz entered Monahan's office building. A private security guard nodded to them from the lobby desk and a few minutes later a secretary led them into the conference room where Vic and Liz had interviewed Erica. Mary Monahan sat at the head of the table, the entire room in front of her, while Erica sat with her back to the Allegheny River, which today had settled lower into its banks and moved less swiftly than the past Sunday. They both rose as Vic and Liz entered the room.

"Started work already?" Vic asked Mary. Vic had the feeling she absolutely belonged in the room.

"Might as well." She rose and came around the table to shake hands with him, her suit a shade of bright blue that complimented her brown hair. The lines were clean and tailored to her body, in a way that showed but underplayed her curves. When they finished the greetings they all sat down and Mary turned her large brown eyes to Vic. Vic noted how natural it all felt, as if Mary had taken over months ago, not just a few days earlier. But Vic was taken with something else, the way Mary walked around the table to shake hands with them. He sensed the action was important.

Mary broke the silence. "I understand that you have another investigation underway."

Vic gathered himself. "We do, although that was only part of the reason I wanted to talk to you. So maybe we can get a couple of things out of the way?"

"Alibis?" asked Erica. "Since Mr. Leaner ran a company we invested in."

"We can start there," said Liz. "From about ten to one last night?"

Erica smiled. "I was here until eleven. With David Conover. He works for me. We were getting a presentation together. Then we went out to Kaya to get something to eat. We left there about twelve-thirty. I treated him, since I made him work so late. So there's a credit card receipt from Kaya."

They waited as Liz finished taking notes, then Vic looked at Mary and raised an eyebrow.

"I was here until about seven, then went out to dinner with a friend. That lasted until about eleven. Then I went home. I have an apartment now in Shadyside. You can check what time I turned off the burglar alarm, and what time I set it again once I was inside. That will tell you I stayed there."

"Very precise answers," said Liz as she finished writing. She looked up. "From both of you."

Mary answered steadily. "We're trying to save you some trouble, Detective."

Liz smiled. "I didn't mean it in a suspicious way. I appreciate the precision."

Mary returned the smile and nodded. "Then you and I are going to get along."

Vic cut in. "Okay, before we all sing 'Kumbaya,' who did you have dinner with?"

Mary turned to him and he caught of glint of humor in her eyes. "John Silver, our COO. I needed to clarify a few things about how things will work with me in charge."

Vic wanted to ask how that conversation went, because something in Mary's tone made it clear that her COO now had marching orders and possibly an ultimatum, but he couldn't think of a way to make it relevant to the investigation. Instead he said, "So, the main reason we're here. With Leaner out of the picture, you have a gap at the head of his company, and you're deeply invested in it and the company is having problems. We were wondering what your plans are?"

Erica started to say something but Mary motioned with her hand and Erica closed her mouth.

"I'm sorry, Lieutenant Lenoski," said Mary. "Yes, we now face some business issues due to the death of Mr. Leaner, but surely our company's concerns aren't part of your investigation."

Vic scratched his stomach, wanting a drink of water. "Yes and no." He gave Erica an exaggeratedly long look to help Mary understand that she might want to dismiss Erica.

"I promoted Erica this morning," said Mary. "She is senior enough to hear this discussion."

"New COO?" asked Liz.

"I think that position requires a few more years of experience," said Mary coolly. Her eyes stayed on Vic. "Perhaps you should reword your question. A bit more, let's say, precision, might help."

"Okay. Did you decide yesterday or earlier to fire Leaner as CEO and replace him with Gaspare, the old CEO of PipeSafe?"

"I don't understand how this is relevant."

"It speaks to motive," said Liz. "And could support an alibi."

"Whose?"

Vic shifted position. He didn't want to bring up Thuds yet, and he wasn't sure if Mary knew of Thuds's arrest. "I'm not sure that matters, but it would be helpful to know if that is the plan."

Mary copied his slight shift of weight, as if she wanted him to know she had spotted the way he dodged the question. "Well, Lieutenant, you should know that these kinds of discussions are confidential. Second, until a decision like that is voted on and approved by the company's board, they are just speculation. Can we count on your department to keep this confidential?"

Vic nodded. "It won't get repeated or made public by me. And I think I speak for my partner on that as well."

Liz nodded.

Mary moved her head slightly, nodding to herself. "All right, I suppose that is the best I can hope for. Then, yes, I had a discussion with one of the company's major investors and we decided to take an action on Mr. Leaner and remove him. It should have happened several months ago, given the company's cash flow. I spotted that when Erica gave me the company financials a few days ago. However our board meeting was postponed, given that the major investor is a guest of your jail at the moment. We'll need to set another time for the meeting."

"I think that answers our question. But was Mr. Lombardo sent to tell Leaner that he was going to be replaced?"

"Yes. He and I decided last night. He was to go over first thing this morning and tell him. The plan was to hold a board meeting by phone later today. Our company is the largest shareholder in Mr. Leaner's company, with Mr. Lombardo the second largest, so we felt it appropriate to warn Mr. Leaner."

Something moved in Vic's gut. "Weren't you worried that Leaner would try to rally the other board members behind him during the phone call? Stop you from replacing him?"

A small smile crossed Mary's lips. "Yes. That was my hope."

The room fell silent. Liz glanced at Vic. Vic turned over Mary's words in his mind. "You mean you told Leaner in advance of the meeting because you wanted to see which board members would take his side?"

"Well, it was his company and he was unlikely to just walk away if we asked. So it follows that he would reach out to board members he believed would support him. So, yes, I was interested to see who those board members would be and what kind of a stand they would take. How they would operate. I need to know who I am dealing with so I know what to do in the future to make the company successful."

"But Mr. Lombardo isn't on the board of Leaner's company, right? He's just a major investor."

"Right. But he had an existing relationship with Mr.

Leaner. So the plan was for him to tell Mr. Leaner I was planning to call an emergency board meeting to remove him, kind of give him a head's up, then watch to see what he did and who he reached out to."

"But couldn't that backfire on you?"

Mary smiled but there was no humor in it. "Well, that's possible. But I had already made an arrangement with Mr. Lombardo to buy all his shares in Leaner's company, making our company not only the largest shareholder, but also the one with the majority. That transaction meant I could outvote the other board members. That was something I only planned to announce during the meeting if I needed to."

Vic found himself smiling. "You know, Mrs. Monahan, I'm not sure I'm cut out for the business world."

She watched him, her eyes steady. "Actually, Lieutenant, I think you would be very good at it. From what I've seen you can spot a rat the moment he walks into a room, and you understand that if you define people's motivations, then you can predict their movements. At this level, that's the game."

"I just want to know about Gaspare. Is the plan to make him the CEO?"

Mary glanced at Erica. "That's still under discussion. I have two strong votes that way, but I haven't made up my mind yet. I don't know him very well. I need to spend time with him and make sure he's the right fit. There's no question that he has the technical skills for the job, but CEO is a different role than inventor or entrepreneur."

Vic smiled slowly. "Well, by your definition he'd make a good board member."

"What do you mean?" asked Erica quickly. From her defensiveness Vic knew her vote was for Gaspare.

"We found some of Gaspare's mechanical drawings at Leaner's house. Gaspare confirmed that Leaner stole them a couple of years ago. He also told us that before they were stolen, he discovered Leaner sneaking around looking at the drawings, so he made small changes to them and left them out for Leaner to find. Leaner took the bait, stole the drawings and ended up building robots that contained Gaspare's design flaw. That's why Leaner's business is in trouble now. So, if Gaspare tells you he can fix the problem quickly, yeah, he can."

Mary sat back, her face tight.

Vic nodded. "I have a hard time deciding if that makes him a bad guy or just a smart guy. Some might say he was only protecting his ideas."

"It makes him devious, that's for certain," said Mary softly.

"Something to think about." Vic glanced at Erica and saw that her face was flushed and somewhere between angry and embarrassed. He turned back to Mary. "You know, we talked to Gaspare this morning. He mentioned that you were going to interview him. Is that today?"

"We haven't set a time. I saw no reason not to, given what happened to Mr. Leaner and how that delayed the board's decision. Do you need anything else?"

Vic noticed that Mary had shifted upright in her chair, her shoulders back.

"I think that's it."

"Good, then I have something I'd like to ask you."

Vic spread his hands in an 'ask away' motion.

"My husband's office. It's still off limits as a crime scene. We can't get in. To be honest, I don't think I can use that office under the circumstances, but that means we need to gut it and turn it into offices or a conference room or something. The sooner we start on that the better, and I think everyone here would rather close that chapter of our lives. I looked into getting out of our lease, but my husband signed on for ten years and we have six more to go. Moving isn't really an option."

"We can look into it," said Vic. "Usually it takes a few weeks to clear a crime scene like that. I know they've cleaned it. I get that people want to move on. And that you have a business to run."

"Thank you, Lieutenant." Mary rose and waited beside

her chair, followed by Erica a moment later. Vic and Liz followed suit. Vic fought the urge to shake hands all the way around again and turned for the door. He heard Liz say something to Erica and Mary as he let himself out into the hall. A moment later, Liz joined him. Vic stood uncertainly for a moment, then headed to Monahan's office. The door was still blocked with crime scene tape. Vic removed it and opened the door.

"What are you looking for?" asked Liz.

Vic paused, his hand on the door knob. "I don't know. I haven't been in here in a few days. Just wanted another look."

Liz didn't reply, so Vic stepped into the space. He felt the silence of the room at the same time the smell of industrial cleaners filled his nose. He took a couple of steps farther inside, Liz close behind him. Someone had stood up the chair and cleaned up the top of the desk, returning the cigars to the inlaid box. Vic remembered the scene the first time they entered, then counted the steps from the door to the desk.

"Twelve steps," he said out loud, more to himself.

"Takes a long time to cover that."

"Yeah." Vic moved behind the desk and looked back across the length of the office to the door. "He would have plenty of time to react to someone coming at him."

"But he went down at the side of his desk."

"Right. Like he knew the person and came around to shake hands with them." Vic stepped out from behind the desk to the lighter, cleaned portion of the rug and extended his hand, mimicking what he guessed Monahan had done, replaying the scene with Mary earlier in the conference room. "Business etiquette. So we have to assume he definitely knew the guy."

"Him or her," said Liz, watching him.

"Him," said Vic. "How often do women stab people? Especially like that."

"Jayvon White," Liz said softly.

Vic instinctively clenched his jaw muscles, the image of Jayvon, his head on his plate of food and the paring knife sticking out of his eye, clear in his mind. "Jayvon White," he agreed.

"Still. Chances are better it's a guy."

"Just keeping our options open."

"Just because you want to stick a knife in me sometimes, that doesn't mean a woman stabbed Monahan."

Liz stared down the length of the office. "Ain't no knife sharp enough to get through your hide."

"Okay." Vic glanced though the window at the river. "I'm good. You ready?"

She nodded, her eyes roving the office. "Yeah. But what the hell is that?" She pointed at the bookcases.

Vic followed her gaze. Sitting on the end of the bookcase near the desk, exactly where it had sat originally, was the robot prototype that disappeared after the murder.

Vic tried to keep the disbelief out of his voice. "You're kidding me."

They stepped over to it, neither one touching it. Almost in unison they leaned in close to examine it. It was the same bullet-shape robot with the large tracks on the side, the same brass name plate on the front.

"You got a bag?" asked Vic.

"Damn right, I do," said Liz. As she reached into her large handbag Vic took several pictures of the robot with his cell phone. Liz filled out the information on the front of the bag and, together, they eased the prototype inside and sealed it. It was lighter than Vic had expected.

"Kevin interviewed everyone in the office, right?" Vic asked.

"Yeah. He said no one knew anything about this."

"Okay." Vic held up the bot and stared at it through the plastic of the evidence bag. "Well, let's see if it can tell us where it's been roving."

CHAPTER 30

When they arrived at the station, Vic gingerly carried the prototype to the evidence locker and asked for fingerprint and DNA tests, then hiked the length of the building to the Tech Center. He hadn't visited since the day the department opened and was surprised to see the grey metal shelves in the center of the room filled with bagged electronic evidence. He spotted Craig standing at one of the workbenches, his eyes locked on computer screen.

"Hey, Craig," he called.

Craig straightened and spun around, blinking, his unruly hair tangled over his forehead.

Vic grinned at him. "Sorry, I just wanted to let you know about something."

"Yes sir, Detective Lenoski."

Vic crossed to his workbench, took out his smartphone and found the photos of the prototype. "See this? It's a robot for cleaning large pipes and stuff. It was in a murder victim's office, then disappeared and then reappeared. So, we bagged it and it's down with evidence right now to get processed. But can you take a look at it when they're done?"

"What do you want me to do with it?"

"Maybe for now just tell me everything you can figure out about it. I know it's outside what you guys normally do, but something is going on with it. You okay with that?"

Craig stared at the photos, his forehead wrinkled in concentration. "I'll give it a shot. Can you email me those photos?"

"Sure."

Craig spelled out his email address and Vic forwarded the photos to him. Craig clicked through a couple of windows on his computer to confirm they'd arrived.

"And something else," said Vic. "Stay on top of those guys in evidence, make sure they don't back burner it. Tell 'em you need it."

Craig nodded, his concentration on the photographs of the prototype.

Vic added, "And anything on that laptop we gave you earlier?"

He looked up. "I just checked the file creation and watched the video. Kinda the same as the last one, the file was opened and stayed open for about four hours. A little shorter than the other one, but that's the deal."

"And he was working on in the whole time?"

"That's what I need to figure out. I want to get into the program itself and see if there's any data in there I can use. I'll have more to work with. I should have a report tomorrow sometime." He pushed his tangled hair out of his eyes.

"Okay. Send the report when you've got it. And if you see anything that's unusual, anything at all, let me know right away. Thanks."

"Yeah. I'd be glad to."

Vic hesitated. "Also, next time you see your dad, tell him we could use him back here. But that I know he's too smart for that."

Craig broke a large grin. "Yeah, I'll tell him. That'll start him telling stories. He's got a ton of them."

"Work here long enough, and you will too."

Vic tapped Craig on the shoulder, left and returned to his desk, thinking about the laptop. It wasn't the content of the videos that bothered him, he decided, it was the fact that Gaspare had basically the same alibi each time.

The desk area was quiet. Liz had gone home and the small glimpse of sky he could make out through the high window was a bruised grey. He didn't know where the day had gone. He sat at his desk and rubbed his cheek where Lorna had hit him before moving his mouse and opening his email program.

CHAPTER 31

It was after eight when Vic pulled his car into his garage. He flipped on the kitchen lights and looked around, trying to remember the last time he had taken a damp cloth to anything, anything at all, anywhere in the room. The sink was a Jenga of unmatched dishes and bowls. Two frying pans sat on the stovetop, the bottom of one covered with a cataract of bacon grease. *How the hell did I get to here?* he thought to himself. His brain and stomach heavy, he turned to the card table and its cluster of squat bottles. He started toward them but hesitated, then moved into the living room and up the stairs to the second floor. In his bedroom the stripped mattress stared at him like a cornered rat. After a moment he removed fresh sheets from the linen closet, dropped them on the armchair and slogged down to the basement for a spray bottle of Febreze. Back in the bedroom, he spritzed the mattress until he was convinced Lorna's smell was gone. He then made the bed, squirting down the bedcover when he was finished. He stepped back to consider his work, the bottle dangling from his hand. It felt like it had taken him an hour, although he knew that it wasn't more than ten minutes. Then, his head still heavy, he opened the dresser drawers until he found an old pair of sweatpants and a sweatshirt. He knew what he had to do. He felt the way he did when he was fifteen, when his father was suffering the first chest pains of Mesothelioma, that entire decade of the eighties, when the mills along Pittsburgh's rivers flickered closed one by one like dying bulbs on a string of Christmas tree lights. They'd called those years the Big Suck, because as the mills shuttered every one of Vic's friends was drawn from Pittsburgh to the rigs off Galveston and the drilling sites of Alaska, to the refineries of Texas and California. As Vic watched his entire generation leave the city, he decided two things before he was even old enough to drive. First, he would stay in Pittsburgh and make sure it didn't collapse. He would protect it. And second, doing that meant he needed to know how to fight, so he had better learn how.

He stripped off his pants and shirt and shrugged into the sweats. They fell into place like an old skin. He hiked down to the basement.

If I started here once, I can start here again, he thought to himself.

From the bottom of the steps he crossed to the heavy boxing and speed bags. The smell of mildew sifted around him. He picked up his boxing shoes, light in the sole and high on the ankle, and held them upside down for a quick shake to make sure nothing had taken up residence in the two years since he last wore them. His Everlast gloves sat on top of the bag. Same procedure, he shook them out and slid them on, feeling the elastic at the wrist scratchy on his skin. A whiff of old sweat came to him, overpowering the mildew. He breathed and stared at the bag, then reached out his glove until it touched the heavy bag and repositioned his feet so he was the correct distance. He rolled his shoulders a few times, dropped into stance and soft punched the bag then glided back and forward again, punched a little harder, remembering the feel, punched again and followed with a light left. He danced back, his feet falling into the old rhythm, his arms salvaging the technique of holding up his guard. He danced in again and brought more commitment to each punch.

It took him a minute of light jabs and foot movement until he felt ready to unleash a body blow to the bag, the whump of contact like electricity up his arm to his shoulder. He dodged and weaved, timing the swing of the bag and hit again with his left, the shock to his arm so strong he coughed out a breath. Again and again he punched, danced back and drove in again, until his lungs burned and his face was slick with sweat. He closed on the bag again and threw the 1-2 combination. Jab, right hook. Danced back, his breath like a stone in his mouth. He darted forward and worked the one-two again before feinting the back step and driving forward to throw a one-one-two, his sweat splattering the bag with the final right hook. His hands ached, his upper arms were heavy and knees mushy, but he kept at it for a standard three minute round, the seconds ticking down in his head. With ten seconds to go he raged forward and worked the one-two-five-two. Jab, right hook, uppercut, hook. Left, right, left, right. It was his signature, that charge at the end of the round when he hoped his opponent was tired and counting down the seconds to the bell. He danced back, hearing the round bell in his head, dropped his arms and rocked on his feet for a moment, before walking around the basement with his arms on his hips, his chest heaving like a bellows and sweat drops darkening the concrete floor. The chain holding the heavy bag creaked as the bag twisted on the rafter hook, before it finally came to rest.

He lifted the bottom of his sweatshirt and wiped the sweat from his face, his heart thudding in his chest. He was stunned at how out of breath and tired he was after only three minutes. Where had his conditioning gone? The years of road-work, the core exercises, the hours spent drumming the heavy and speed bags, his hands growing used to the punishment. That strength was no longer there. Gone.

He slid off his gloves, bent over and unlaced his shoes. When he stood up, he had a small headache. He climbed upstairs, found a clean glass and took a long drink of tap water. He needed to get back on track. He knew it. He decided to see how his muscles felt tomorrow, then do another round, then work it up to two rounds. Then three. Keep working it.

Maybe give Crush a run for his money on who is more in shape. It was time.

As he drank down a second glass of water he stared at the

bottles on the card table. He wiped his mouth on his sleeve and placed the glass on the only uncluttered corner of the counter-top, then crossed in front of the bottles. He stared at them a moment longer, then picked up the two with the most inside and carried them to the sink. He dumped them out, the whiskey splashing on the dirty dishes, the smell roiling his stomach. He then emptied the rest, collected them in a blue plastic recyc-ling bag and moved them into the garage, aware that his arm muscles were already stiffening. He went upstairs and stood in the shower until he felt renewed, then searched the refrigerator for leftovers he could make into a dinner.

He watched television as he ate, catching the B roll of Crush calling through the bullhorn on a street that was appar-ently outside Thuds' house. He glimpsed Thuds being led to a squad car, his sport coat covering his handcuffs. He looked be-mused. Vic slowly shook his head.

Enough of this, he decided. *Tomorrow we start fresh and fig-ure this thing out.*

CHAPTER 32

Vic was at his desk by seven o'clock, despite how his aching calves and hamstrings slowed his walk. He lowered himself into his desk chair gingerly, his arms like deadwood. His computer was barely working when Crush appeared next to his cube.

"Vic!" He bounced on his toes, his eyes hooded. "My office. Right now." With a quick pivot he shot down the aisle.

Vic grimaced as he rose, forgotten muscles complaining, glad that Crush missed his reaction. He knew that Crush would have misunderstood his grimace for annoyance. *Which would only be sixty percent true.* A moment later his legs found their stride. He grinned at the stiffness, liking it. As he approached Crush's office he looked for Lorna, unsure how she would react to him, but she wasn't in her seat.

Crush's desk was bare except for his telephone and computer. He sat with his back straight and hands folded in front of him. A woman Vic didn't recognize was in one of the two chairs facing Crush's desk.

"Close the door," said Crush as Vic stepped into the office.

He did, then took the empty seat. The woman next to him was in her fifties, her black hair cut in a severe page boy, the corners of her dark eyes heavily wrinkled and filled with makeup. She had positioned the jacket of her navy pants suit around her waist carefully, as if she wanted to camouflage her waistline.

"Do you know Leslie Summeri?" asked Crush.

Vic reached out a hand and they shook. Her hand was dry and he felt that if he squeezed he would break the bones. "I'm from Human Resources," said Leslie, her voice slightly hoarse.

Vic nodded, trying to piece together the reason for the meeting.

"Okay," said Crush. "You're probably wondering what this is all about?"

Vic nodded. "Well, yeah."

Crush reached into his desk drawer and placed a file in front of him. He moved slowly, as if he enjoyed everyone watching him. He flipped the file open and studied the top sheet. Vic saw that his close-set eyes were jumpy in a way he hadn't seen before. Crush tapped the top page and looked at him, but Vic didn't feel like Crush actually saw him. "The short point is this. You are suspended barring an internal investigation into your behavior."

"What?" The word was out before Vic could stop it.

From his right Leslie said, "We don't make these kinds of decisions lightly." Vic looked at her, then at another file folder that had appeared in her lap from somewhere. He had the irrational thought that she must have been hiding it when he came in. "We've had a variety of complaints about your behavior," she continued, "And I'm afraid that it's reached the point where we have to take action."

"What complaints?" Vic watched Crush, noting how his eyes refused to meet his gaze.

"Insubordination," said Crush. He looked down, as if the top page in the file held all the answers.

"Well, there's been a variety of complaints," Leslie said quickly. "Insubordination is clearly one. Apparently you didn't follow a direct order from your commander related to bringing a suspect in for questioning. Instead the department had to arrest him at his house, which meant SWAT had to be activated and you know that is a costly thing to do."

"There was no need for SWAT, and the arrest was unfounded."

"That's for an inquiry board to decide. But the fact is you disobeyed a direct order. There was also an episode where chain of custody was not maintained on a piece of evidence, a laptop, I believe?"

Vic sat back, dragged his sore arms up to his chest and folded them together. All he could think about was his discussion with Kevin about the laptop containing Gaspare's alibi video. He turned to Leslie, waiting to find out if there was more. She glanced at a piece of paper that held a letter. In the body of the letter he could see four bullet points.

"We also had a complaint lodged by a witness or possible suspect, a Mr. Gaspare, who said you intimidated him yesterday. But the most concerning complaint is from a department employee who says you invited her to your home and then forced yourself upon her. She is a subordinate in this department and you know that relationships between coworkers is against policy, and in truth her statements are concerning. She may decide to file formal rape or assault charges."

Vic closed his eyes as she spoke. He didn't say anything, just felt a burning from the spot where Lorna's slap had landed. "Does the union know about this?" he finally heard himself say. His mind suddenly slid into gear and he remembered that one of the union reps was Sergeant Wroblewski, who was at the Barking Shark when Lorna came in, and knew when Vic had left. Without Lorna. But he had also seen Lorna slap him the next day.

"The union will receive a copy of this letter, as will you."

"And how long does this last?"

"It usually takes a couple of weeks to gather statements and prepare for the hearing."

Crush broke in. "You need to stay out of the office, and hand over your badge and service weapon."

Vic looked at him. He wanted to shout something but the words died in his throat. He tried again. "You know you're chasing the wrong guy for Monahan's and Leaner's deaths, or are you too hung up on your career to give a shit? Or is this you finally getting me out of your department because you couldn't find my daughter and it's slowing down your career?"

Crush lifted his palms and looked at Leslie. "See what I mean?"

Leslie turned to Vic. "Detective Lenoski, I'd advise you to keep your comments to yourself. This investigation is already underway and you can't stop it. The suspension is effective immediately. Your comments will only add to the evidence against you." She held out the letter to him.

Vic took it without looking at it, folded it twice in half and stuck it in his shirt pocket.

Crush leaned forward. "Now, where are your service weapon, badge and access card?"

"My desk. Badge is in my coat pocket with the access card, weapon is in the top right hand drawer of my desk."

Leslie looked at Crush. "If you could retrieve them, I will wait here with Detective Lenoski."

Without a word, Crush unwound himself from his chair and left the office. Vic looked at Leslie. "Anyone interested in my side of the story?"

"You will be interviewed and statements taken on all of the charges," she replied. Her eyes were steady. Vic knew she was used to this kind of conversation and he wondered if she ever tired of it.

"Tough job you've got," he said after a moment.

She held his eyes without blinking. "You should talk to your union rep," she said finally. "The most damaging charge involves your female colleague."

"Of course it does. If it were actually true."

Vic broke eye contact and stared out of the window. He could make out a sliver of the Ohio river between the casino and stadium. The surface was flat, dingy grey and appeared to be motionless, as if the river itself had stopped running for some reason. He uncrossed his arms and dropped his hands into his lap. They waited in silence until Crush reentered the office, carrying Vic's weapon, badge wallet, and sport coat. He placed the weapon and badge in his top desk drawer and lay the sport coat on his desk in front of Vic.

"So I just leave the building?" asked Vic.

"I'll escort you out," said Leslie as she rose.

Vic stood up and shrugged into his sport coat, turned his back on Crush and left the office. Lorna was still missing from her desk, but a uniformed police officer waited for them, and he fell in behind them as they moved toward the lobby.

"Who tells my partner?" he asked.

"Commander Davis will inform Detective Timmons when she gets to work." They pushed through the metal doors into the lobby as Liz stepped in from the outside. Her eyes brightened in recognition of Vic, but as quickly tightened as she saw Leslie and the officer. She stopped, waiting for them to reach her.

"Vic, what's happening?"

He started to slow to talk to her, but the officer put his hand in the small of his back and urged him forward. As he walked by he said, "Suspended. Not allowed on the premises."

"That's crazy!"

He passed her, the officer's hand still on his back. "It's chicken shit and revenge," said Vic over his shoulder. He pushed through the door and stepped outside, the officer's hand falling away. The air was cooler than he remembered from the ride to work. He heard the door click behind him and turned to look.

Liz stood just inside the lobby, a frown on her face. She lifted her thumb to her ear with her pinkie extended to form a telephone and mouthed 'call me.'

He nodded, turned and headed for his car, wondering how long it would take Crush to realize he drove a pool car and ask for it back. He slid behind the wheel and sat for a few moments before looking up. Crush was standing at his office window, hands on hips, watching him. He thought about giving him the finger but couldn't summon the energy. He just felt tired and disgusted. *Screw you and your investigations*, he thought. *You go after Thuds and you come up empty.* He started the car and backed out of the space, barely aware he was driving.

As he cleared the parking lot his cell phone rang. He fished it out of his jacket pocket and pressed the talk button.

"Detective Lenoski?" It took Vic a second to connect the voice to Craig.

"Yeah," he answered, the word coming out gruffer than he had expected.

"Listen, wow, you know that prototype you gave me? The one from the dead guy's office?"

Vic knew that he should tell Craig that he was suspended, but his voice was urgent and excited.

"Yeah," he said quickly, encouraging Craig to speak. "The Monahan case."

"You wanted me to look at it, so I took it apart. To begin with, it made no sense. It's lighter than you would expect, turns out that's because the motor is missing. The back end of the tube is empty. But the front end, where that plastic nose bubble is?"

"Yeah," said Vic, picturing the bullet shape of the prototype in his mind.

"So that's got more stuff in it than I first thought. I couldn't figure it out for a while. Then I got it."

Vic heard pride slip into Craig's voice. "Got what?"

"This is the cool part. See, there's a high quality microphone and a wide angle video camera. Right up in the nose. So they can shoot video through the thing. Record what's in front of it. I figured that might be what they used it for, but that makes no sense. Then I figured out that the back end is empty for a reason. They took out the engine on purpose, I think. So they could put the components and antenna they needed to stream video to a server? You get this? The video streamers I've seen are all boxes. But someone took the box apart and fit the components inside the tube. I had to take apart a video streamer to understand it. Totally cool. But then it gets even better. Cutting edge. You want to shoot video through the thing, what's the problem? I mean it's sitting on a shelf for months."

Vic slewed the car over to the curb and hit the emergency flashers. "Craig, just explain it to me. A McDonald's drive through is high tech for me."

"What do you have to do with your phone every day?"

Vic closed his eyes for a second. "Charge it?"

"Yes! Exactly! You're gonna shoot video, you have to stream it. For that you need batteries, but they run down."

"It wasn't plugged into anything."

"Right, this is why it's so cool. The camera batteries use a Wi-Fi signal to recharge. Totally cutting edge. So the thing can shoot video with sound whenever, using the office Wi-Fi to recharge the batteries and stream the video at the same time. This thing is off the hook. Whoever came up with it really gets video and Wi-Fi. I haven't seen anything you can buy that's configured this way. Someone totally made it out of thin air."

Vic held the steering wheel, trying to wrap his mind around what Craig was telling him. He pressed his phone closer to his ear.

"Wait, you mean this thing is always streaming video? I mean twenty-four seven?"

"No, no. I forgot to mention. There's a motion detector built in. It only records when there's movement. If the office is empty, it turns off and just recharges. You get that? Wow, someone thought this through."

"So let me understand. This thing sits there recharging, then when someone comes into the office the camera fires up and records what is happening, including voice. And it sends the video to some computer somewhere?"

"Yeah, well, most likely a server. It's got some storage, but not much. Not for eight or ten hours of video. You need a server for that. This thing is amazing. I gotta steal this technology."

"No, wait, it's evidence. I mean, listen, go find Detective Timmons and tell her what you told me. And Craig, one other thing?"

"Yeah."

"Go to Detective Timmons on everything related to this

case from here on in. I'm suspended."

Vic closed his eyes for a second, hearing the silence on the phone.

"That sucks," said Craig after a few moments.

"Tell me about it. Also, did you look at that laptop we got from Gaspare? His alibi?"

Craig's voice slowed, the excitement draining away. "Doing that next. I got too fired up with the bot. I slept here last night. That's some amazing tech."

"Okay. Tell Detective Timmons what you found as soon as you can. And listen. We never had this conversation. If they found out you gave me case information while I'm suspended you'll get reprimanded. So you called me, but before you told me anything I told you I was suspended and we talked hockey. You got it?"

"Yeah, I get it."

Vic could tell from Craig's tone of voice that he wanted to ask why he was suspended, but didn't feel he could. "Take it easy."

Vic's phone went dead and he sat behind the wheel, the emergency lights clicking loudly. Occasionally a car rocketed past. He stared out of the windshield. Finally he smiled. "You sly dog, Leaner," he said. Because Leaner had made the gift of the bot to Monahan, and in doing so had planted a spy right in the center of Monahan's office.

"And why would you want to do that?" said Vic out loud as he slid the car into drive and clicked off the emergency flashers. He checked his mirrors and started driving.

CHAPTER 33

Vic drove without thinking, finding himself in Pittsburgh's Lawrenceville neighborhood and then underneath the brick arch that led into Allegheny Cemetery. He followed the curve of the access road, the sunlight bright on the dashboard. The smell of moist earth rolled in through his open window. He parked and crossed to Dannie's memorial, the ground squelching with each step. Vic hadn't wanted a memorial, but Anne did, and the front was engraved with Dannie's birth date and a line from scripture.

He that endureth to the end shall be saved. Matthew 10:22

Bile rose inside him. There was nothing about the line he liked, from the 'He' that started the quote to the meaning of the message itself. He read it as a promise Anne was making to herself, not something for Dannie. Wind rolled over the top of his head and his skin prickled. He had no one to blame but himself. When Anne first raised the idea of a memorial, he had refused to take part. Most of the time he'd been drunk. And this was the result. He turned back to his car.

As he worked his stiff muscles into the front seat, his phone vibrated with a text message from Liz.

Asshole talked to me. He goes after Thuds, Kevin and I gotta chase down other leads and do what Crush says. Where are you for lunch?

He thought about it and responded with the name of a sandwich place in Pittsburgh's Strip District, then sent a second message telling her to see Craig. He started his car and headed home. He decided to get his muscles working again and do another round with the weight bag.

More than that he just wanted to punch something.

^ ^ ^

At noon he settled gingerly onto a stool at the counter of a narrow sandwich shop. For a time, while he worked the weight bag, his muscles had loosened and turned warm and stringy. But within fifteen minutes of his shower the tightness was back. He pulled the straw out of the paper cup, tossed it on the counter and sipped the ice water, glancing at the door, then watching the cook palm French fries and coleslaw onto sandwiches before topping them with a slice of Italian bread. Liz entered wearing wrap-around sunglasses and dropped her purse on the counter without saying a word. She radiated anger. Vic waited while she ordered. It was only after the waitress placed a cup of orange soda in front of her that she peeled off her sunglasses and dropped them on the counter. She looked at him, her lips tight. "What the hell, Vic?"

"How much did Crush tell you?"

"Just that you were suspended. I'm not supposed to gossip about it or talk to you." She looked him up and down. "Like that's gonna happen."

"You could follow orders on the gossip part." Vic sipped his drink, astounded at how much his arm muscles ached. "They had four things. Insubordination because we didn't bring Thuds in."

"I figured that one."

"Screwed up chain of custody on the laptop."

"That piss ant Kevin must have told Crush about that."

"Gaspare filed a harassment complaint."

"Oh please."

"Right. But the big one is that Lorna charged me with unwanted sexual advances. And technically, she's a subordinate."

Liz sat back, staring at him, then stabbed a straw through

the plastic lid of her cup. She went to drink and stopped, her eyes never leaving him.

"You slept with her?"

He shrugged, his shoulders complaining about the effort. "Yeah. She came over to my house and sat on my lap and somehow that translated into me forcing myself on her."

"She's been trying to get into your pants for weeks. And she accused you?"

"Well, the next morning I told her I didn't want anything to do with her. Pretty sure that had something to do with it."

"Jesus, she's been sleeping with anyone who has more than twenty years in."

He stared at the dirty pressed tin ceiling. "How is it everyone knew that but me?"

"You were looking at the wrong parts of her. Jesus, I hope she was worth it."

"She slept over and the next morning Anne walked in on us."

"Vic," breathed Liz, and closed her eyes. The cook slid his sandwich in front of him. Liz opened her eyes. "I guess you decided that since you're going to hell anyway there's no point waiting?"

He tugged the corner of the wax paper underneath his sandwich so it was square in front of him. "Yeah. I shoulda figured trouble when I saw Lorna's tramp stamp was a skull and crossbones."

Liz looked away but after a moment looked back, a softness in her face. "Okay, Vic. I guess you can joke about it. What the hell else can you do?" She studied him. "You gotta fix this with Anne. I mean today."

"I already tried. She didn't have much to say to me."

"Keep trying. How long are you out?"

"They figured two weeks to the first hearing. They'll want your statement."

"I'll make sure the union is all over it. That shit old sergeant with the bent nose you know, Wroblewski, he's one of the union reps, isn't he?"

"Yeah, and he saw Lorna and I at the Barking Shark the night before, and knows I left before her. And he knows Lorna. So talk to him."

The waitress returned and slid a sandwich in front of Liz. They both stared at it for a moment as if it might offer some kind of answer. She looked at him. "Three of the charges are bullshit. It's Lorna you got to worry about."

"Yeah, I know."

Vic took a bite of his sandwich, the corned beef rich on his tongue. Liz bit into hers and some egg yolk dripped onto the wax paper. They chewed in silence for a few moments, then she put her sandwich down.

"I talked to Craig. That is some crazy shit with the camera in the robot. Why the hell would Leaner need that?"

"I was thinking about that." Vic sipped his water, liking how cold it was on his tongue. "I'm thinking that if he's paying Monahan not to invest in Gaspare's business, then the camera was his insurance policy. He could make sure Monahan held up his end."

"If Monahan tried to deny it later, you mean? Wish I knew where those video files were streamed to."

"Yeah. Leaner's laptop was missing from his house. Now I'm starting to think maybe that wasn't an accident."

Liz nodded. "That's a question for Thuds."

"Right, but Crush will never think to ask it."

Liz took another bite.

"There's another crazy possibility," said Vic carefully.

Liz looked at him, her eyebrow arched.

"Maybe, just maybe, there's video of the perp stabbing Monahan. If the motion detector starts recording when the perp walked into the office, someplace the whole thing might be on video. Whoever killed Monahan found out about the video and had to get Leaner before he saw the tape."

Liz stopped chewing. "But why wouldn't Leaner give us that video? It would clear him right away."

"Right. Unless somehow he didn't know he had it."

"You mean he wasn't checking the video?"

"Think how much he has. Hours and hours of it. I'm thinking he put the bot in there to keep track of Monahan, then realized it was a full time job watching the video, so he just quit watching and forgot about it. Erica said Leaner gave Monahan the prototype when they did their deal, that's more than a year ago."

"So why did the prototype get taken out and put back?"

"Beats me. Maybe the perp thought the video might be stored in it. But then the question is how the perp found out about the camera."

Liz poked her sandwich. "But how do we even know that prototype is the same one we saw originally?"

"Why would someone return a bot configured for video? Makes more sense they would steal the bot and replace it with one without the video stuff. Then we'd never know about the filming. Also, did Craig look at Gaspare's alibi video?"

"I get that." She dabbed her lips with a paper napkin. "Craig's looking at the alibi video now."

"So let me know what he finds."

"You're suspended."

Vic shrugged. "Doesn't mean I'm dead. It's weird. Now I want to solve the case more than I did before. Also, if Thuds didn't know about the video, then he's the wrong guy to be chasing. You need to keep Crush from screwing up the investigation."

"Oh, sure. Like he listens to me. Or anybody."

"He listens to Kevin."

"We're just born lucky."

They both bit into their sandwiches and chewed for a time in silence. Finally Vic put his sandwich down and looked at her. "I like this Craig guy," he said. "Beats me why. But I like how he thinks."

Liz nodded. "Yeah, and he works like a dog. You know he worked all night? He took apart a unit that streams video to be sure about the components inside the bot. You don't see people working that hard much anymore."

"Not sure we saw it a lot back in the day, but there's always some people who are workhorses. And you know what to do with them?"

"Ride 'em." Liz dabbed the corner of her mouth with a paper napkin.

"Yep," said Vic. "Ride 'em." He bit into the sandwich again, liking the taste of it. He chewed, thinking about that. It had been a while since food tasted good to him.

CHAPTER 34

It was early evening when Vic's phone rang. He dried his hands on a dish towel, looking around the newly clean kitchen. Even the dishes were washed and put away.

"Detective Lenoski?" asked Craig's raspy voice.

"Craig," he said quickly. "I told you yesterday. I'm suspended, I appreciate you calling but you should talk to Detective Timmons."

"I checked, but she left already."

Vic glanced through the window. "Well, yeah, it's dark out. It's almost seven. Most people have left already."

"And I called you from my personal cell phone."

Vic found himself smiling. He took a new tack. "Is Kevin around?" He hesitated, trying to remember Kevin's actual rank and title, unsurprised that he didn't know them.

"He is, he was down talking to me earlier. But I thought I'd call you. I'm in my car in the parking lot."

"You know if it gets messy, they'll check your personal phone as well."

Craig was quiet for a few moments, then said carefully, "When *Kevin* came down earlier he was bragging about how he blew the whistle on you about the chain of custody on the laptop. Got you suspended for screwing up. He's a dick."

Vic stared at the ceiling for a moment. "Yeah, well, I did screw up the chain of custody on the laptop. But it's something we can work around. Look, since you called, what's up?"

"I had to tell someone. I went through the video file on

the laptop. That guy's alibi?" Vic heard excitement sift through Craig's voice and his words ran together like stampeding horses.

"You mean Gaspare's video file? I thought you said it looked like the other one."

"Yeah. But there was something about it I didn't get. I had to play it like fifty times before I got it. I needed headphones."

Vic tilted his head, interested, and pleasantly impressed with himself about the cleanliness of the kitchen.

Craig's words tumbled out. "So the first few times I watched it, I just played it at a regular level on my computer in the lab. There's other guys in here so it was loud, and I put on headphones, and that's when I got it."

"Got what?" asked Vic into the pause.

"The audio soundtrack was screwy. See, the file was open the entire time when he needed an alibi, like the last one? But part of the soundtrack on this one was flat, his voice sounded off, and I realized there's no ambient noise on that part of it. Like none."

"Okay." Vic wasn't sure where Craig was headed. "I guess I'm not sure what this tells us?"

"He did a voice over, the kind that's added after the video is laid in. Right? So you can match up the audio to what you're seeing on video?"

Vic screwed his eyes shut, waiting for understanding to dawn.

"But the part where the soundtrack is flat there's absolutely nothing else on the soundtrack but his voice. Nothing. Like nothing."

Vic opened his eyes. "Craig, I still don't get it. Start at the beginning."

"Sorry. I'm too fired up. My dad always told me to slow down. The only way you avoid ambient noises on a soundtrack is to make it in a sound studio. Insulated and quiet, designed for making soundtracks, right?"

"Right."

"But you said he made these in his basement. Not a sound

studio, it should be pretty quiet, but you would get house noises. Furnace turning on, water in pipes, that kind of thing."

"Yeah, I get that."

"But this new tape, there's this long like three minute stretch when there is absolutely no background noise. He totally suppressed it all. There's nothing there, which is why it sounds so flat. You take *all* the other sound out and it affects the part you want to keep. Has to."

"Could be a million reasons to do that. Someone rang the doorbell, his girlfriend came downstairs yelling at him."

"Sure. But three minutes?"

An idea formed in Vic's head. "Are you trying to say he took something out, as if he needed to hide it? That what's not there could be helpful?"

"Yeah! That's it!"

"Maybe he just wanted a clean soundtrack?"

"Well, yeah." Craig's voice faltered. "Sure, that's possible. But it just seemed so weird that he had to scrub it that hard, that he couldn't let any ambient noise be there."

Vic smiled to himself. "Craig, look. It's late. You've got an interesting idea, but take another look at it in the morning. Sometimes you need to sleep on something before you understand it." He tightened as another meaning of his words conjured a vision of Lorna. "I appreciate you calling but talk to Detective Timmons tomorrow and tell her what you told me."

"You sure?"

"I'm sure. Just tell Detective Timmons, that way you don't need to mention talking to me. We all come out clean."

"Sure Detective Lenoski."

"Thanks, Craig."

He pressed the disconnect button and looked about the kitchen, shaking his head slowly. The case would not leave his thoughts. To distract himself he opened the refrigerator and stared at the empty shelves. All he owned was a half-full quart of milk. Wanting dinner, he took his car keys and backed out of the garage and into the road.

As he pulled away from the house a pair of headlights moved from the curb and fell into line behind him. He watched them vaguely, registering how the headlights took the same turns as he did and remained a careful twenty yards behind him. He headed into the Squirrel Hill neighborhood, then, between a theater and a bank, yanked his wheel right and accelerated up a residential street.

The car behind him sped up to maintain distance. At the first stop sign he waited until the car pulled in behind him, then flipped on his red and blues and hopped out of the car. Automatically he slapped his hip, remembering coldly that his service weapon was in Crush's drawer. He held his hand against the outside of his jacket at his hip as if it was still there and approached the car. A black Cadillac Escalade. The driver side window slid down noiselessly.

"You following me?" asked Vic as he drew closer.

A dark haired young man flipped on the dome light and leaned toward the open window. Vic strained not to react to the man's misshapen face. A purple swollen bruise ran the length of the man's cheekbone to his cut and swollen lips. Dried blood speckled his upper lip below a bent nose. His right eyebrow looked like someone had slipped a golf ball under the skin, and the eye itself was bright red from a broken blood vessel. The man waited as if his face answered the question.

"I'm Pittsburgh Police. You want to explain yourself?" Vic asked.

The man blinked then said, "I'm Mike Turcelli. Thuds Lombardo asked me to find you. Told me not to go into your house, but to meet you someplace public. He wants to see you."

As he spoke spit flew through a gap where one of his front teeth was broken halfway down. Vic thought about it for a moment. "I heard about you. You're his bagman. He couldn't call?"

"He just got out on bail. He wanted to talk to you quick. He called that guy you both know but he was out. So he sent me to find you."

"Where does he want to meet?"

"Same place as last time. But he figured you wouldn't want to be seen with him. So go in the front, ask for a drink at the bar, then say you're going to the bathroom. Go down the hall to the last door on the right. Knock twice."

Vic felt the cold of the evening around him. He nodded. "Okay. When?"

"Soon as you can get there. He has something for you." Turcelli turned his head as he spoke, as if that fact made him angry.

Vic thought about it and nodded. "I'll head over. Just quit following me."

"That's the plan," said Turcelli. Vic watched his face disappear as the tinted widow glass slid into place, then headed back to his car. He flipped off the red and blue lights, waited for an opening in the traffic and headed to the restaurant. He drove slowly, wanting to call Levon Grace from his cell phone, but decided against it. The Cadillac peeled away at the first major intersection and disappeared, but Vic stuck to the neighborhood streets, taking his time so he could think. If he was investigated, he didn't want a lot of calls to and from Levon. Instead, he stopped in Shadyside, turned off his phone and called from a public phone in a Laundromat next to a Japanese supermarket. Voicemail. He didn't leave a message.

He reached the restaurant fifteen minutes later, took a seat at the bar and ordered a bottle of water, then told the bartender to watch it while he went to the bathroom. The bartender nodded, a half smile on his face. Vic passed the glassed-in grill area of the kitchen and headed down the narrow hall. At the last door on the right he knocked twice. The door was immediately opened by Turcelli, whose swollen and lopsided face looked worse in the bright light. Vic stepped inside and Turcelli thumped the door closed.

The office was small, with just enough room for a cluttered desk and a couple of visitor chairs. A file cabinet was crammed into one corner, one drawer partially open. The walls were fake wood paneling from thirty years earlier and the smell of fry oil wafted from the dingy and wrinkled carpet. Thuds rose from behind the desk and worked his way between the side of the desk and wall. He wore a light green suit and black t-shirt, his eyes black and bright under the steel grey of his close cropped hair.

"Appreciate you coming," he said.

"Appreciate you not calling me about it."

Thuds held out his hand and they shook. There was a single knock at the door and as Vic glanced that way, Turcelli opened it and accepted a small tray from the bartender. On it were a bottle of Pellegrino and Vic's bottle of water from the bar. Vic noted that Turcelli's hands were unmarked, unlike his face, as if he hadn't defended himself. Thuds settled himself into one of the chairs facing the desk and waved for Vic to take the other. Turcelli placed the waters on the desk in front of each of them.

"Go okay today?" asked Vic.

Thuds shrugged. "I thought I might meet you or that hardass partner of yours in the interrogation room, but they sent in some rookie. Made no sense to me."

"Yeah, well, I thought Crush would keep you as long as he could. I'm surprised to see you out so soon."

"Good lawyer, no real evidence. Maybe a phone call or two in the right places. I told them I was at Leaner's, saw the body and called it in. No law says I have to stick around." He looked Vic up and down. "And it helps when someone gives you a heads up. Lets your lawyer get his ducks in a row."

"I talked to Mary Monahan. She said you were supposed to go to Leaner's this morning. As far as I care, your narrative holds." Vic took his water and sipped. "Doesn't mean you weren't there the night before, but dragging you in this morning wasn't going to prove that. Crush has an agenda with you. It's more about his career than catching a murderer."

"And I heard you got suspended. Also heard it's bullshit. Some woman tripped you up?"

"That and not doing what Crush wanted me to do with

you."

"Yeah, well, like I said, I appreciate that."

They looked at one another for a moment and Vic had the feeling Thuds was weighing something in his mind. He waited.

"Okay," said Thuds. "I need some advice on how to handle something. I felt like you were the right guy to ask."

"Try it."

Thuds turned and looked at Turcelli, who bent over and lifted a small shopping bag from one side of the desk. He held it open so Vic could see a silver laptop with a couple of stickers on the case. Vic turned to Thuds and waited.

Thuds gently scratched his cheek. "I'm guessing you expected this to be in Leaner's house?"

"If that's his laptop, yeah."

"Well, Mike here has a bad habit. He likes to lift shit. He was with me when we found Leaner and I didn't know he grabbed it until after." He looked at Turcelli. "Can't help yourself, can you?"

Turcelli stared at the desktop, his eyes brittle. His lips were so swollen that he looked like he was puckering up to kiss someone.

"So when I found out, Mike and I had a little talk." He nodded at Turcelli's face. "Mike is now reformed. But I'm thinking that you guys could use this laptop more than I can, or more than the hundred bucks Mike might get for it on eBay."

Vic glanced at Thud's hands and saw bruising around the knuckles. "Yeah. That would be true." He wondered why Turcelli needed such a beating just for lifting a laptop on the way out of Leaner's house. "But I don't think I can just show up at work with the damn thing under my arm."

Thuds nodded. "I didn't think so either. That's why I wanted to meet. I figured maybe between the two of us we could figure something out."

"You could tell Crush you have it. That Turcelli stole it."

"Yeah, but that ain't taking advantage of the situation. I learned a long time ago that when shit goes bad, you gotta up the bet. Take it up a level. Turn it into an opportunity."

Vic thought of the three dead Columbians in the empty garage next to the eighteen-wheeler loaded with coke. He wondered if they had seen themselves as an opportunity. He sipped his water and placed the bottle on the edge of the desk. "Maybe I do have an idea."

"I'm looking for solutions," said Thuds. He took a swig of his Pellegrino. Vic had the feeling that Thuds was enjoying himself. He glanced at Mike and then back at the bag, which now sat on one corner of the desk.

"I guess most people would expect the laptop to be in Leaner's house or his office. We sent a detective down to his office to look for it. Same rookie who interrogated you. Crush has a big shine on the guy. So maybe tomorrow my partner decides to double check Leaner's office, goes down there and finds the laptop in the lower right desk drawer, under some shit."

Thuds nodded. "Yeah, but that would make the cop who went down to Leaner's office the first time look like an asshole. Or screwing incompetent."

"Yeah," said Vic, a smile creeping onto his face. "It would." He took a longer swig of water.

Thuds sat back. "I like it. Your partner, what's her name? Liz? She checks tomorrow morning early, finds it in the bottom right desk drawer." He looked at Turcelli. "You on board, Mike? Any problems making that happen?"

Mike shook his head quickly, a look of relief struggling to emerge from his misshapen face.

"And one other thing," said Thuds. He rearranged himself in his chair. "Since we worked this out in a way you like, maybe you can let me work something out the way I like?"

Vic waited. He wasn't surprised there was a condition.

Thuds' eyes turned electric. The air thickened and Vic carefully placed his water bottle back on the desk.

"Here's the thing," said Thuds. "Like I said, Mike here likes to lift shit. He also runs errands for me. Like handing over envelopes of cash to our friend Leaner."

Vic nodded.

"And the thing is, while Mike and I were having our discussion earlier about what a dumbass he is for stealing the laptop, he decided it was a good time to mention that he was a moron in another way. Turns out that he did some freelancing. All on his very own."

Vic guessed where the story was going and fought back a smile. "Stupid idea to freelance when you're working for someone," he said quietly.

"You know, I said the same thing to him. It's one of my rules." Thuds flexed the fingers on his right hand. "Anyway, it turns out that when Mike heard Drake Monahan was dead, he remembered all those cash envelopes he'd delivered to Leaner. He already knew Chris Leaner was passing the envelopes along to Monahan. That's when Mike here figured there might be a pile of the envelopes in Monahan's house. He saw a payday."

"And he freelanced," said Vic, running his tongue against the inside of his cheek to keep from smiling.

"Exactly. So, apart from the laptop, we had a discussion about not freelancing. Like I said, that's one of my rules. And you understand my rules now. Right, Mike?"

"I got it. Crystal. One hundred percent. Somepin I never do now," Mike said in a rush. A fleck of spit escaped under the broken tooth and arced across the room.

Thuds nodded and looked at Vic. His dark eyes turned hard. "Okay, I handled that one in my own way. I'm hoping you're good with that. Mike never did find the money at Monahan's. Only you were smart enough to do that, so I'm thinking Mike's now reformed, you have the money, Mary has moved out of the house, no harm no foul."

Vic made a show of studying Mike, who tried to meet his eyes and failed. After a few moments he said, "Reason we send people to jail is to get them reformed. If Mike's already jumped to the reformed step I'm good with it."

"I'm there," said Mike quickly. "Ain't doin' it again." His eyes jumped about.

Thuds nodded, lifted his Pellegrino bottle and clinked it against Vic's water bottle. "Good. And I'll make sure Mike don't make that mistake again. I'll be like his parole officer."

"I'll drink to that," said Vic, and lifted his bottle from the desk and swigged down a mouthful. Thuds matched him. He re-arranged himself in the chair. "I'm guessing that's it?"

Thuds rose, the cords in his neck like steel cables. "Yep. Although if you want to stay at the bar and have dinner, it's on me."

Vic rose. "Thanks, but I gotta keep my nose clean."

Thuds smiled, his capped teeth large and white. "Just like Mike here." He held out his hand. "I hope you figure out that suspension, Vic. Force needs more guys like you."

Vic studied Thuds' face for a moment. "They think I'm a god-damned dinosaur. So maybe it's a good wake up call."

"Sleep late. Get some bag work in," Thuds said slowly. "You were Golden Gloves, right?"

He wasn't surprised that Thuds knew Pittsburgh's boxers, given the amount of betting around the matches. "You got a long memory."

Thuds shrugged. "Not a lot of white guys come through. I watched some of the tournaments back then. Wanted to know who might take a shot at the pros. I saw you a few times. You liked to press late in the round. Run 'em when they were tired. I like guys who get better late in the game. You used your brain."

"Using your brain isn't what gets people into boxing, usually. And then I found out there were guys who didn't get tired, or were so desperate they wouldn't let themselves get tired."

"You had a good run. And you got into the ring." He looked at Mike. "Most guys don't have the balls."

"Till next time," said Vic.

Thuds stuck out his hand. "Until next time."

They shook, and Vic left the office and walked back to the restaurant, where people were two deep against the bar. Somehow his stool was still empty. He crossed to it and the bartender appeared instantly. Vic threw a ten on the bar. "For my water, you keep the rest."

The bartender nodded and the bill disappeared into his hand as if it was the size of a molecule. Vic worked his way through the crowd to the sidewalk. Parked directly in front of the bar was a cream-colored Cadillac Escalade with the rear window down. Bandini watched him, a phone pressed to his ear, his large eyes missing nothing. As Vic stared he said something quickly into the phone, lowered it from his ear and gave Vic a quick salute. A moment later the window slid up soundlessly and the Cadillac maneuvered away from the curb, as if the traffic had parted just to let the car out.

CHAPTER 35

The next morning Vic rose at seven and worked out on the heavy bag, forcing himself through two complete rounds. Afterwards he stood in the kitchen, sweating and drinking ice water, knowing he needed to call Liz about where to find Leaner's laptop, but not wanting to use his own phone. As he thought about it, his cell phone rang, and Anne's name appeared on the screen.

"Vic, are you around? I want to stop by."

He blinked, trying to remember the last time Anne had actually called him. "Sure," he yanked himself back into the present. "Any time."

"Right now?"

"Yeah. Absolutely. I just worked out, so I'm sweaty, but I'll take a shower."

"You worked out?"

"Yeah. Downstairs. The bags are still down there."

"Mmmm."

Vic was alert in a way he hadn't felt in a long time. It was the tone of Anne's voice, something he hadn't heard in years, her no-nonsense 'time to get things done' signal. "What time will you get here?" he asked.

"You said now?"

"Yeah."

"So I'm outside waiting for you to open the door."

"Ah." Vic launched himself into the living room, his muscles complaining with every movement. When he opened the door Anne was waiting for him. She lowered her phone from her ear and pressed the disconnect button.

"Wasn't quite expecting that," said Vic.

She looked at him steadily. "I learned my lesson last time about just walking in on you."

He knew there was no answer to that. He held the door open for her to step inside. "I told you that's over."

She looked at him for a long moment then glanced around. "You cleaned up?"

"It's time I did."

"Yes it is. Too bad you had to get yourself suspended to figure that out."

Vic felt himself nodding. "Right." He was impressed. The wives' network still moved at lightning speed.

"Right nothing. Liz called me and told me what happened. So I talked to some of the other wives. You need to get your job back."

Vic blinked, her energy confusing him. "Well, yeah. I'm working on it."

"You could start with a shower."

"Anne, I'm lost. You've wanted absolutely nothing to do with me for months. Then you found me with Lorna. If you never wanted to talk to me again, I would understand. But you show up today like this, after I cheated on you. I don't get it."

She stared up at him, her eyes sharp, her mouth a tight line. Vic realized he was supposed to fill in the blank.

"Because I got suspended?"

Anne put her hands on her hips. "Vic, for all the cases you've solved you can be really dense. You really can. Listen to me. If you lose your job you'll have lost everything. I don't think that's right. Not over some gold digger like Lorna. She went through the unattached guys in the department like some kind of stomach bug. She accused you because she's angry at you and the other stuff is political garbage, right?"

"I think so. But Crush sees it as a way to get me out of his department. Every day I'm working for him I make him look bad. I'm the walking, talking reminder of the case he couldn't close."

"So you need a plan. Solve the case you're on and keep your nose clean."

"I was just saying that to someone last night."

"Don't joke around. Now what are you going to do?"

"Well, I could borrow your phone, for starters."

She stared at him.

"I need to talk to Liz, but I can't call her on my phone. I'm not supposed to be talking to anyone. I learned something about our case last night. If I use your phone, they can't prove I made the call."

"Good, that's better." She held out her phone to him and went into the kitchen. As Vic dialed Anne called out, "Oh my, you even cleaned up in here."

Vic listened to the ringing until Liz answered. "Anne?"

"No, it's me. I borrowed Anne's phone."

"Makes me want to ask a million questions."

"Yeah, but not now. Listen up." Vic walked Liz through the meeting with Thuds and how she would find Leaner's laptop in the bottom desk drawer. He then talked her through his best understanding of Craig's discovery on Gaspare's audio file.

"Yeah, Craig was waiting for me when I came in this morning," said Liz, when he was finished. "He told me about the audio. If the laptop is where you say it is, I can't wait to make Kevin look like an asshole."

"It should be. Get it to Craig. We need to know if Leaner was the one bugging Monahan's office. If he wasn't then we got other problems and there's someone out there we don't know about."

"Okay."

He told her about Turcelli searching Mary Monahan's house for the cash.

"We let that go?" she asked.

"I think so. Maybe we get a favor later. And we got the laptop back."

"Unless Thuds is using that story to give you back the laptop. Like after he stole it because he needed to delete something."

"Tell Craig to check that. If no one used the computer after Leaner died, then we're clean on that, and so's Thuds."

Liz was silent. Vic waited, knowing she wanted to speak her mind. "Listen," she said after a few moments. "You always got an answer that puts Thuds in the clear. You get that he might be the guy, right? There's motive there. And he's smart and cocky enough to act nice to you so you look someplace else."

"I said at lunch. I'm not seeing it."

"Maybe because that's what Crush is seeing?" Her voice hardened. "Maybe it's got more to do with you wanting Crush to be wrong, instead of you figuring out who actually killed Monahan?"

He closed his eyes and rubbed his forehead with his free hand, the muscles in his arm heavy. "Maybe," he said finally. "I'll think about it."

"You do that. Because this is about solving the case, not making your boss look bad. Now, can you keep using this phone so I can reach you?"

"I'll try. Anne is here now."

Liz was silent for a beat. "Like I said, I got questions about you two. But right now you need to figure out this case and get ready for your suspension hearing. Get your story figured out."

"Or I could say what actually happened."

"Yeah. Because that always works out so well for you. Just get on it. I ain't working the rest of my life with that asshole Kevin."

"If there's a problem with me using this phone I'll let you know."

"And I'm going down to Leaner's office to get his laptop. Mostly because I want to see Kevin's face when I walk in with it."

"And get it to Craig."

"You think I didn't hear you?"

"I'll believe it if you give me a full description of Kevin's face when you show up with the laptop."

He heard what sounded like a strangled laugh. "You got it." The line went dead. Vic looked up to see Anne standing in the doorway, a dish towel in her hand.

"See what I mean?" she asked. "You're better when you're working on something."

"Like a shower?"

"Before you do that, you need to explain something to me." Her voice was tight. "After Dannie disappeared, I understand why you weren't on the task force. Conflict of interest, they would never let you anywhere near it. I understand that. What I don't get is what happened afterward. Did you ever look for her yourself? I know you, Vic. You aren't the kind to let things lie. The guy I married wasn't like that, I wouldn't have married him if he was. But you did nothing. Except not to care about anything but drinking, which you never did before. And now here you are suspended."

"I do look for her."

She shook her head. "You need to do better than that. If you mean sitting outside Jenny's house hoping she'll show up, that's not doing anything. Do you think her mother hasn't seen you out there and called me? Or driving by her school? What is that? Do you think she's just going to show up one day like nothing happened? That's not looking, that's hoping, and it's desperate but mostly sad. You need to take it seriously. Investigate her case."

He wanted to answer but nothing came to him. "I couldn't look at the file," he said after a few moments. He looked about the room. "I tried. I even have a copy of it in my desk. I just can't open it. I pulled it out a bunch of times and tried to get started, but I just can't."

"Why not, Vic? She's our daughter. Why not?"

He felt himself clutching Anne's cell phone as if it was some kind of talisman. He closed his eyes and opened them. Made himself look at her. She stared back, her brown eyes unwavering.

"I was scared," he heard himself say, his voice a whisper. And he knew in that moment it was true. "I was scared if I looked I would find out what really happened. All of it. I mean everything. I didn't know if I could stand it. What it might make me do."

"You don't think I'm scared of that too? I'm her mother. I carried her. I gave birth to her. But where are we now? Both of us. You tell me. Would it be better for us to know or not to know? I've tried not knowing. It doesn't work for me."

"Would knowing really make a difference?"

"No. She would still be gone. But I can't keep going this way. I just can't. I need to try the other way. I need to know what happened and try living that way. And you're the only person who can help me do it. But you're suspended, and that's why I'm here. You need to beat the suspension. And then you need to investigate and find out what happened to Dannie."

Vic looked around the small living room. It was as empty as he felt. He searched inside himself and looked at her. "The task force chased every lead. One of the guys got a two week suspension because he beat up a guy he thought had more information. Liz put the barrel of her Glock in a guy's mouth to make him talk. She got three weeks and a permanent note in her file. They tried. All of them are good cops. They didn't miss anything."

"I don't blame them at all, Vic. None of them. But you need to look. *You* do. You know her better than they do. There has to be something there." Her voice faded and they stood in silence. Vic found that he was breathing hard, not fast, just deep and slow as if his chest was too tight to let him absorb oxygen. She raised her eyes to him again. "It won't fix what's wrong between us, Vic. But I need this. You need this as well. You do this and we might get things a little better between us."

Vic nodded slowly, his chest relaxing.

Anne looked around the room, her eyes settling on the front door. It was as if she was talking directly to it. "It'll take a different kind of courage, Vic. Not the getting into the ring and going ten rounds kind of courage. That takes guts, no question, and you've got that. But this is different. This is the courage you need to walk into a burning house because you know it's the only way to save yourself." She turned to him. "And if it means anything, I'm scared too."

"Okay," said Vic carefully. He wasn't sure if he was agreeing to search for his daughter or just responding, but at the same time he did know.

Anne held up his phone. "I'll keep your phone, you keep mine. Now fix that suspension and then go find what happened to our daughter." She turned and walked over to the front door, stopped to look at him, then let herself out.

The screen door slammed. Slowly, he turned and climbed the stairs. He put Anne's phone on the bedside table and undressed, then crossed into the bathroom and started the shower. As he waited for the water to warm he thought about the file in his desk drawer. The whole four or five inches of it, and the rubber bands. The simple weight of it. And how that same heaviness just wouldn't leave him.

CHAPTER 36

L ater that afternoon, Vic placed supermarket shopping bags against the right side of his car's trunk, using a first aid kit and rain slicker to wedge them in place. An apple rolled free and he caught it and stuffed it back in a bag. He wanted to cook a meal, to actually eat vegetables. As he climbed into the driver's seat Anne's phone rang.

"Vic?" Liz asked.

"Yeah."

"Leaner's laptop was exactly where you said it would be. I pulled it out during the case update meeting. Everybody got to hear how Kevin missed it when he searched the office."

He smiled, enjoying it more than he should. "How'd Crush react?"

"Swept it under the rug. What do you think? But everyone got it, and Kevin was too slow to say someone put it there after he searched."

"He'll get there."

"Yeah. Craig has it and he's working on it. You need to understand this. Craig also told me someone used it early in the morning after Leaner was killed. Leaner was too stupid to password protect it. Craig is figuring out if any files were deleted. So Thuds might have been after the laptop."

Vic massaged the back of his neck. "I hear you. And you told Craig to look for video files?"

"Yeah. We're getting a warrant to search Leaner's cloud files as well, but that will take some time."

"So we wait."

"Vic, you need to think about Thuds being the suspect. Or this Turcelli guy who works for him."

"Step at a time. Can you do me a favor?"

"Right. I'll add it to the list."

"Yeah." Vic stared through the windshield at shoppers pushing carts across the parking lot or lugging blue shopping bags to their cars. The sky was low, grey and worn. "Top right drawer of my desk. There's a couple of files with rubber bands around them. Can you drop it off sometime?"

"Tomorrow good? I got plans after work."

"School stuff?"

"Something like that."

"Yeah, tomorrow is fine."

They fell silent for a few moments, then Liz said carefully, "That's a copy of your daughter's case file."

Vic placed his right hand on top of the steering wheel and picked at the plastic with his thumbnail. "Well, I got some time, thought I'd take a look."

"You need me to go through it with you? I can do that."

"Thanks. I thought I'd try reading it cold first. See how that goes. I know you can add a lot."

In the silence Vic listened to each thud of his heart, then Liz said in a voice just above a whisper, "Lorna was in Crush's office for a while this afternoon with that HR lady. I'm guessing she was giving a statement."

"I'm sure I'll hear all about it."

"Yeah, but it was real short. Five minutes, tops," Liz added. "I'll drop off the file tomorrow. I'll call you."

"And let me know as soon you hear from Craig."

"Vic, I got plans tonight. Personal shit. I'll call you tomorrow."

"Okay, okay." Vic disconnected the call and dug at the steering wheel again. He knew she was right. He didn't want Thuds to be the murderer because he didn't want Crush to be right. He knew it. *I need to get past that*, he thought. *If Thuds is the guy then I go after him.* He tamped down the feeling and started the car.

^ ^ ^

Later that night, stuffed on green beans and meatloaf, Vic washed the dishes, his mind running through the details of Leaner's crime scene, trying to spot evidence connecting Thuds to Leaner's death. The dishes put away, he circled through the living room, dining room and kitchen remembering his interviews with Thuds.

Nothing stuck out or connected.

He stopped in the half dark living room. But no one had asked Thuds for his alibi the night of the Monahan murder. Or for Turcelli's. Suddenly those two facts bothered him like a splinter under the skin.

Lost in thought, he took a bottle of water from the refrigerator, opened it and sipped. As he walked he remembered a piece of advice Craig's father had given him fifteen years earlier. *If you can't find proof connecting someone to a crime, then find proof disconnecting them.* He sipped again and carried the bottle into the garage and his car. He took a right at the end of the driveway, headed toward Leaner's house. There was something he didn't remember anyone checking.

Fifteen minutes later he stopped in front of Leaner's house, cut the engine and stared at the yellow crime scene tape fluttering at the top of the entrance stairs. The sound was lost in the dull roar of a passing train. Carefully, he got out of his car and walked the sidewalk toward the South Side bars and restaurants, staring at the houses on both sides of the street, trying to spot a security camera. He reached the location where the police officer had climbed out of his patrol car and identified the first few numbers and letters of Thud's black Escalade. The road was straight and well lit. He shook his head. There was nothing he could use to disprove, or prove, Thuds being there at the time of Leaner's murder.

As he walked back to his car, he dug Anne's cell phone out of this pocket and thumbed in Craig's number. On the second ring Craig answered with a guarded 'hello?'

"Craig, this is Detective Lenoski, sorry, I'm using my wife's phone. I was wondering how things were coming with that laptop that belongs to Leaner, the murder victim?"

"The one Detective Timmons brought in today?"

"Yeah. Liz told me that someone accessed the computer, but I was wondering if the person who accessed it deleted any files?"

Vic heard papers shuffling as Craig looked for something. "She asked me the same thing. Some, I'm reconstructing them now. So far it just looks like they were trying to clean off the hard drive. Also, I got the warrant for his cloud accounts a little while ago and I'm waiting for the server company to give me access."

"When you get in look for video files."

"Yeah, I know, but I was thinking about that. Do you remember the way that robot was set up to stream whatever video it recorded over the office Wi-Fi? OK. That's fine, but that's a shitload of video. Sorry."

Vic pressed his phone closer to his ear as he slid into the driver's seat of his car, glad to be out of the cold. His sport coat wasn't warm enough. "Craig, no problem. I thought the same thing. I actually figured that Leaner might have given up checking it. So what are you saying?"

"Suppose he didn't want all that video? Maybe he only wanted specific meetings. I assumed that he recorded all the video someplace because the bot transmitted constantly, but suppose he didn't? Suppose his plan was only to collect video at certain times? And that got me wondering if you can pick up the office Wi-Fi signal outside."

"You mean like somewhere else in the building?"

Craig hesitated. "Maybe, but I was thinking the parking lot. Then he could sit outside and collect video in real time anytime he wanted. Or just leave his laptop in his car as he recorded."

Vic shifted in his seat. Craig had a point. "So how would we check that?"

"I was thinking after work I'd drive down to the Monahan office and check the parking lot, see if I can pick up their Wi-Fi. If it isn't accessible from the parking lot then I guess all the video is on a server someplace."

Something moved inside Vic. "Craig, I tell you what, I'm out already. I'll drive over and check it out. You keep going on Leaner's cloud account."

"Oh, sure," Craig sounded surprised.

"Don't worry about it. I need something to do anyway. I have my wife's smart phone, so I can see what Wi-Fi networks it can access from the parking lot."

"Yeah, sure. I should hear from the server company by then anyway, so it's better if I'm here." Craig told Vic the name of the Wi-Fi network Monahan's company used and he wrote it down.

"I'll let you know," said Vic, "and contact me when you get into his cloud account."

"You got it. This phone?"

"Yep. Absolutely."

He started the car, did a three point turn and worked his way over the Smithfield Street Bridge and through Pittsburgh, dropping onto Penn Avenue. He slowed as he entered the Strip District, wary of the couples walking arm in arm on the sidewalks and how they darted across the road headed to different restaurants, nightclubs and bars.

Two blocks down he turned left and glimpsed the Allegheny River, as black as oil, the shore lights shimmering orange on its surface, then bumped over the railroad tracks and into the parking lot of the Monahan's office building. He passed the loading dock and it's access door before swinging around in front of the building and parking against the yellow curb. He cut the ignition and the car engine ticked in the silence. He searched the parking lot. Nearby was the janitor's tired Toyota in its usual spot under a light pole. He didn't see Erica's white BMW, but he did see a Mercedes sedan parked in one of the office building's reserved spaces. He frowned, sure that it was the same make and model he had seen parked in the Monahan's garage: Mary Monahan's car. He doused his headlights and swiped through Anne's phone to the Wi-Fi networks screen.

The Wi-Fi network for Monahan's business appeared. He thought about that, then started his car and drove to the far end of the parking lot, backing into a space that faced the front of the building. Anyone who wanted to steal the signal, he reasoned, would park somewhere inconspicuous. The network was still available, although the signal was weaker. He dialed Craig.

"How's it look?" asked Craig.

"You can read it. Better by the front door, but also at the far end of the lot."

"Yeah. I thought so. So maybe someone sat in the parking lot and stole the signal."

"I get that, but they would need the password and to know when and what meeting to film."

"Password would be easy. If they ever visited the office I bet it was given to them. Hey, I just got access from the server company, I'm gonna look at Leaner's cloud files now."

Vic hung up and looked around the parking lot, a thought forming. One type of person wouldn't need to see the schedule of meetings, and that would be anyone invited to the meeting. He wondered if Leaner wanted a record of his payoffs to Monahan. *Nothing like some video as insurance in case Monahan denied receiving the payoffs. Or better yet, use the video for blackmail, to keep Monahan's investments coming.* It would be easy enough to start his laptop recording as he sat in the car, then leave it on when he went inside for the meeting.

He smiled to himself. From everything he knew, Leaner was a guy who would think that way. He started his car and rolled forward, his eyes first pulled to a car parked in the lot on the side of the building, and then to a large SUV sitting in the far corner of the lot, away from the pole lights, the black vehicle backed into a spot against some shrubs. A late model black Cadillac Escalade. He went warm all over, pulled his wheel and headed toward it.

As he cleared the corner of the office building something moved among the shrubs on his left, a shadow. His heart jumped. He looked at the loading dock and saw Calvert, the janitor, pushing his wheeled can of garbage bags toward the dumpsters. Vic looked back at the loading dock door, just in time to see it bump closed against the brick that propped open the door. He wheeled his car into a space and sat, staring at the door, unsure what he had actually seen. But it lived in his memory: the moving shadow, the bump of the door closing too long after Calvert exited.

He grabbed Anne's phone and tapped in Liz's number. As it rang he clambered out of the car and jogged across the parking lot. Calvert was dragging the wheeled can up the ramp toward the door, his head bobbing to the music from his headphones.

Liz was suddenly angry in his ear. "Vic? What the hell?"

"Liz, listen, I'm at Monahan's office building. Can you get over here? Something's going on."

"I told you I have personal stuff tonight."

Calvert reached the door, swung it open, shoved the can inside and hooked the brick out of the door jamb with his foot.

"Wait!" shouted Vic as he bounded up the loading dock steps, knowing Calvert wouldn't hear him over the music from his ear buds. As the door swung shut he lunged and caught the handle just before it closed.

"Vic! What the hell is going on?" Liz's voice carried from the phone.

Vic pulled the door open and stepped into the hallway. Calvert was already at the far door, his headphones so loud Vic could hear the music. He jammed the phone against his ear as the outside door thunked shut.

"I'm inside Monahan's offices. I saw someone sneak in through the side door, the same way Monahan's perp got in. I got a black Cadillac Escalade in the parking lot. Looks like the one Thuds owns. Mary Monahan is here, I recognized her car from the time we were in her garage."

"So what if Thuds is visiting her?"

"By sneaking in through the side door? I'm worried it's Turcelli. Look, I need to check this. I'll leave the loading dock door open. Come in that way."

"I'm at dinner. What are you even doing there?"

Vic kicked the brick into the door jamb and checked the door was ajar. "Working with Craig."

Silence spun through the phone and made Vic stop. He waited a beat then said, "God dammit, then just call back-up for me. I'm going up to Monahan's office." He pressed the disconnect button.

When he entered the lobby he found only the wheeled garbage can. Calvert had vanished. He glanced about desperately, wanting Calvert's office keys. He walked down the hall past the elevators, trying doors, but they were all locked. He stopped and looked around, breathing hard, then walked slowly back toward the lobby, listening. When he reached the front desk he heard faint music. He circled the desk, still listening, and finally spotted a narrow door inset into the wall around the side of the receptionists desk. Stepping in front of it he heard music from the other side. He tried the handle but the door was locked. He knocked. Nothing. Clenching a fist he pounded on the door and the music was suddenly louder. Calvert had removed his earphones.

"Calvert," he shouted at the locked door. "This is Detective Lenoski. I need your help."

The music stopped but Calvert stayed silent.

"Calvert!" shouted Vic again. "Remember I interviewed you a few days ago? Someone snuck into the building while you were dumping your garbage bags. It just happened a few minutes ago. I think they're headed to the fourth floor. I need to get in there and I need your keys."

"How do I know that's you?" his voice wavered.

"Open the door. You'll see it is."

"Slide you badge under the door."

Vic uselessly patted his jacket pockets. His ID was in Crush's desk drawer. He closed his eyes, controlled his breathing and tried to moderate his voice. "Calvert, I'm off duty. I left it at home. Look, open the door. I just need your keys so I can get into the offices on the fourth floor."

"I ain't giving you nothing. How'd you get in?"

"Through the loading dock door." Vic glanced around the lobby desperately. "Look, if you don't want to come out I don't care, but slide the keys under the door."

"Un-uh. I'm calling the cops right now."

"I am the goddamned cops!" he shouted. He grabbed the doorknob and shook it, then kicked the bottom of the door. "I need the keys!"

"I'm not giving you shit!"

Suddenly a thought came to him. "Wait, are you still using a garbage can to prop open the doors upstairs?"

From the silence, he guessed the answer was yes. He controlled his breathing. "Listen. When you come out stay in the lobby. More cops are coming, let them in." He jogged to the elevators and pressed the elevator button, hoping fourth floor doors were still propped open. The elevator took what felt like five minutes to arrive.

The fourth floor was silent. Vic looked down the hall and with relief saw the door propped open by a garbage can. He stepped toward it but his phone rang and he stopped again.

"Detective Lenoski, it's Craig."

"Right," whispered Vic, stepping to the partially open door and sneaking a look inside the Monahan offices.

"This is crazy! You won't believe what I found!" Craig's words ran together, the same way they had the night before.

"Craig, I have two seconds. What is it?"

"I got into Mr. Leaner's cloud account. You won't believe what I found."

"Just tell me, I'm in a situation."

"Yeah. You're whispering. Um, first thing I did when I got into the account was check to see who accessed it. And when. And I found this one computer logon like every three or four days for the last two weeks. But it was the computer address that was crazy. It wasn't Leaner's laptop. It was this other computer that accessed the account, and I thought I recognized the computer address, so I checked."

"Yeah," said Vic quickly. He slipped through the door and, ducking down, worked his way along the row of cubicle walls. He heard a voice ahead. Orienting to it, he knew the sound came from the glass-walled conference room that Mary Monahan used as her office.

Craig rushed ahead. "It's the laptop you brought me that has the alibi on it. For that Gaspare guy? He'd been accessing Mr. Leaner's cloud account."

Vic closed his eyes, trying to process the information. "How is that possible?" He slid around the corner of the work station, focused on the voice. As he did someone started shouting. He took another step, and through the glass of the conference room wall spied Mary Monahan standing on one side of the conference room table, Gaspare across from her, jabbing his finger at her. His face was red and spit flew from his mouth. Vic ducked and shuffled a work station closer to the conference room door. "Craig, I gotta go." He tapped the disconnect button, watching Gaspare, his mind reeling from Craig's information.

"I will never make you CEO," said Mary into a sudden silence from Gaspare. "You're completely unfit for it."

Gaspare pounded his fist on the conference room table. "I called that Erica today. She said you still hadn't decided. I knew it right there. You and your husband planned this. You stole my company and gave it to Leaner. This is all your fault!"

Vic darted for the door, reaching for his Glock under his sport coat, but there was nothing there.

"David Gaspare!" he shouted from the doorway, straightening and holding his hand against his hip as if he had a weapon under his sport coat.

Gaspare spun to face him, his lips pulled thin, his eyes bright and twisted. Vic glanced at Mary Monahan. She was standing across the table from Gaspare, her arms slightly away from her sides as if she was ready to defend herself, her face pale. She mouthed a thank-you toward him.

"David," said Vic. He realized he was blocking the door and Gaspare was stuck between the table and the outside windows. He watched Gaspare rock on the balls of his feet, his eyes darting about, the realization he was cornered burning in his eyes. Vic purposefully dropped his voice to a conversational level. "David, we can talk this through. We all go home tonight."

Gaspare turned so his back was to the windows. His right hand moved near his waist. Mary's eyes locked on his hands.

"Show me your hands," said Vic quickly.

Gaspare hesitated, still rocking. Vic raised his palms toward Gaspare. "Look. I'm not drawing my gun, but I need to see both of your hands. Make a good decision here."

"It's a knife," said Mary from the far end of the room, her voice strangled.

Vic hesitated, searching for a way to distract him. "Look, David, we know you got into Leaner's cloud accounts. I bet you knew his password from the days he worked for you. We know what you were looking for. And why you had to sneak in here and take your prototype from Monahan's office. You had to make sure there was no video of you stabbing Drake Monahan." Out of the corner of his eye he saw Mary Monahan grab the edge of the table to support herself.

Gaspare's eyelids scrunched tight. "Bullshit." He snapped off the word so hard it sounded like an explosion.

Vic kept his palms up. "David. Let's talk about how you got in here. Without anyone knowing. Using the door the janitor left open. Like you did the Saturday night you came up here to see Drake Monahan." And Vic understood it then. The pieces fell together. He cocked his head as if he and Gaspare were old friends. "Goddamn Leaner, huh? He screwed up all your plans. You figured that with Monahan gone and Leaner's company going down the tubes, you'd cake walk back to running your company. And then you saw the tapes Leaner made of his pay-offs to Monahan. You knew they were meant to drive you out of business. Wow, that pissed you off so much that Leaner had to go too. Am I right?"

Something moved in Gaspare's eyes and Vic didn't like it. "Look, David, you need to understand something. Mary didn't know anything about any of this. I found the cash from the pay-ments. She didn't know about it. It was something her husband did without telling her."

Gaspare charged him. The speed of it caught Vic off guard for a split second, his eyes locked on the knife in Gaspare's right hand. He realized instantly that it was a garden trowel, flattened and sharpened, absurdly wide, and his mind leaped to the trowel handle he'd seen sticking from the plant pot on Gas-pare's front porch. Gaspare was half the distance to him when Vic snapped his fists up into a boxers stance. As Gaspare closed, Vic hopped to his left, his hip banging the conference table, and in the same movement danced to his right as Gaspare stabbed for his waist. Something seared on Vic's left side as he threw a jab at Gaspare's nose, the punch landing with a crack. Gaspare stumbled back with a grunt, blood splattering the tabletop and coating his chin. Vic's side felt as if someone had slapped a red hot branding iron onto him. Gaspare stumbled back another step then feinted toward him. Vic hopped back, and as he did, Gaspare, trailing blood and a guttural roar, stumbled up onto the table, found his footing and charged across the tabletop at Mary Monahan. Vic started down the aisle next to the windows to catch him. Halfway to Mary one of the windows facing into the office shattered with a bang and Gaspare spun sideways off the table, landing face first in a heap of overturned chairs. Vic glanced at the window and saw Levon Grace sighting down a handgun.

"Vic," shouted Liz, coming through the doorway, her sil-ver .38 held diagonally across her chest.

"Get Mary out!" Vic yanked chairs out of the way, reached

Gaspare and kicked the knife under the table. Gaspare was on his side against the outside wall of the room, his left hip a mass of blood.

Vic glanced back and saw Levon advancing behind him, his pistol clasped in two hands and pointed at Gaspare. Levon was light on the balls of his feet as if he had done it a thousand times before, and Vic knew in that instant he had. He heard Liz talking to Mary Monahan, urging her out of the room. Levon reached him and held his pistol out for Vic to take, and when he did, patted Gaspare down, then slid out of his windbreaker, bunched it up and pressed it against Gaspare's hip.

"Get an ambulance," Vic shouted. He searched for Liz and saw her on the other side of the broken window, her phone to her ear. Mary Monahan was sitting near Liz in an office chair, pale and staring straight ahead, her back so straight Vic thought it must hurt.

Liz dropped her arm. "Back-up is close."

Vic gingerly touched his left side, where the pain was getting worse with each heartbeat. His fingers came away soaked with blood.

"Get pressure on it," said Levon, watching him from the floor beside Gaspare, his eyes unnaturally calm. "Use your sport coat."

Vic nodded, starting to feel lightheaded. "How'd you guys get here so fast?"

"We were eating dinner in the Strip," called Liz. "Like two blocks away when you called."

Through the doorway two uniformed officers appeared, swinging their weapons about. Liz raised a hand so they could see her badge. "Police," she shouted. "I called it in."

CHAPTER 37

As paramedics trundled Gaspare away on a gurney, a second team finished wrapping a bandage around Vic's middle so the large wad of gauze against his side was firmly in place. The pain killer they had given him felt just fine.

"You're lucky," said the lead paramedic. "Another inch over and you'd be gut stabbed. Those are bad news. A bunch of stitches to fix this up."

"Lucky me." Vic watched a detective escort Levon to the bathroom to wash the blood off his hands. Mary Monahan still sat in the chair by a cubical, her face tight, a female paramedic monitoring her blood pressure. Mary's eyes studied the flow of cops and technicians moving about, then strayed to the long furrow of a scar on the top of Vic's shoulder. Vic looked at the paramedic. "Can I get my shirt back on?"

"Sure." As the paramedic helped him into the sleeves of his shirt Levon returned,
pulled over a chair and sat next to him. Vic nodded toward Levon's pistol, now sitting in a plastic evidence bag on the conference table. "You always carry on a dinner date?"

Liz cut him off. "In the trunk of his car. He's got a carry permit."

Levon smiled slowly, his eyes calm. "She freaking asked if I had the permit when I got it out of the lock box in the trunk."

"Thank you again." They all looked toward the voice. Mary stared back at them from her chair. Some color had returned to her cheeks. She managed a smile and Vic saw confidence in her eyes.

"Glad I was nearby," said Vic.

Levon said, "You punched him? You brought a fist to a knife fight?"

Vic felt a bit giddy from the medication. "Screw you, my boss has my weapon. Best I could do. It wasn't going to work a second time. He just didn't expect it the first time."

Levon turned to Liz. "See, that's the hard ass Vic I always knew. I'm surprised the knife even cut that hide."

Vic struggled to maintain focus. He stared at Liz. "All your dates this exciting?"

She rolled her eyes. He noticed that her blouse was unbuttoned a couple of buttons from the top and she was wearing a light shade of lipstick. He couldn't remember her doing either, at least around him.

"Not much of a date for you guys," said Vic. "And I've got more bad news. A weapon discharge? Liz'll be doing paperwork all night."

"Thought you were the lead detective?" cut in Liz with a smile. "You should do the paperwork."

Vic spread his palms. "Hey, I'm suspended. You know it was Craig who got the right idea. No way someone kept video of every moment in that office for a year. But recording specific meetings from the parking lot? That makes sense. I bet Leaner only wanted video of his Monahan meetings. That way he has tape to use against Monahan if he needed it."

Liz shook her head. "Yeah, but we need Gaspare to make it. I'm not sure we can prove he committed both murders."

Vic drifted for a moment on some porous wave of the pain killer. "I don't know, Craig found something in one of his alibis, and now we got a weapon."

"Oh yeah, I figured out his alibi."

Vic and Liz turned to find Craig standing in front of them, his eyes bright under his unruly thatch of hair. "I heard all this on the scanner and knew you were here. You remember I was saying about the sound being wrong in the video? I went back through the program and found that it auto saves like every half hour. I have every version of his alibi video. The noise he took out was a train. Lasts like three minutes."

"The train outside Leaner's house?" asked Liz.

"So he edited the video sitting in his car outside Leaner's house?"

"Yeah. I got meta data on each save of the video. Includes GPS location. And I know exactly when he was working and when the file was open but not being worked on. I guess he didn't know about the auto-saves. When I get back I'm gonna check the first alibi video as well."

"Bet it turns out he made it in the parking lot here." Levon pointed at the evidence bag with the knife inside. "And what the hell is that thing?"

Vic shook his head, trying to clear it. "Trowel. He flattened and sharpened it. We walked right by it. It was sticking out of a plant pot on his front porch."

A movement at the door made Vic glance that way. Crush walked in, his bald head gleaming in the light, his white uniform shirt perfectly starched. Sergeant Wroblewski shambled in behind him. Crush looked about, bouncing on his toes, then crossed to Vic, his face angry. "You're suspended, Detective Lenoski. Explain to me why you're here."

Vic took a breath to calm himself before he spoke, but Mary Monahan cut in. "His job. Detective Lenoski saved my life. I'm very fortunate Vic was nearby, as I was fortunate that his partner and Levon Grace were nearby." She rose, stepped over to Vic and placed her hand on his shoulder, over his scar.

Vic nodded at Crush. "This is Commander Tompkins Davis, my immediate supervisor."

Crush glanced from Mary Monahan to Vic and back again, his eyes wide. "And who the hell are you?" He leaned forward, trying to use his size to intimidate her.

She leaned right back at him, invading his space. "This is my company. And, since you look like the kind of person who only shows up at the end of something to take credit, I'd appreciate it if you left my property. You bore me. Or do I need to call the mayor?"

"You're Mrs. Monahan?" Crush's eyes widened and he stepped back. For the first time that Vic could remember Crush wasn't in motion in some way. And he seemed smaller.

"I'm not Joan of damned Arc."

Crush reddened and took another step back. He looked at Vic. "I want you on duty tomorrow. But you need to make your statement. Tonight." He closed his eyes and opened them, gave Levon a long and confused look, then turned sharply on his heel and left the room.

Mary squeezed Vic's shoulder. "A little over the top?"

Vic looked at her, deciding that he liked her hand on his shoulder. "Not with that jerk. He's the one who arrested Thuds and wanted to go after your Dad. He figured if he could make charges stick he would make deputy chief. He didn't give a shit what the evidence said."

Mary removed her hand and sighed. "That's the thing about my father. Someone always wants to take him down. Even I did once. Everybody really needs to grow up." She leaned over and gave him a lingering kiss on the cheek. "Thank you, Detective Lenoski." She straightened.

Vic nodded, unsure what to say, and finally managed to squeak out, "Glad I could help."

Mary nodded, and Vic watched Liz draw her over to another detective to get her statement. He turned to find Sergeant Wroblewski staring down his bent nose at him.

"I saw the perp when they were loading him into the ambulance," said Wroblewski. "He's gonna have a nose like mine." His bloodshot blue eyes looked Vic up and down. "Good job, rookie."

"He got a piece of me."

"The good busts always do." Wroblewski then added softly, "Crush needs you back tomorrow because Lorna dropped her charges. And the other shit doesn't matter now. Your suspension is over, once you get that thing stitched up." He nodded at Vic's side.

Oddly, Vic didn't feel any elation, only a hard tiredness, masked by the drugs. "What made Lorna change her mind?"

He shrugged. "I reminded her that I was with you at the Barking Shark when she came in, and that I saw you guys leave at different times. And I knew you went back to the office, I checked your computer log-in times. Then I reminded her that I would testify to all that, as well as how she's been dating half the damn department, including some of the married guys. And how she accessed your personnel file without permission to get your home address."

"And then she had a change of heart."

"Oh yeah."

Vic was quiet for a moment, then looked at Wroblewski. He somehow seemed taller than anyone. "Thanks, Sarge."

He nodded, then said quietly, "And next time you see Bandini, tell him I said hello."

"You got that."

Wroblewski turned to Craig. He leaned close to him and Vic was glad to see that Craig didn't back up.

"You're Luntz's kid, right?"

Craig nodded. "Yes sir."

Wroblewski nodded slowly.

Vic said quickly, "Craig blew up this case. He figured out the evidence. We should have enough to nail Gaspare."

Wroblewski glanced at Vic and then looked Craig up and down. His eyes lingered on Craig's thatch of hair. "Wouldn't expect it any other way." He held out his hand for Craig to shake, and when they were done headed toward a group of crime scene technicians.

The paramedic placed a hand under Vic's shoulder. "Let's get you stitched up."

Vic nodded, grateful for the support, and for the way the paramedic guided his arm over his shoulders. He glanced at Liz to say goodbye, but she was lost in conversation with Mary Monahan and the detective. He looked at Levon. He was sprawled in his chair, silent, his head down. Vic followed Levon's eyes to his lap and saw a tremor in Levon's left hand. As he watched Levon slowly covered his left hand with his right, raised his head, his eyes closed, and breathed through parted lips. It was timed breathing, a kind of meditation, he realized. A coping mechanism. *This is what the assholes of the world do to good people,* he thought. *Why the fuck can't I do anything about it?* A tear slid down his cheek.

"Whoa," said the paramedic, seeing his face. "Too much pain?"

"No," Vic answered. "I'm good."

The paramedic chuckled. "Sure, tough guy."

No, thought Vic. *Nowhere near tough enough.*

CHAPTER 38

A week later Vic and Liz finished the interviews and paperwork related to Gaspare's shooting. It was close to six when Vic's phone rang. He glanced at the caller ID, but the caller was blocked. He answered.

"Vic, it's Mary Monahan. How are you?"

"Getting there, just getting ready to leave, why?"

"I have a couple of friends coming over. They want to talk to you. I was hoping you could stop by my apartment. I think one of them has something for you."

Vic closed his eyes. He could guess the identity of the visitors. "What time?"

"It's six now. Eight thirty?"

"I'll be there."

He sat back and saw Liz watching him from her desk across the aisle.

"I'm guessing that wasn't Lorna."

Vic shook his head. The grapevine had said Lorna was working at the vehicle impound. "Mary Monahan. She wants me to meet someone."

Liz frowned. "Careful who you start hanging out with."

"Mr. Careful. That's me." He stood up, opened his desk drawer, removed his Glock and clipped it to his belt. He stared into the drawer for a moment, then lifted the thick files bound together by rubber bands, and hefted the weight of it all.

"Whenever you're ready," said Liz quietly. "I'll give you the background."

"Thanks. Like I said, I just want to read it cold first. See how that goes. He slid gingerly into his sport coat to avoid the dig and pull of the stiches in his side and carried the files to his car. He thought about it for a moment, and then placed them in the trunk.

∧∧∧

After dinner at Ritter's Diner he parked a block down from Mary Monahan's apartment building. As he hiked to her apartment building he checked the cars, and halfway there reached a black Cadillac Escalade. As he approached, the passenger window slid down and Mike Turcelli nodded to him, his face still bruised in places. He was healing, but sections of his face were still the color of an old prune. Vic nodded back.

Mary Monahan answered the front door of her apartment when he rang the bell. The side panels of her skin tight black cocktail dress were white, calling attention to the curve of her hips. There wasn't a hair out of place on her head. She rose on her toes and kissed him lightly on his cheek.

"Thank you for coming. How's your side healing?"

"On target, from what the doctor says. Stiches out soon."

He stepped into a living room of low, modern furniture. Thuds lounged in a corner of one of the couches wearing his usual suit and black t-shirt. Bandini rose from an armchair that faced the door. He wore grey flannel pants and a sport coat over a white silk shirt. They could have been wealthy businessmen, which Vic conceded they probably were.

"What can I get you to drink?" asked Mary.

He glanced at the coffee table. A small bottle of Pellegrino sat in front of Thuds, a low crystal tumbler of something brown in front of Bandini. A glass of red wine sat across the coffee table from Thuds's Pellegrino.

"Water is fine," said Vic, and crossed to Bandini, who stuck out his hand. They shook and Vic nodded at Thuds, who stayed seated.

"Have a seat, Vic," said Bandini.

Vic took a seat on the couch facing Thuds, who picked up his water and sipped. Vic could see Mary in the kitchen, twisting the top off a bottle of Pellegrino.

"I saw Mike outside," Vic said to Thuds. "He looks more reformed."

Thuds smiled, but it was Bandini who answered. "He's young. You heal faster when you're young. I'm thinking you'll need a couple more weeks, though."

Mary placed the Pellegrino in front of Vic and gracefully sank down on the couch next to him.

"Now, Vic," said Bandini, and waited until Vic looked at him. "I want to thank you for what you did the other night. Showing up at Maria's offices when you did. It could have ended a lot worse."

Vic remembered Mary's comment that her father still called her Maria. "We got lucky. I was doing something related to the case and was nearby."

"That asshole going to live?" asked Thuds.

"Yeah. Levon knew enough first aid to keep him together until the paramedics got there. He'll never walk the same, but he won't be doing much of that the rest of his life anyway."

Bandini leaned closer, his large brown eyes bright. "And did he confess to Leaner's murder?"

Vic glanced about the room, stalling, knowing it wasn't information he should pass on, but he also knew it would be on the news the next day. Crush had already held two press conferences about the case and had the last planned for the following day. "He did, but you didn't hear it from me. When he heard our evidence, he gave it up." He looked at Thuds. "Guess that makes a mess of how you handle PipeMine."

"We'll figure that one out," said Mary.

Bandini raised his glass to Vic. "To good friends," said Bandini. Everyone raised their drinks, but Vic hesitated before he took a sip. He didn't like the toast.

"Just so you guys know," said Vic, wanting to build some

space between himself and Bandini after the toast, "I only went into Mary's offices because I saw what I thought was Thuds's Escalade hidden outside. I guessed Turcelli was paying Mary a visit and I didn't like that idea."

Thuds cocked his head slightly. "Do I need to say it wasn't my car?"

"Well, if I'd gone over to it, I would have seen the driver's side window was smashed. Turned out someone carjacked it a few days earlier and just dumped it there. Just so you know where my head is."

"Fair enough," said Bandini. "I know you can't really associate with Vince and me, I get that, but I appreciate how you've handled things." Vic noted how Bandini ignored Thuds's nickname and called him by his given name. "And having a mutual friend like Levon is useful." He paused, and Vic understood that if he wanted to contact Bandini or Thuds again, Levon was the conduit.

"Not just because he knows how to use a gun," added Thuds.

Bandini's face suddenly turned serious. "But we thought you might find another piece of information useful." He paused and sipped his drink before returning it to the table. "I don't know how to be delicate about this, Vic, and really I ain't that kind of guy. So I'll just say it. We know your daughter disappeared not long ago. About this time of year."

Vic tensed. He nodded carefully, waiting.

"As it turns out, Marie, or Mary, I guess," he gave her a pointed look, "she's shown me the error of my ways in how I've treated the women who work in my clubs and other businesses." Vic wondered if Bandini was going to start calling Mary by her preferred name from now on. "Vince and I were talking about that the other night, and between us we remembered something we thought you might find interesting."

"Related to my daughter?" asked Vic.

Bandini shrugged, his large eyes never leaving him. "Possibly." He nodded to Thuds, who reached into his suit coat and produced a large brown envelope and placed it on the table in front of him. Bandini picked up the conversation. "Right around the time your daughter went missing, three girls who worked in our clubs disappeared. Maybe there's a connection, maybe not. But they both specialized in looking young. You know, pigtails and stripping out of Catholic school uniforms, that kind of thing."

Vic felt a movement on the couch and knew Mary had tightened up.

"Did you guys report it?" he asked, watching the envelope out of the corner of his eye.

Bandini and Thuds exchanged a glance. "Yeah. For all of them. We gave it a couple of days to see if they were going to show up, then checked their apartments, talked to their roommates, but they were gone. One was eighteen, the other two nineteen."

"And you filed police reports on them?"

"Yeah, but the cops didn't do anything. They figured the girls had found boyfriends or just run off. Turns out guys like us aren't the only ones who treat strippers like shit. Plus they disappeared over five weeks, so it wasn't easy to connect. But the timing with your daughter going missing is interesting, given the kind of show they put on. And Mary is pissed we didn't do more about it at the time."

So it was going to be Mary. "Okay." Vic was skeptical. "Bit of a stretch."

Bandini was quiet, watching him. "It is. But you never know, do you?"

Mary shifted next to him. "I know it sounds like a long shot, Vic, but it might be worth a look. Those girls never turned up. One day they were there, the next they weren't. We should know what happened."

Thuds pointed at the envelope. "That's their employment files and some pictures, so you got something to go on."

Vic nodded, picked up the envelope and slid it into his jacket pocket. "Okay." He finished his water and stood up. "I appreciate you letting me know."

Thuds and Bandini rose and they shook hands all around.

"By the way," Vic added, looking at Bandini. "Sergeant Wroblewski sends his regards. Told me to pass them along if I saw you again."

Bandini smiled. "Yeah, now there's a guy who knows how to play a hand. Tell him I said hello."

Mary walked him to the door and followed him into the hall.

"Vic? Okay if I call you for lunch every once in a while?"

Vic nodded. "Yeah, that would be nice. I heard from Levon you like to do that."

She smiled, her brown eyes warm. "Only with the people I like and trust." She reached up and kissed him lightly on the cheek. "Take care of yourself. I'll be in touch." She dropped her hand onto his wrist and gave him a gentle squeeze.

Outside, Vic walked to the black Escalade and tapped on the window. Turcelli lowered it and Vic bent over and leaned on the window frame. He stared at Turcelli. "We gonna have a problem, you and I?"

Turcelli shrugged. When Vic stayed in place waiting, he said, "No."

"Okay. Because your boss told you the rules, right? His rules. And you get that the rules are different than the law?"

Turcelli stared at him. "I get that," he said finally.

"Good. And I got rules, too. You want to take a guess at my first rule?"

Turcelli frowned and stared at the windshield. After a moment he pursed his lips and turned back to Vic. "Don't free-lance?"

Vic shook his head. "No, my first rule is don't break the law." He held Turcelli's stare for a moment, then straightened and tapped the bottom of the window frame with his palm. He continued down the sidewalk to his car.

From his trunk he lifted the thick files bound by the rubber bands, carried the bundle inside his car and placed it on the passenger seat. After looping his seatbelt in place he took the envelope Thuds had given him, lifted the rubber band and slid it underneath. He snapped the band back into place, sat for a moment, then started the car.

As he drove away he rested his right hand on top of the file folders.

The End

Peter W. J. Hayes was born in Newcastle upon Tyne, England, and lived in Paris and Taipei before settling in Sewickley, a village just north of Pittsburgh. He spent many years as a journalist, business writer and advertising copywriter, but it was a six year stint on Wall Street as Chief Marketing Officer for a global investment company that really prepared him for crime writing. His short stories have appeared in a variety of mystery magazines and anthologies and he has won or been shortlisted for several awards by the Crime Writers' Association (CWA) and Pennwriters. He is currently working on the novels of his Vic Lenoski Mysteries.

Mystery
HAyes
2018

1624717

Made in the
USA
Monee, IL